# LOVE INSTINCTS:
## The Romance of Sex

*A love story about how human
sexual instincts influence
romantic relationships*

## Jan McBride, M.D.

# CONTENTS

This story is dedicated to you, the Reader,
and to humans of all ages who
play the male vs female game
of romance and love.

# Prologue

"I can't make it for lunch," he lied. "I have to finish a paper."

"Oh, okay...but may I ask you something?"

"Sure."

"Can we go to Sequoia this weekend?"

He stared at her, dumbfounded. Had she no clue what a punch in the gut she had given him last week? Yet from somewhere in his mind there flashed a spark that an opportunity was presenting itself. "Do you trust me?" He scowled.

"Hmm...not completely...but I think I can handle you." She smiled mischievously, ignoring his ill humor.

That smile ignited the spark, and it flamed in his brain. Did she have any idea what she was doing to him?

\* \* \*

## Chapter 1

# New sweets in the candy store

Until that moment it had been an ordinary day. School had been in session for two weeks, and the students sitting in their second period government class had not yet become restless with the teacher's lecture. They had finally shed their free spirits of summer and settled into their academic routines.

Suddenly the door quietly opened and she appeared.

The vision she presented was so unexpected and stunning that Mr. Walford stopped talking in mid-sentence and held a frozen pose, as the class followed his astonished gaze. Floating layers of white blonde hair drifted around her shoulders as she stepped into the room and closed the door behind her back, as she scanned the class with a passive expression.

The students held their breaths and stared, waiting for her to step lightly and seductively in slow motion, her hair billowing in a soft breeze, as they would expect from any similar beauty in a Hollywood movie or a sexual fantasy. Instead, her movements were purposeful—too rapid to comply with the air of mystery suggested by her exotic allure. She crossed the room with determination, carrying her electronic pad in the crook of her hand the way the boys did, rather than cradled in her arms in girlish fashion. She carried no purse or other visible object.

Neither her boyish motions nor her simple attire could hide the feminine sensuality that emanated from her image. A plain white top hugged the generous curve of her breasts; it could have been an ordinary t-shirt except for the neatly finished jewel neckline and sleek, almost shimmery fabric.

She turned and paused in front of Mr. Walford's desk as she retrieved a slip of paper that had rested between her hand and her computer. She handed him the schedule slip as she looked into his eyes and spoke a soft "hello." Her foreign accent was exposed by the single word and the students strained their ears to hear more, but she did not speak again.

Time seemed to pause as the classroom eyes behind her drifted up and down the willowy figure that had not been in their world, then suddenly was.

Wispy tips drifted around the white cascade of hair and glistened in the overhead fluorescent lighting like flickering sparkles on sunlit snow. The slightly raised heel of her sandals enhanced the curve of her calves; from there the creamy smoothness of her legs extended upward to mid-thigh, where the flare of her light blue skirt interrupted the image as it draped the narrow roundness of her hips.

She waited patiently as Mr. Walford looked at the paper, then at her, then at the paper again.

"Cla—" he coughed, cleared his throat, then looked up.

"Class, this is Vindi... Jo..."

"Yo-hahn-son," she pronounced for him.

"Oh, yes...Vindi Johansson," he then pronounced correctly, replacing the *J* sound with that of a *Y*. "She will be joining our class for the semester."

He recovered his professional demeanor as he handed the schedule back to her and directed her to choose one of the two open seats at the front of the classroom. She moved more leisurely this time. Boys held their breaths and girls gaped in frozen silence as her slender limbs and body appeared to glide to the desk nearest the window.

Before taking her seat she surveyed the classroom again, scanning each pair of eyes that she had captured. Her expression remained passive, providing no hint of her thoughts. She turned and sat with unfeminine carelessness, betrayed by the curve of her hips as they slid into the sculpted chair.

Rays of morning sunlight streamed through the glass and got caught in her hair, turning the icy white sparkles into a yellow halo of reflected light that shifted and glimmered with every movement of her head, attracting the eyes around her like a sun shining on its orbiting planets. She appeared oblivious to the spectacle she presented, and focused her gaze on Mr. Walford as he continued his lecture about the Bill of Rights.

The droning voice was the only clue that time was passing in the suspended mini-universe of the classroom until the bell rang, instantly reanimating its inhabitants.

Several boys jumped from their seats and dashed to Vindi before she could get to the doorway. They were immediately captivated by the liquid blue eyes, perfect pink lips and creamy complexion of her fashion-model face, enhanced by the slightest hint of natural-looking cosmetics.

Unperturbed by the clamor for her attention, Vindi was calm and friendly as she sought the name of each admirer and exchanged greetings with a warm smile. She gradually made her way out the door, with the boys circling around her.

When the introductions were finished, Quinn, the tallest and best looking of the group, waved his muscled arm at the others. "I've got this handled, guys...you can move along now." His dark blue nylon shirt covered a broad chest and shoulders, and the open V-neck displayed scattered brown curls. Despite these signs of maturity, the wavy brown hair that played over his ears emphasized the boyish face and smile of a teenager.

"No," Vindi stated. "That is not how we are doing this. My next class is chemistry in room one-oh-four. One escort is enough, so anyone who wants to play can join in now with rock-paper-scissors. Who is playing?"

As the other students wove their way around the small group, they strained to hear her lilting accent, so unfamiliar to their ears. Most proceeded down the hallway to get to their next class in the time allotted. Quinn stayed at

Vindi's side, as did Ansel, shorter and less muscular than Quinn but dressed with more flair, as the golds and browns in his plaid dress shirt reflected the auburn color of his short, professional haircut.

"I'm in," Ansel declared.

"I'll play," said Jared, who stood behind Ansel. He was thin, with straight light brown hair, angular face and a shy smile that displayed a thin retainer wire across his well-aligned upper teeth.

Vindi looked to her right, where Matt hesitated awkwardly. He was obviously not in the same social circle as Quinn and Ansel. Barely reaching Vindi's height, his plain blue t-shirt was covered with a light brown zip-front jacket; his dark brown, slightly curly hair was neatly groomed and accented by the brown frames of his sturdy glasses.

"What about you?" Vindi asked him.

"Sure."

"Why are you asking *him*?"

Vindi looked up at Quinn. "How is he any different from you?"

Quinn opened his mouth but nothing came out; he shook his head. "Okay, fine…you guys go."

Ansel won, and Matt moved away as Vindi smiled and said, "Bye, see you later."

Quinn beat Jared, who offered Vindi a waving salute as he turned to leave.

Next Ansel beat Quinn, who waved his hands with a shrug. Vindi met his puzzled gaze with a smile. "Don't worry, Quinn. It is just a game."

Ansel snickered, and as they started down the hall he tried to take Vindi's arm, but she calmly pulled it away. "No. We are just walking."

"Okay, sorry!" He jerked his hand away with exaggerated alarm, then flashed a confident smile. "By the way, I'm Ansel, and I'd be happy to show you around the area sometime and help you get acclimated."

"No, we are not doing that either," Vindi said flatly. "You did not win any prize except a walk to class, so you need to get out of pursuit mode."

"Oh! Well..." This time his surprise at her directness appeared genuine. "How about this? I'm in your chemistry class, and we have lunch period after that, so I can show you where the cafeteria is...how about that?"

She peered into his eyes and paused, as if considering her reply. "That depends...on whether you can win the rock-paper-scissors again, and if you don't get disqualified for being too annoying."

"Right." He nodded, then grinned. "So...where did you say you were from?"

Less than an hour later Doug Goodwin made his usual rounds in the cafeteria, teasing and flirting with the girls, and talking sports and school events with the boys. As usual, he started with the table of juniors who were finishing their lunch shift and preparing to proceed to their next class.

The giggling girls welcomed his attention, returning his winks and smiles with their own, and observing whose fries and saved tidbits he chose from the plates on their trays.

At times he rested his hand on the back of a chair, flexing his biceps as he leaned in to speak in a low seductive voice, following with a twitch of his dark eyebrows, then a flash of his even white teeth.

He greeted the boys with hand slaps or claps on the shoulders, demonstrating camaraderie as he stood over them, manifesting his social and physical superiority that was evident at a glance. Through no effort of his own he was the recipient of exceptional genes that produced pleasant and symmetric facial features, a strong jaw, and straight black hair that he wore neatly trimmed around the ears and topped with a careless wave at his forehead.

The same genes had initiated the flow of testosterone throughout his body at an age earlier than the average male, and stimulated his muscles to respond vigorously with added bulk and strength in the appropriate places. The muscles in his face had responded with equal precision, creating a sculpted, masculine appearance that matched the sonorous pitch of his voice.

Nature had wrapped Doug's genetic gift with the bow of intelligence, giving him the ability to use his assets to his advantage. His sense of fairness and humility made him popular with his male classmates, who privately coveted his social position. His plans for college and a future career were easily in sight. But he practiced his art of charm with daily dedication in order to achieve his most important goal in life at age seventeen—that of getting laid.

As the juniors sauntered away from their tables, Doug moved to the other side of the room, where he greeted fellow seniors as they settled into their usual places. He repeated his maneuvers with the chosen classmates who merited his attention. These were the best looking and the best dressed, who shared varying degrees of his genetic gifts.

The small private school the students attended attracted upscale families from the surrounding neighborhoods, and many of the students had been classmates since the first grade. The elegantly designed and decorated buildings had multiplied over the years to provide additional classrooms and amenities as the student body grew and matured. The grounds were manicured with precision, including the paved and tree-lined high school student parking lot, where many new and slightly used sports cars spent their days basking in the California sun.

The cafeteria Doug commanded was orderly and efficient, designed to seat in shifts the students from grades nine through twelve who occupied the building each day. Each grade was composed of thirty to forty students, who shared some classes across grade levels to facilitate flexibility in scheduling and advancement.

Quinn and Doug had both attended the school since grade one, and had become best friends by the third grade. Quinn now approached, and joined Doug's remaining social rounds, sharing in Doug's aura without challenging his status, like a faithful sidekick. While Doug pulled out chairs to seat the girls as they arrived, Quinn cut out early to join the food line, then made his way to the empty table near the center of the room.

Quinn's arrival at their table was Doug's cue to withdraw from his adoring public, and he strolled to his chair, polishing an apple on his red polo shirt. As he sat down, Quinn looked at him expectantly.

"What?" Doug asked.

Quinn gestured with his hands. "You don't know?"

Doug sat back in his chair and bit the apple with a loud crunch. "Know what?" His words slurred around the firm chunk that occupied his cheek.

Quinn leaned toward him, speaking softly. "There's a new girl in school today. She was in my government class. She. Is. A. Babe."

Doug raised his eyebrows and leaned forward. "Yeah? Tell me more."

Quinn glanced at the cafeteria entrance, then turned back to Doug and continued. "Man, wait 'til you see her...she's gorgeous! But she's no pushover! She shut us down, like that..." he snapped his fingers, "like she knew exactly what was in our minds and wasn't buying any of it!"

"So, you got nowhere with her." Doug leaned back with a sly smile, then bit the apple again.

"That's right! She even set 'Blind-as-a-Bat Matt' up against me...can you believe that?" Quinn looked behind him again, then leaned back in his chair. "Of, course, I'm sure you won't have any trouble with her."

Doug chuckled. "Why do you say that?"

"You know why. Girls have been coming on to you since we were ten! I don't know how you do it, but you can throw a little of it my way once in a while."

"I've tried to tell you, it's my animal magnetism." He grinned, as he finished his apple.

"Yeah, that's why you can get away with dating so many girls at the same time and not getting your teeth kicked in." Quinn paused. "I don't know, though, I think this new girl might be different. She's obviously been around." He glanced at the doorway again. "Oh, here comes Maggie." Doug understood, and the subject was dropped.

Maggie bounded toward them, her short light brown curls bouncing with each step. She greeted Doug, then gave Quinn a quick kiss and a "Hi, baby!" as she sat down beside him and accepted the salad he handed her from his tray. She was tall with a medium build and light complexion; a few faint freckles sprinkled over her cheeks danced when she smiled.

Shortly afterward Jenna and Alisse brought their food trays to the table, and sat on each side of Doug. They were friends with each other but competed for dates with him, fully aware that they were not his only options. He was certain that they compared notes after each encounter, which he accepted as an unspoken challenge.

Jenna was of medium height and slender, with dark brown hair that covered her shoulders. She wore expertly applied makeup—heavy on the eyeliner and mascara—at all times except when she was sleeping. Alisse was slightly taller and thinner, with long, straight yellow blonde hair. Their California summer suntans were complimented by the latest clothing fashions, which they maintained with great effort and discussion.

"So, has anyone seen her?" Jenna asked.

"Who?" Quinn asked innocently.

"The new girl!"

Quinn and Doug looked at each other without speaking, knowing the conversation would continue without them, which it did.

"No, but I've heard that she's from Sweden and has all the guys panting after her like dogs!" Alisse snorted.

"What else," replied Jenna, leaving off "would you expect" that was understood. "Sara was in government with her, and said that when the guys crowded around her after class she made them play rock-paper-scissors to see who got to walk her to her next class!"

Doug looked at Quinn, who returned a blank stare.

"Uh-oh, you'd better watch out, Maggie." Alisse leaned forward. "A girl like that will dish it out to every guy she sees!"

"A girl like what?" Doug asked.

"Like a slut!"

"Wait a minute!" Doug protested. "She's only been here a few hours, and you're already calling her a slut? Why? Just because guys are attracted to her? Are you so worried about the competition?"

"Hmf!" Alisse stabbed at her salad.

"What else!" Jenna said sarcastically. She had sliced her hamburger in half and carefully covered one portion with ketchup and mustard from small packets. She topped the gooey surface with pickle slices from the other half, replaced the bun and handed the sandwich to Doug.

"Well, I'm not worried about competition!" Maggie leaned her head against Quinn's arm and looked up at him with pouting lips. "Right, baby?"

"Right, baby." He gave her a quick kiss on the lips.

Maggie turned her head. "So, what's your plan, Doug? How is the senior class playboy going to compete against rock-paper-scissors?" The other three looked at Doug, interested in his reply.

He shrugged. "I don't intend to compete against anything. If she's interested in me I'm sure she'll let me know." He took a bite of his half burger as he accepted the napkin that Jenna held out to him.

Quinn nodded. "I'm sure she will."

Jenna looked over Maggie's shoulder across the room. "Catch that! That's got to be her!" Quinn and Maggie turned around to look.

Doug's eyelids snapped open at the image of beauty he could not have imagined, and he barely kept himself from blurting aloud the *wow!* that exploded in his brain.

"Oh, whoopee, a blonde Swedish girl," Jenna sneered, but her gaze followed Vindi's movements, interrupted only when she looked down at her plate to slice her naked half hamburger with a knife and fork, one bite at a time, as if she were eating a steak in a high-class restaurant.

"What's Ansel doing with her?" Maggie scowled. "Ooh, wait until Carleigh finds out."

"I told you!" Alisse shook her head, flipping her hair around her shoulders. Suddenly she huffed. "Look at her! Can you *believe* what she's wearing?"

"*Seriously*," Jenna agreed. "She must shop at the plain white t-shirt store!"

"How boring. I'll bet she has one in pink, too."

"I think it looks pretty great on her." Doug scanned Vindi with lustful interest.

"You would," said Jenna. "You guys have no fashion sense at all!"

"Of course we don't," Doug agreed. "All that fancy stuff you girls buy is just to impress each other. You both would look better to me if you wore nothing at all." He hugged them simultaneously, as he looked from one to the other with a flirtatious smile.

"Stop it!" Alisse giggled.

Jenna gave him an exasperated look as she punched him in the shoulder.

"You're a pig!" scolded Maggie.

Doug smiled and winked at Quinn, then continued to watch Vindi as he rested his arms on the backs of the girls' chairs.

Ansel and Vindi went through the food line, then approached the group with their trays.

"Hello gentlemen...and ladies." Ansel bowed slightly. "This is Vindi. Vindi, this is Maggie...you know Quinn..." Maggie looked at Quinn with a combination of surprise and alarm. Not noticing, Ansel continued, "Jenna...Doug...and Alisse."

Vindi smiled briefly at each one as they were introduced.

"Ansel, where's Carleigh?" Alisse asked sweetly, as Vindi sat down next to Maggie.

Ansel took the chair on the end next to Vindi. "She's in broadcast media lab, you know that. Don't make a big deal out of it."

"Vindi...where did you get that beautiful shirt?"

"Jenna, stop it," Doug scolded, finding it difficult to avert his eyes from Vindi's stunning image as the overhead lights danced in her hair.

"No, I mean, it's nice...and I was just wondering where you do your shopping?"

Vindi looked at her with no sign of antagonism, as if she did not recognize the syrupy sarcasm. "I ordered some things online after we moved here. Most of my clothes are for cooler weather, and I had trouble finding what I wanted in the stores." She emphasized every few words slightly with her accent.

"Oh, and this is what you wanted?" Jenna continued. Doug nudged her under the table, his eyes still on Vindi.

"Ja, this is what I would wear in the summer in Sweden." She maintained eye contact with Jenna, ignoring Doug's interest.

"What's this I hear about rock-paper-scissors?" Maggie interrupted. "What is that all about?"

Vindi chuckled, meeting her questioning gaze. "Oh, I saw the boys doing that to settle arguments when I was at university in Sweden, so I thought I would try it. I think it worked very well!"

"So that's how you pick a guy?" Jenna asked.

"Oh, no, I'm not picking anyone, and they are not picking me. Obviously, we do not even know each other! They are just following their instincts, you know…the new girl, and all that. It's just a game, so I used a game to make it easy, and have some fun."

None of the girls had a reply to that, which was rare.

Doug accepted a cookie handed to him by Alisse. He leaned forward on his forearm and stared at Vindi. "So, you've been in college?" he asked in a low sensuous voice, lifting one eyebrow.

Vindi's eyes met his, her face passive except for a slight amused tilt on one side of her mouth. "I lived on campus for a few months, but I was not a student there." She held his gaze for several seconds.

"How was that?" Doug finally asked. He took a bite of the cookie and chewed as he continued to stare at her.

Vindi glanced at Alisse, who was scowling at her, then at Jenna, who scowled at Doug. When she looked back at Doug, his lips parted into a slow smile and he winked at her. Her face became passive. "It's a boring story." She broke off eye contact and began to cut at the oddly shaped white meat on her plate, ignoring Doug's continued stare. "What kind of fish is this?" Vindi looked at Maggie.

"It's chicken."

"Oh." She took a bite and chewed slowly as she studied her plate.

Doug leaned back in his chair and exchanged surprised glances with Quinn. This was unexpected behavior in response to Doug's charm. She should have been smiling and flirting with him by now. *So, she wants to play a bit. We can do that.* He sat up straight and puffed out his chest as he took a breath. "So, Vindi…" He paused.

Vindi looked up at him as she chewed, then dabbed her lips with her napkin, waiting.

"What do you think of the school so far?" PING.

One side of her mouth twitched upward again but her eyes remained serious. "I think it's great." PONG. She returned her gaze to her plate as she cut another bite.

"Have you met any guys that you like yet?" PING.

She looked up again. "The guys I have met are all right." PONG. She held his eyes, her face passive, as she took a sip of her juice.

Doug leaned forward with a half-smile and spoke softly, "If you need any help learning who's who just let me know." PING.

Vindi squinted slightly as her pale eyebrows lowered into a glare. "No, thanks. I can see who is who already." PONG! She returned her gaze to her plate.

Doug's jaw dropped slightly as he straightened his spine. He glanced at Quinn, who suppressed a smile.

Jenna giggled as she shoved her plate toward Doug. She began to speak, but stopped when she saw Doug scowling at her. She then addressed Alisse and Maggie. "Oh! You won't believe the purse I found Saturday! It's exactly what I was looking for. Remember that buttercup leather we saw downtown?"

"Don't tell me you found the shoulder bag!" The three of them pounced into an enthusiastic discussion about accessories and an upcoming sale at the mall. Vindi did not participate, but observed the girls' excitement with curious interest. She did not look at Doug.

As if knowing better than to lean around Maggie to speak to Vindi, Quinn challenged Doug with his thoughts about the local college football team. Doug hesitated, as he chewed on the fries from Jenna's plate. *It's rude for us to exclude her from the conversation. But she seems pretty satisfied with the way she shot me down, so what does she expect? Maybe she thinks she's too good for us.* Vindi was not looking at him, but was speaking to Ansel. *Wow...she's beautiful enough to do whatever she wants. And she knows it.*

Doug tried to talk to Quinn, but was not sure what he was saying because he could not keep his eyes from darting past Maggie to Vindi. The ordinary gleam of the ceiling lights was converted into a hundred searchlights that flashed from her hair and shot into his left eye. Quinn's smirk became a grin, as if he were enjoying Doug's distraction.

Ansel had not taken his attention from Vindi throughout the entire lunch period. Now he checked the time and stood up. "Vindi, I have to go meet Carleigh. I'll see you later."

"Okay. Thanks for your help."

He turned and left with a satisfied smile.

Vindi consulted her schedule. "My next class is algebra, in room two sixteen." She spoke to no one in particular.

Maggie peered over her shoulder. "Oh, Doug, that's your class!"

Doug gave her a deadpan look. "So?"

"So, you can show Vindi where the class is!" She held her hand around Quinn's arm as she spoke.

Doug turned to Vindi with an expression of indifference. "I'm sure you can find it by following the sequential room numbers…but you can walk with me if you like." He waved his hand. "Whatever you prefer."

Vindi met his gaze. "Thanks so much. I'll let you know." She stood and lifted her tray. She scanned each face, addressing no one in particular, "I have enjoyed meeting all of you." She turned and headed to the tray return window across the room, the edges of her skirt fluttering with her long strides.

"Well, that was interesting," Alisse commented loudly before Vindi was out of hearing range. The others were silent.

Doug did not try to conceal his overt observation of Vindi as she dropped off her tray. His expression turned to one of surprise as she was approached by Matt and his friend Kenneth, whose name did not conceal his obvious Asian heritage. He was slight in build and stood several inches shorter than Vindi.

"It looks like the brainiacs are going to try their luck," Doug remarked. All eyes at the table watched to see how Vindi would handle them.

"They have some nerve," snorted Alisse, "to even think that she would have any interest in them!"

"You're such a snob, Alisse," Quinn scolded.

"Oh, and I suppose you hang around with the geek boys?"

Before he could answer, they were all stunned into silence as the trio approached the table.

"Doug, Matt and Kenneth are in algebra too, so they will show me where the class is." Vindi held her chin up as she looked down at him with her eyes. "You don't have to bother. Thanks anyway." Her voice was flat. She glanced at the others with a partial smile. "I hope to see you all later."

After they left, the group exchanged bewildered glances. Doug made a questioning gesture to Quinn, who shrugged in reply.

"What was that about?" Doug finally asked, shaking his head.

"Yeah," Jenna smirked, "she didn't even let you play rock-paper-scissors!"

Quinn snickered. "She's already got you figured out."

"Right, and she'd rather be with a couple of geeks than with you!" Maggie tittered, then became silent at Doug's scowl.

Jenna rose from her chair. "Let's get to class."

As they scattered, Doug heard Maggie ask Quinn, "What's this about her knowing you?"

As they made their way down the crowded hallway, Matt and Kenneth talked in turn about the material that had been covered in algebra class. Vindi heard their voices, but was involved in her own thoughts.

*I suppose they all thought I was pretty rude, but I'm not going to play his game. So proud of himself. Thinks every girl is just dying for his attention. Hmf! Just like...Olof.*

An image appeared in her mind, of a young man with broad shoulders and a confident smile lighting his handsome face, but with blue eyes and a wave of honey-colored hair.

*A slightly younger Vindi, with snowy white bangs covering her forehead, jumped and waved her pompoms as she cheered. The honey-haired teen ran toward the group of girls with the elation of victory, his muscular chest covered with a large number twelve on his lightweight soccer shirt. His hair was disheveled and sweaty after the game.*

*Olof hugged each of the girls in turn, then flashed Vindi a flirtatious smile as he tugged on her pigtail. She turned her face upward and his lips met hers.*

*The scene changed. This time Vindi's hair floated loosely around her shoulders as the boy gazed into her eyes. They were sitting on a sofa, and he wore a dark green shirt. He kissed her lightly, then more passionately as he pressed himself toward her. She began to resist, pushing her hands against his chest.*

*"Don't stop me," he whispered into her ear, pulling her into him.*

*She continued to struggle. "Stop..."*

*"Don't you love me?"*

*"Ja, but..."*

*"Then come on..." he murmured, pushing her back forcefully against the sofa. He took a deep breath and moaned, "I want you so much..."*

SLAM!

The images disappeared at the sound of Vindi's notebook hitting the floor where she had dropped it in front of the doorway. Kenneth quickly picked it up and handed it to her with a smile.

"Well, here we are!" he said cheerily.

Doug entered the classroom as the teacher was directing Vindi to an empty seat. He chatted briefly with Ariel, and then with Krystal as he made his way to his usual spot on the opposite side of the room. As he sat down he looked at Vindi, but when she turned her head toward him he averted his gaze. *Two can play at this game. We'll see how she likes being ignored.*

Yet throughout the class session every time he stole a glance at her out of the corner of his eye he was surprised to note that she was ignoring him.

## Chapter 2

# She must be ignoring me just to get my attention

Throughout the rest of the week it appeared to Doug that Vindi wanted to become acquainted with everyone in the senior class except for him. Carleigh's lab was on Monday and Friday; Ansel escorted her to the cafeteria on the remaining days.

On Tuesday Doug saw Vindi enter with Todd and join his table of students that Doug had shared classes with for years, but had not spoken to since grade school. *What is she doing with them? They're definitely not at her level on the social ladder. Hmpf! She's just making a point of snubbing me.*

The following day Vindi sat with a group that Doug did not even know. She seemed to be purposely associating herself with students Doug ignored when he visited his domain in the cafeteria. Yes, she definitely was taunting him.

The gossip about Vindi throughout the school diminished as her classmates became acquainted with her. She exhibited no snobbish behavior, but appeared pleased to speak with everyone; she even sought out and spoke to the shyer students in her classes. Doug learned that she disposed of rock-paper-scissors after the second day, but maintained control of her interactions with the boys who felt compelled to pursue her.

They discovered quickly that she did not accept any invitations, and would not even give out her phone number. Her answers were always the same—no excuses, just brief and to the point, and always beginning with a firm "no."

"No, we are not doing that now."

"No, I'm not ready to do that."

"No, you need to get yourself out of pursuit mode."

They accepted the straightforward but polite rejections without trauma or animosity, and continued undaunted in their quest for her attention. The girls were less enthusiastic; most of them treated her with the cool indifference of a rival.

"So, have you gotten anywhere with Vindi yet?" Quinn asked Doug later in the day.

"Hmpf! I'm not falling into that trap!"

"What do you mean?"

"Oh, she's playing her little game of avoiding me. The only class we have together is algebra, and I'm not going to compete with the jerks who mob her after class. I'll just let her make the rounds and find out what's out there. She'll come back around eventually."

"Interesting strategy. You know, this is the first girl I've seen resist your charm and your 'animal magnetism.'" Quinn smirked.

"Just wait. She'll be back."

On Thursday Vindi saw Matt and Kenneth heading out the door with their lunch trays. She followed them, and discovered the outdoor seating area of the cafeteria. It was smaller than the indoor lunchroom and consisted of eight round tables, each with six attached seats. It was surrounded on three sides by small trees planted purposefully in a row and skirted by smaller vegetation. On this day only a few of the tables were occupied.

She approached the two boys with enthusiasm. "Hi, guys. Are you going to eat out here?"

"Hi, Vindi. Sure, we sit out here every day…unless it's raining, of course."

"Oh, how great it is to sit in the sun! Why doesn't everyone come out here?"

"Hmf! Most of them are afraid they might break a sweat and ruin their fancy clothes!"

"Well, I'm going to get my lunch and join you! Is that okay with you?"

"Sure, if you want to."

When she returned, the boys abruptly stopped conversing as she slid into the seat next to Kenneth.

"Mmm…this is wonderful." She lifted her face toward the cloudless blue sky as her hair captured golden yellow sparkles from the sunlight. She then arranged the food items on her tray as the boys watched silently. She looked at them. "What do you usually talk about at lunch?"

"Oh, different things…"

"Nothing in particular…"

Vindi smiled. "I know…things you think I will find boring, or will not understand. But don't worry about me…I like listening, and I'll let you know if I have a question about something."

"Why don't you tell us about Sweden?" suggested Kenneth.

"What would you like to know?"

"I have a question." Matt adjusted his glasses. "With the long winters and lack of sunlight, is vitamin D deficiency a problem?"

On Friday Doug saw Vindi enter the cafeteria with Ansel, and waited in anticipation for them to approach his group. Throughout the week she had not given him more than a quick "hi" if they happened to pass each other entering or leaving algebra class.

He was surprised when she veered away from Ansel and joined two girls sitting at a table by themselves. One he did not recognize; the other was Marie, whom he had known since elementary school. Both of her parents were research scientists, and she was named after Marie Curie, "the mother of modern physics." Because of her intellectual drive and ability, her classmates frequently called her "Madame Curie" in a condescending manner.

Ansel arrived at the table and sat down in front of Doug, obviously annoyed.

"What happened with Vindi?" Doug asked.

"Can you believe it? Here's my chance to have lunch with her, and she wants to talk to the geek girls!"

"Hunh!" *Now that's just crazy. How far is she going to take this game?* Doug feigned disinterest, but observed the girls in what appeared to be a congenial conversation. While pretending to listen to Jenna, Alisse and Maggie talk about who-knows-what, he saw Vindi and the two girls finish eating, drop off their trays and then exit to the outdoor seating area.

The following week Vindi settled into somewhat of a routine as her classmates became accustomed to her presence and amiability. She walked between classes with various individuals and groups, and greeted others with a smile as she passed them in the hallway. For her midday meal she favored sitting outdoors with Matt and Kenneth. As a result of Vindi's introduction, the boys were frequently accompanied by Marie and Liz, and they shared lively discussions on diverse topics.

There was one group of students Vindi did not approach—several rough-looking boys who congregated at the furthest end of the outdoor cafeteria on most days. In contrast to the other students, they sported radical hair styles and untidy attire. They were frequently loud, but kept to themselves. None of them were in any of her classes, and they were ignored by the other students. She observed them without much interest until the day she saw *him*.

He was slightly taller than the other ruffians, with a wiry build. He had disheveled light brown hair, and wore an oversized military jacket despite the warmth of the season. He was not with the group every day, but when he joined them he appeared to be their leader. On several occasions Vindi furtively watched him, and on the day she saw him sitting by himself she asked Matt who he was.

"Oh, great," he said sarcastically, "he's back again. That's Blake, who used to be Barry in grade school, but then he started making everybody call him Blake, and I heard that he legally changed his name. He's a bully and a troublemaker, and got suspended from school last year. I was hoping he wouldn't come back."

"I second that," Kenneth added. "I've been harassed by him and his group too many times."

"I'm going to talk to him," Vindi said.

"Why do you want to do that?"

"Because he reminds me of someone I used to know…a guy who was tough on the outside, but had a rough life and needed a friend."

"I recommend against it," warned Matt. "If he gets nasty with you we're not going to be of any help."

"No, no, I don't want you guys to get involved. I'll walk around the other tables so he will not even know I'm coming from here."

"Are you sure you want to do this?"

"Yes, it will be fine...just stay here." She got up and walked toward the building, then circled around several tables and approached Blake, standing where his view of her would not include the table she had just left. It was a fairly warm day and the few students that were outside were clustered near the entrance out of hearing range. Only Matt and Kenneth noted Vindi's approach to Blake's table.

"Hi, Blake." Vindi remained standing several feet from him.

He turned his head toward her, looked her up and down, then his closed lips widened into a lewd smile.

"Hey, babe, come on over and join me."

"No. Your guys are not here, so you don't have to impress anybody. I just wanted to say hi, and if you want to talk sometime...like between two people...we can do that."

"You talk cute. What's your name?"

"Vindi."

"Well, Vindi," he scanned her again, "there's a lot I'd like to do with you, but talk isn't one of them. How 'bout we go for a ride?"

"No. No games, no lines, and no pursuit. Maybe we can talk another time." She turned and walked toward the building, entering the far side door.

Vindi walked leisurely across the cafeteria. She glanced across the room of lunching students, and was surprised to see Doug staring in her direction with a scowl. She made no response, but continued through the exit to the corridor and made her way to her locker. She retrieved her computer pad and notebook, then closed the metal door. Suddenly a hand grabbed her wrist.

"Let's go for a ride now," Blake said firmly in a low voice. "My car's right outside." He started to pull her forcibly down the hallway.

"Stop it!" she commanded in the deepest voice she could muster, but her struggles only tightened his grip.

"Don't make any noise or it'll be worse for you," he warned through clenched teeth, as he continued to maneuver her down the hall.

Suddenly a larger hand seized Blake's wrist and held it immobile as another hand clasped a fistful of hair on the back of his head.

"Let go of her." Doug's left hand was pulling Blake's head backward, causing his back to arch. Blake had no choice but to release his grasp. Vindi stepped back, breathless, rubbing her wrist.

"Hey, she's the one who came on to me, struttin' her…"

"Shut up!" Doug curled Blake's right arm behind his back, maintaining a hold on his hair as he spoke into his ear. "Hey, *Barry*…if I remember correctly, there's a restraining order forbidding you to come into this school, which means if I take you to security you'll be arrested and thrown into jail. Or maybe I'm wrong…shall we go find out? Or do you want to leave now and never come back?"

Blake did not attempt to struggle. "Fine. I'll leave."

Doug steered him several paces down the corridor. "If you'd prefer, we'll find a quiet spot outside and go head to head right now."

"I said I'll leave!" Blake snarled.

"Do that! And if you ever bother her again you'll *want* to be in jail to avoid what I'll do to you!" He shoved Blake forcefully and released him.

Blake stumbled forward, then turned around and held both middle fingers up as he backed the rest of the way to the exit door at the end of the hall. Without another word he slipped through the door, and it closed behind him with a click.

As Doug returned to Vindi, she stood stiffly in the center of the hallway and crossed her arms over her chest, looking up at him with a wary expression. Doug glared at her sternly for a few seconds, breathing heavily from the adrenaline rush.

"Is it true that *you're* the one who approached *him*?"

"Ja…yes." She cut both words off sharply, in contrast to her usual lilting speech pattern.

"Why?"

"I had a reason."

Doug waved his arms and glanced upward, then scowled down at her again. "Vindi, you've got to have more sense than that! It's great that you're friendly to everybody…but don't you know what guys think about when they look at you?" He shook his head. "Some guys aren't going to back off just because you tell them to!"

She lifted her chin and stood silently, her face passive and her eyes coolly returning his glare. After several seconds his expression changed from anger to exasperation. The corridor began to buzz with activity as chattering students clanged locker doors and headed to their classes.

"Come on…I'm walking you to algebra whether you like it or not!" He attempted to take her hand, but she pulled away from him. She started down the hall without a word and did not look at him as he strode beside her.

As they walked side by side in silence, Vindi contemplated Blake's reaction to her attempt at friendship. *I guess it's not the same after someone is grown up…and when I'm a girl.*

Later that week Ansel met her at the door as she was leaving first-period English, which was unexpected, since she usually did not see him until they arrived separately at Mr. Walford's government class.

"Vindi, are you coming to Doug's party?" He walked down the hall beside her.

"I don't know anything about that."

"Oh, well, he has one every year for his birthday since…forever…and it's going to be on Saturday. I know you don't go on dates, but this isn't a date; it'll be with the whole group, and you've got to come!"

She thought for a moment. "It sounds like fun."

"Great! I know it's not a date or anything, but if you like, I can drive you there."

"No, thanks. I will drive myself."

"Oh, okay." He paused. "Oh, and one more thing." He lowered his voice. "Your geek friends won't be invited."

She turned sharply toward him, then nodded. "Ja, sure, just the cool people...I understand." She took a breath and continued down the hall. "I guess I'm considered one of the 'favored' persons," she added thoughtfully.

"Are you kidding?" He ignored her introspection. "Will you come anyway?"

"Yes. I know I cannot change the world."

"By the way, why do you hang around with them? The geeks."

She stopped walking and looked at him. "Why should I not? They are not that different from anyone else."

He snorted. "No, they're very different...their looks, their dress, their interests..."

"Ja, you are prettier, have a more expensive haircut and fancier clothes. They are smarter and interested in things that you don't understand. So, everybody is different in some way from everybody else. They are different too, which means...there is no difference!" She chuckled at her unintended joke.

"But you have nothing in common with them!"

"Ja, I do. I used to be a...geek."

"When were you ever a geek?"

"Actually, I still am one," she almost whispered as she resumed walking.

"No, you're not," he argued. "A geek is someone who doesn't fit in, and that definitely is not you!"

"No, you only see what is on the outside of me." She glanced around the corridor as if contemplating her surroundings. "There are many ways that I do not fit in…"

Before he could reply she turned and started down the stairs as a group of students pushed their way in front of him, separating them. After leaving the stairwell Vindi continued on without waiting for him. She joined the flow of students that entered the classroom, not looking at any of them as she made her way to her desk and sat down, lost in her thoughts.

Saturday was a California perfect day, sunny and comfortably hot. The sparkling pool was the center of activity as it sprawled lazily behind a multilevel house that clung to a sloping hillside of trimmed green grass. The classic contemporary design of the structure belied its age; it was one of the few properties of its size that remained in a region that sprouted several new tightly packed housing developments every few years.

Vindi arrived late; cars were lined along the curved drive and the adjacent road. One side of the driveway was open except for a lone car; she parked behind it. As she approached the stony face of the house she could see that the inside front door was open. She stepped into the foyer, and was startled when she turned and found Ansel standing beside her.

"Ansel! What are you doing?"

"Just waiting for you." His short swim trunks and mesh shirt showed off a wiry muscular frame that had not been evident under his usual school attire. "There's a bathroom down here where you can change." He stepped into the living room, but she did not follow.

"Where is everyone else?"

"Oh, they're downstairs."

"Well, then, I'm going downstairs." She headed to the stairway. Ansel caught up with her and tried to take her bag, but she held on to it. "No, that is okay."

The stairway opened into a large recreation room as they descended. A hallway stretched in front of them, but Vindi's eyes were drawn to the large glass doors to her right that seemed to magnify the bustle of activity in the bright sunlight of the outdoor patio. Shouts and laughter sharpened their focus as she stepped through the door.

Several teens splashed in the pool. A group of boys sat and stood around tables and benches that surrounded the barbecue grill at the far end of the tiled patio.

"Vindi's here!" someone shouted, and several boys crowded around her with enthusiastic greetings, which she met with a friendly smile and brief chats.

After the fuss dissipated Vindi looked around. Doug was still standing near the grill, watching her. As she approached him he moved forward to meet her, his expression passive.

"Hi, Vindi."

"Hi, Doug. I hope you don't mind that I'm here, since you didn't invite me." She looked at him somberly, with a sudden thought that he might ask her to leave.

"Well, I would have invited you if you had let me say more than two words to you in the past three weeks." His tone was friendly, but his face serious.

She lifted her chin and gave him an innocent wide-eyed gaze. "What was stopping you?"

"Huh!" His jaw dropped in surprise, then he saw her lip twitch in a sly smirk. "Oh, you're wicked!"

"Sorry!" The amusement in her eyes matched her sarcastic tone.

Doug led Vindi to the grill area where his father and brother were arranging items, and introduced her to both of them. Dave was a year younger and had a thinner, more angular face, but the same black hair and captivating smile. Their father, a family doctor, was an older version of Doug's rugged features, with attractive streaks of gray that accentuated the dark hair around the edges of his tanned face.

Vindi greeted each of them with a cordial smile. Dr. Goodwin, who laughed frequently and seemed to be enjoying himself as much as the teenagers were shook her hand, exuding a warmth that made her feel instantly welcome and comfortable. After a brief chat Doug pointed out the cabana at the opposite end of the pool, which the girls were using as a dressing room.

Jenna, Alisse, Maggie, and Carleigh occupied a row of padded lounge chairs in front of the cabana, displaying artistic bikinis while assuming optimal positions for sunbathing. Vindi's greeting received nothing more than a brief glance of their dark sunglasses and a cool "hi," so she continued past them. When she reached the door she turned and found that Ansel was standing behind her.

"Why are you following me?"

"I'm waiting for you to get undressed so we can start having some fun." He grinned as his neatly styled auburn hair glinted in the sun. "How about I come in and help you?"

"Not so funny. Isn't that your girlfriend over there?"

"Not any more. We had a big fight yesterday, so we're not together now. I'm all yours today." He spread his arms and puffed out his chest.

"Oh, is that so? Come here." She walked past the cabana toward an empty space near the fence that crossed behind the small building, then turned to face him. "Look, we are not on a date, and I would appreciate that you give me some space here."

"Well, gee, if that's the way you feel about me..."

"Oh, don't play with me the game of the hurt puppy. If you want sympathy, try it on someone else."

He chuckled and nodded. "You're good. All right...for now. But I'll be seeing you later." He winked at her, then turned and left with a confident stride.

There was no sign of Ansel when Vindi emerged from the cabana. Her bikini was modest and plain compared to the designer suits displayed on the lounge chairs, but her reappearance was welcomed with renewed enthusiasm by Chad, Jared and Adrian, who climbed out of the pool and approached her as she walked along the water's edge.

"Hey, Vindi, do you need any swimming lessons? I'm a certified instructor."

"Don't be stupid! Of course she knows how to swim!"

"Vindi, you'd better be careful or you'll get a sunburn. Let me put some lotion on you."

"Vindi, do you know how to play Navy seal?"

Vindi stood and smiled, waiting for them to expend their efforts. "Maybe later. I would just like to enjoy the water by myself for a while, okay?" They reluctantly backed away, as she stepped lightly past them, her creamy complexion contrasting with Chad and Jared's suntans and Adrian's natural dark brown. She stopped and braced herself, then suddenly pushed Chad and Jared into the pool. As she went for Adrian he grabbed her shoulders and they fell into the water, their laughter turning into gurgles as they submerged in a shower of sunlit spray.

Vindi scuffled with the boys as they chased after her; she responded by leading them in a challenge of grabbing the opponent's ankle and pulling him under the surface. Their rowdy amusement brought others into the fray, until someone threw a beach ball into the pool, instigating a game of keep-away between impromptu teams.

As the frantic splashing continued, Vindi climbed the side ladder and strolled to the deep end. When the way was clear, she cut through the disordered ripples in a shallow dive that barely made a splash. Ignoring the chaos around her, she slid through the glistening water, savoring the caress of the cool liquid on her skin and the warm sunlight that surrounded her when she emerged.

After exiting the shallow steps, she watched Quinn and Doug stretch a low net across the pool. The game changed, and the beach ball became a volley ball. She joined the play with enthusiasm—jumping, splashing, and struggling along with her teammates for every point. She was disappointed when the boys finally took down the net and replaced the beach ball with a football.

Vindi dodged the first pass and the frenzied splashes that followed it as she and the other girls exited the water. She tried to stay with the girls, but they dispersed without acknowledging her presence, and she could think of nothing to say to any of them. She did not see a vacant chair, so she found a spot on the sun-warmed tile away from the splattering rowdiness. Breathless with exhaustion, she stretched out on her stomach, savoring the radiant sunlight that enveloped her skin and hair.

Her body warmed as it dried, and it did not take long for the rigid surface beneath her to feel hard and uncomfortable. She sat up and looked around, viewing the scene outside her cocoon of sunlit warmth with sudden unease. Boys wrestled and splashed in the pool, while the stylish girls in the lounges and chairs chatted about shopping and clothing.

*I don't belong here...I should not have come. These people have known each other for many years, and I don't really know any of them. Would it be rude to leave now?*

She stood, found her white cotton cover-up and put it on, flipping her damp hair over her shoulders. She walked toward the cabana, then stopped and scanned the grounds beyond the house and pool. Her eyes paused at a low wooden building that beckoned a welcoming white in the spotlight of the afternoon sun. She glanced around her then slipped through the low back gate, stepping lightly on her bare feet as she hurried down the warm sidewalk.

*Chapter 3*

# She wants me...she wants me not

Doug had just climbed out of the pool when he caught a glimpse of Vindi as she entered the stable door. *Aha! She figures I'll follow her. She wants to be alone with me. I knew she'd come around.*

When he entered the stable she was petting and whispering to a white mare. "Her name is Sugar," he said quietly.

She glanced at him, then returned her attention to the horse. "She is beautiful."

"Are you familiar with horses?"

"Ja. I started riding when I was five. My family would take riding holidays together."

"Would you like to go for a ride?"

"Oh, yes, absolutely!"

"Walk her on out and I'll get the saddle."

"Would you mind if I rode her without the saddle? I will be gentle."

"Sure, if you want to. Can you manage okay?"

"Ja, sure." Doug passed her a bridle which she placed over Sugar's head, murmuring to her as she adjusted it, then she walked the horse toward the door of the stable.

"There's a trail to the left. I'm coming with you, you know."

"Okay." Without another word she slid easily onto the mare's sleek back and prompted her to move forward.

By the time Doug had positioned the bridle and guided the ebony stallion out of the stable Vindi had disappeared into the tree-lined trail, and he had a momentary flash of apprehension. He knew she was safe on the property, but did not know how well she could handle the powerful animal. He also had not ridden bareback for some time, but did not want to take time to saddle his horse, so he quickly mounted Vader and pursued Vindi down the pathway.

The winding route was short and ended in a large open clearing that was hidden from the house by a thicket of trees. Vindi was waiting, and turned to Doug as he emerged from the trail.

"This is so beautiful," she said softly.

"Yes, it's always been one of my favorite places." He pointed to a cluster of large trees at the far side of the hill. "The secondary trail starts there. Do you see the faded red ribbon on that tree?"

"Ja, I see it." The white mare pranced with energy and Vindi circled her around but held her back. "Sugar wants to run...I'm going to let her go." She shifted her weight slightly and gave the horse freedom to move at her own desired pace. The mare began with a light trot, then broke into a gallop as she approached the top of the hillside.

Vindi became oblivious to Doug's presence, elated in the moment...the ride...the green surroundings...the rays of the bright afternoon sun on her warm body. Memories of a ride in a similar green meadow rushed into her head.

*A much smaller and younger Vindi with snow white braids, and a young beautiful woman with wavy yellow-blonde hair smiled at each other. They each sat upon a horse, one light brown, the other white. In front of them a man and a young boy, both with white hair, faced them atop brown horses. Then the man and boy grinned and waved, turned their horses around and galloped away, laughing.*

Doug stayed behind, impressed with Vindi's expert handling of the animal, and appreciating the spectacle of the long slender legs and flowing snowy manes of both the horse and rider. A mystical glow surrounded them as they shimmered in the sunlight. Vindi did not turn to look for him, but appeared to be caught up in her enjoyment of the ride.

"I know, boy, I feel the same," he murmured to his stallion, feeling him quiver with excitement. "We're going to hold off just a little more. Any minute now she'll stop and look back, to see if I'm playing her game. We'll make her wait for us."

Vindi arrived at the ribbon-marked tree, then passed into the trail and vanished without glancing behind her.

*Damn!* He nudged Vader and the horse galloped across the hill to the trail entrance, eager to catch up to the white mare.

After less than a minute of riding down the cool, shaded pathway, Doug heard an odd noise before him. As he neared the source, he was startled to realize that it was the sound of Vindi crying. Suddenly concerned, he prompted Vader, who bolted forward and found the pair easily.

Vindi was still atop Sugar, leaning forward into the horse's mane. Her shoulders shook with each sob, which she tried to muffle with her hands. Her hair flowed around her, hiding her face; her slender legs and bare feet hugged the animal's broad body.

"Vindi, what's wrong? What happened?"

"Nothing! I...I'm fine." She kept her face hidden. "Please...go away!"

"But..."

"Go away!"

He turned Vader around and guided him back to the meadow, where he paused. What was he supposed to do now? He slid off Vader's back and allowed him to walk around freely, while he sat on the warm grass. He was still wearing his swim trunks, now almost dry, and the tapered tips of the thick grass felt like dull needles on his bare legs.

He could no longer hear Vindi but he waited patiently, watching purple-black birds flit through the trees and soar high into the blue sky. He recalled the many times in years past he had lain on the velvety grass in this meadow, watching the clouds and birds. How long had it been since he had done that?

Suddenly he became aware of voices in the distance, and he perceived an aroma that was undoubtedly emanating from the barbecue grill. Just as he wondered how much longer he should stay away from his own party, Vindi emerged from the trail. She appeared composed and serene, and her head was bowed, allowing her hair to fall over the side of her face. She guided Sugar toward where he sat.

"I thought you would wait," she said calmly.

"Sure. Is everything okay?"

"Ja. I'm fine, thanks."

"We should get back to the party."

"Okay."

Doug whistled, and Vader trotted over and nuzzled Sugar as Doug slipped onto his back. He followed closely behind Vindi across the hill and then through the short path to the stable. He was determined not to ask her anything, but was surprised that she was silent throughout the ride. Even as they brushed down the horses she did not speak. It was not so much that he expected an explanation, but he was accustomed to being with girls who seemed compelled to fill any silence with constant chatter.

They guided the horses to their stalls. The sunlight that filtered through the windows seemed to direct an otherworldly performance of light and shadow throughout the cool dampness, which was enhanced by lingering scents of straw and tack leather.

Doug paused near the side of Vader's stall as Vindi gave Sugar a parting caress and murmured something to her in Swedish. She then stepped to Vader and did the same, after which she glanced sideways at Doug and said, "Thank you for the ride. I know it didn't look like it, but I had a great time."

"I'm glad you did. You can come over any time you want to ride. I don't even have to be here."

She looked at him directly, then suddenly smiled, as if amused at the serious expression on his face. He realized it was the first time she had smiled at him since her arrival at the school, and the sincerity it emanated aroused an instant surge of attraction toward her. His pulse broke into a sudden gallop and a flash of heat burned his face. In the surreal glow that surrounded them her expression gleamed with an innocent exuberance that erased all traces of the distress she had experienced earlier.

Doug stood motionless, trapped in her smile, suddenly uncertain about what to do next. Was this part of the game she was playing with him? Did she want him to move toward her, or did she want to play the aggressor? Why had she been crying on the trail? What was he supposed to do about that?

Vindi interrupted his confusion by turning around and moving to the door. He had no choice but to follow her out into the bright sunshine that exposed the ordinary world.

"Race you to the pool!" she challenged, as she took off running. Caught off guard, he chased after her. He could have easily caught up but he lagged behind, mesmerized by the cascade of golden sparkles that danced around her shoulders in the brilliant sunlight. When she arrived at the pool entrance Vindi passed through to the patio, then looked back and flashed a sly half-smile as she headed toward the girls' cabana.

Doug was aware that his heart was pounding and he was breathing more heavily than should be necessary after the brief run. He paused for a moment at the gate, trying to figure out what had just happened, as he watched Vindi walk away from him.

Hamburgers were being served by Dr. Goodwin and Dave. Most of the girls had already dressed into casually elegant party attire, but the boys were content to wear their swim trunks or shorts with t-shirts.

Doug exhaled vigorously and shook his head to clear it, then joined his father at the grill where a small group gathered, filling their plates.

"Sorry, Dad, I didn't mean for you to start without me."

"No problem. I was planning to do the cooking anyway, and I've been getting some help."

Jared approached with a sly grin. "Hey, Doug, I see you've been out getting some private Swedish lessons!"

"Yeah! Tell us about it! How was she?" Adrian asked.

"You guys are morons!"

They began poking and jabbing at each other and soon ended up in the pool. Others joined in, and they wrestled and splashed in a testosterone-charged display. By the time they had gotten out and back to the barbeque grill, Doug observed that Vindi already had a plate of food and was sitting on the swing next to Ansel, talking and laughing with a group of mostly boys. She was wearing khaki shorts and a silky lavender sleeveless top; her hair glimmered around her shoulders in the slanting rays of the sun.

As the afternoon brightness transformed into the golden aura of pre-twilight, the teenagers made their way through the open patio doors into the large recreation room, where the vibration of the deep bass of the music was palpable. Small groups chatted; some danced now and then. Doug's father assumed his secondary role of chaperone, chatting and jesting with the teens as he moved about and observed that drinks were not spiked, illegal substances were not in use, and couples were not engaged in improper activity.

The boys had finally changed out of their swim trunks and many were now gathered around the pool table in the adjoining room. Jenna, Alisse and Ariel competed for Doug's attention while simultaneously flirting with the other boys.

Doug leaned against the wall where he could see the pool entrance while observing the game. He watched for Vindi, and finally saw her enter and pass through the sitting area with a disinterested glance. She stopped abruptly at the billiard room. Ansel was following close behind and bumped into her. She turned and met his grin with a glare as she stepped away from him.

Quinn noticed the movement also. "Hey, Ans," he called from across the table, "what's up with you and Carleigh?"

"Oh, we had a big fight yesterday. I suppose she's around here somewhere, but I really don't care."

"Ah," Quinn nodded, as he took his shot and missed. The other three players—Doug, Adrian and Chad—took their turns. Vindi watched the game attentively as the striped and solid balls were gradually cleared from the table over several rounds. Finally the eight ball was pocketed.

"Now can I play?" asked Alisse.

"Noo," protested Jared, "wait until the guys are done, then you girls can have the table."

"You guys will be playing all night!" Alisse complained. "Just let us play one game, then we'll leave you alone for the rest of the night to play pool...*if* that's what you want to do." She looked suggestively at Doug.

The boys looked at each other, then at Doug.

"All right, one game," he consented.

"But it has to be with one guy and one girl on each team," Jared countered, "otherwise it will take forever!" The other boys voiced their agreement.

"Good idea," Doug agreed. "Who's playing?"

"I am!" said Alisse, "I'll be your partner."

"Who else?" He looked at Jenna, Ariel and Maggie, all of whom declined.

"How about Vindi?" Adrian suggested.

"Yeah, I'll take Vindi as a partner," Jared offered. "How about it, Vindi?"

"Ja, sure, I'll play!"

"Do you want to play, Ansel?" Doug asked.

"Oh, no, I'm not very good. You guys go ahead."

As Jared racked the balls, Vindi asked, "How do you decide which balls you shoot at?"

Jared explained that the first ball pocketed determined whether that team was assigned to clear the table of either the striped or solid balls. The other team had the opposite ball style, with a player shooting until he either sank the white cue ball, or failed to sink one of his designated balls into any pocket.

"So, you don't look at the numbers?" Vindi asked.

"No, except for the eight ball, which has to be the last one you pocket after all your other balls. If you pot it before that, you lose."

"Hmm, that is interesting."

"Okay, who's going to break?"

"I will!" Alisse positioned the white ball on the table and aimed her cue stick at it in the direction of the triangular cluster of balls at the other end. After several practice movements of the stick, she hit the ball energetically. It rolled forward and hit the foremost ball of the triangle, shifting and spreading the cluster negligibly.

"Good job, Alisse!" Quinn teased. She made a face at him.

"Okay, Vindi, you're up," Jared said. "You have to take the shot from where the cue ball is now."

"Ja, okay." She paused to pull her hair into a high pony tail, winding a segment around it and then tucking it underneath. She scanned the table as she chalked her cue tip, then leaned over, positioned the stick and hit the cue ball with controlled force. It rammed into the cluster of balls, scattering them in all directions, and two balls fell into separate pockets. She stood and watched the balls come to their resting places, displaying no reaction as the boys sputtered with surprise.

"Whoa! Great shot, Vindi!"

"Beginners luck!"

"You sank a stripe and a solid, so you can pick which one you want," Jared told her. "See where you have your best shot."

Vindi chalked her cue tip again as she studied the table. There was an obvious easy shot with a stripe, so they were all surprised when she selected solids and took the more difficult shot. She pocketed that ball, and as the cue ball came to rest in direct alignment for the next shot, they understood her choice. She potted the ball easily.

"I guess this game might not last very long after all." Jared observed, breaking the stunned silence.

"Let's see how she does with this one," Adrian said softly.

The only shot available was more difficult, requiring banking—or ricocheting—the cue ball off the side of the table before hitting the target ball. Vindi appeared unconcerned, concentrating on the shot. After several experimental angles of alignment she chose one and struck the cue ball gently. It rolled slowly, bounced off the springy table edge and tapped the target ball gently, causing it to slowly roll into the pocket.

The guys hooted and cheered, attracting attention from the adjoining room, and several boys and a few girls came to watch the game.

"This isn't very much fun," grumbled Alisse. No one replied.

Vindi was silent as she made her next two shots, then missed a double bank on the final solid ball.

"Wow, impressive!" Doug remarked. He pocketed three striped balls, then missed his next shot. Jared went next, sank the final solid ball, then missed his attempt to pot the eight ball.

"Oh, I'm finally going to get a turn?" Alisse whined.

"Give it your best shot," Doug encouraged. "I'm counting on you!"

"Hmf!" She shook her head and wiggled her body into position, not really paying attention to which ball she was targeting. She missed the shot, which prompted her to pout even more.

"Okay, Vindi," Jared explained, "you have to call the pocket you're going to put it in; if it sinks anywhere else, we lose. And if you sink the cue ball, we lose."

"Ja, okay." There was no direct shot and she studied the table from several angles. When she called the near corner pocket the onlookers were skeptical, and watched silently as she carefully lined up her shot then tapped the cue ball firmly. It hit the eight ball off center, causing it to bounce first off the side cushion, then the end, then roll the length of the table and drop into the designated pocket. There were shouts of amazement and approval. Vindi's only reaction was to look up with a contented smile.

"Where did you learn to play like that?" Jared asked.

"Oh, I used to live in a pool hall," she answered nonchalantly. Everyone laughed.

Doug asked, "What I want to know is, why did you act like you didn't know how to play? Why put us on like that?"

"We play a different game in Sweden. I have never seen this game before."

"How do you play in Sweden?" asked Quinn.

"Well, the game we usually play is called 'rotation' or 'fifteen-ball,' where you shoot the balls in sequence, by the numbers. You keep score by the total of the balls you sink."

"Can you clear the table?" asked Jared.

"I have done it...but it is pretty difficult."

"Show us!"

"No, not now. Let's play another game your way...I would like to try it again."

New teams were chosen—Vindi and Quinn against Adrian and Chad. Doug resumed his position against the far wall and watched, while endeavoring to be attentive to Jenna, Alisse and Ariel at the same time. Except for Maggie, the other girls left, those with boyfriends dragging them to the sitting area of the party room. The unattached boys stayed to observe Vindi's surprising expertise.

Vindi offered to play last, which was accepted. As Chad racked the balls, Ansel, who had been observing the game from the opposite end of the table from Doug, approached Vindi and murmured something into her ear.

"Stop that!" Vindi scolded.

"What?" Ansel asked innocently.

"You know what! Use your brain."

"Yeah, Ansel, instead of your…"

"Quack!" Quinn made a garbled sound of a duck. The girls giggled.

The game was competitive but congenial, and a friendly banter arose. Vindi participated in passing humorous jabs back and forth, while keeping her focus on the table.

"Vindi, do you believe in love at first sight?" Adrian asked.

"No."

"Okay, then I'll leave and then come back so you can see me again."

"That is funny. Do you know what would be even better?"

"What?"

"You could leave and not come back."

The boys laughed boisterously; her only reaction was a sly smile as she lined up her next shot.

"I might do that, just so you'll miss me," Adrian jested, undaunted. "You know, absence makes the heart grow fonder."

Jared countered, "Yeah, except in your case it would be out of sight, out of mind."

After Quinn made a difficult shot, Maggie gave him a kiss, and he prolonged it.

"Hey," said Jared, "this is a PDA-free zone."

"What is PDA?" asked Vindi.

"Public display of affection," answered Jared.

"Or in this case, public display of assholeism," quipped Chad.

"Well, if that is the case, then there are a few people here who should leave," Vindi jested with a half-smile, eliciting laughter.

"Whoa! Watch out for Vindi." Chad warned. "When she hits a pool table she shows her true colors."

"What does that mean…true colors?" Vindi asked.

"How mean you are," Doug explained.

"Oh, you mean I hurt the sensitive male egos?" She looked across the table at Doug with one corner of her mouth upturned.

He returned her gaze with a smirk. "Some of them, maybe."

She scanned the group. "Well, then, gird your loins, men. Vikings show mercy to no one."

The boys sputtered with laughter, as she nonchalantly chalked her cue tip.

"What did she just say?"

"She said to gird your loins!"

As Vindi watched Adrian plan a shot, Doug noted that she appeared as relaxed and happy at the pool table as she had during her ride across the meadow. She was obviously having fun bantering with the guys, but her wit was droll rather than flirtatious. Between turns at the table her casual stance and relaxed grip on the pool cue mirrored that of the boys. *Ah, I get it! She looks like a beauty queen, but she's a tomboy! Huh!*

Doug also noticed that Ansel had been standing nearby, quietly observing the activities, and called out to him, "Hey, Ans, do you want to get in on the next game?"

"No, thanks. Vindi's too good for me."

"It's about time you learned that!" Vindi suddenly giggled and shook her head, causing her hair to tumble down around her shoulders.

"Touché!" quipped Doug, as the other boys hooted.

"Ow! That hurt!" Ansel pretended to be struck in the chest with an imaginary knife.

"Gird your loins!" Quinn advised.

Vindi broke into laughter as she twisted her hair behind her head. It immediately fell loosely around her neck and face when she leaned forward to shoot at the cue ball. She initially appeared to have some difficulty in setting the angle, then adjusted her position and made the shot.

As she walked around the table to line up her next shot she stopped momentarily and blinked her eyes. Ansel was instantly at her side, and said something to her that Doug could not hear. She shook her head briefly, then leaned forward and tapped the cue ball too quickly, causing it to spin at an angle and completely miss the target ball.

"Uh-oh, we're wearing her down," Chad observed, as he approached for his turn.

Vindi stepped away from the table and leaned against the narrow wall between the patio doors. Ansel followed and stood in front of her with his back to Doug, who watched and listened, but could not hear any conversation between them. Ansel took Vindi's hand as they walked toward the sitting area; he then wrapped his arm around her as they continued across the room and disappeared around the corner that led down the hallway to the bedrooms.

*Chapter 4*

# A damsel in distress needs a chivalrous knight...or two

Quinn was preparing to shoot, and Doug bumped the end of his cue stick as he rushed to the hallway. This behavior was out of character for Vindi, and he had no reason to trust Ansel.

Doug arrived at the bedroom just as Ansel was closing the door, and he thrust his way in forcefully. "Vindi, are you all right?" She blinked at him through glazed eyes; Ansel was practically holding her upright. "What did you give her?"

"Nothing! She just told me she was dizzy so I was helping her in here to lie down!"

"And why did you 'just happen' to be hovering over her when she 'just happened' to get dizzy?" Doug stood in front of Ansel and scowled down at him from inches away. Ansel glared back, displaying no hint of intimidation.

"What? Like it's so suspicious that I would hang around Vindi and try to get her to pay some attention to me?

The question is, why are you watching her when you have three girls after you already? Or were they just getting in the way of your plan?"

As they argued, Vindi pulled herself away from Ansel, curled up on the bed, and closed her eyes.

Doug's father burst into the room. "What's going on?"

"I think Ansel slipped Vindi a rufie!"

"Ha! If anyone gave her anything it was you!"

Dr. Goodwin rushed to the bed and turned Vindi to her back as he called her name. She did not respond, but appeared to be in a deep sleep. He evaluated her breathing and pulse, lifted her eyelids and examined her pupils, then darted out of the room.

Doug and Ansel continued their face-to-face confrontation.

"Sorry I spoiled your plans, Doug," Ansel sneered. Doug grabbed Ansel's shirt front with one hand; with the other he grabbed his wrist and rotated his arm inward, backing him toward the door in obvious pain.

"Get out of here now before I throw you out!" He spun him around and gave him a shove.

Ansel stumbled into the hallway, where a group of students had gathered. Carleigh was among them; he grabbed her hand and pulled her toward the loud music. "Come on, let's dance!"

Dr. Goodwin reappeared in the hallway with his medical bag, shooed the curious teens away from the area, and returned to Vindi's bedside. He performed a more thorough examination, measured her blood pressure and pulse rate, and placed a portable oxygen saturation monitor on her fingertip. He made another attempt to rouse her; she opened her eyes momentarily, then mumbled something and dozed off again.

Doug's brother Dave entered the room carrying an iced drink in a glass. "Here's the soda Vindi was drinking."

Dr. Goodwin sniffed the drink, then set it aside. "If this is the only one that was spiked, she didn't drink much. It must have hit her fast, but she'll sleep it off." He looked at Doug. "Any idea who did this?"

"It had to be Ansel. He was hanging around her for the past hour, and brought her in here."

His father looked distressed. "I'd better call her parents. Do you have your phone?"

"Yes, but I don't have her number."

"What? That's not like you."

"She hasn't given her phone number to anyone, as far as I know.

"Maybe there's a listing on the web."

"I haven't found one," Doug admitted.

"Do you know where she lives?"

"No, and I don't know that anyone else does either."

"She hasn't dated anyone?"

"Not that I've heard, and I'm pretty sure she drove herself here today."

"Hmm. Maybe she has her driver's license on her." Doctor Goodwin carefully checked the pockets of Vindi's shorts. In a back pocket he found a laminated card which was the correct size, but with no resemblance to a California license or identification card. There was a photo of Vindi's face, her name, and two separate sequences of numbers, neither one of which contained the appropriate digits for a telephone number. He handed it to Doug. "What do you think this is?"

After examining it briefly, Doug ran his fingers over the card, noting that it felt thick. He discovered that there was something that looked like a flat black computer chip adhered to the back. Squinting at it directly under the bedside lamp he could see a narrow protrusion on one end that appeared to be in a small slot. With a fingernail he slid the tab across the slot; there was a momentary vibration, then nothing more.

"I have no idea what this is, but it isn't going to help us. He placed the card on the night stand next to the lamp.

Just then Jenna peeked into the doorway and whispered loudly, "Doug? What's going on?"

Both Doug and his father directed her, and the inquisitive onlookers behind her, to return to the party room. Jenna looked relieved to see that Doug was not alone with Vindi, and as she turned to leave she gave him a wink and mouthed, "Later."

Dr. Goodwin followed the students, turned down the music, and called for their attention. "I know you are all curious about what is going on, and I'm very sorry to report that it appears that one of your classmates has been given a drug, most likely in her drink."

There was a murmur throughout the room, and he waited patiently for it to subside.

"For the safety of all of you, I would like you to observe each other and yourselves. Please report to others around you if you experience any feelings of dizziness, blurred vision or sleepiness. If you see anyone who appears impaired, please observe them. You girls especially are at risk, because this type of drug can cause you to engage in activity that you may not consent to under normal circumstances." He was interrupted by nervous laughter, which died out swiftly.

"I sincerely apologize that this has occurred in my home. Once I know that the young lady down the hall is taken care of, I will be available to assist any of you who need it."

Dr. Goodwin returned to the bedroom and checked Vindi's status again, finding her to be in a deep sleep but in no danger. "She should have a cell phone where we can possibly find her home number. We need to find her purse." He nodded at Dave, who left the room. "If we can't find anything, I'm sure the police will be able to find her parents."

"The police!" Doug exclaimed.

"Yes, we have to report this incident. Do you have any proof that Ansel spiked the drink?"

"No, I didn't see anyone give her a drink. He says he just happened to be there and was helping her in here to lie down because she was dizzy."

"Is it reasonable that he is telling the truth?"

"Well, I suppose so. It's just that he was hanging around her constantly the whole time we were playing pool."

"Is that so unusual?"

"Well, no…he's been after her since day one."

"Then we have no idea who did it."

"I'm sure he'll tell the police I was the one who did it. How can I prove I didn't?"

They stood discussing the situation. Within a few minutes Dave reappeared with Vindi's cloth bag. "It looks like Vindi had no purse with her, just this." He handed it to his father, who sifted through its contents: a hairbrush…cosmetic bag…ah, a phone.

"Her home number should be in here," he said, retrieving the object. "Hmm, what is this?" he turned it over and over, then handed it to Doug. "Have you seen one of these?"

Doug studied it from all angles. "It looks like a flip phone but I don't see any way to open it. I have no clue." They looked at Vindi with bewilderment; she was motionless as she slept.

On the adjacent street a black van stopped abruptly. Inside the cargo area a large man dressed in black clothing and a heavy black cap studied a computer screen which displayed white blips that represented heat signatures inside the house. Most of them were clustered in the main room. Another four blinked in a smaller group down the hallway; adjacent to them flashed a single red dot.

He looked up, tapped the tiny object in his ear, and signaled two men next to him who were similarly outfitted. The three of them pulled their black hoods down over their faces, leaving only their eyes exposed, and then silently jumped from the van into the dark night, carrying assault rifles at their sides. In the front seat the van's driver observed their progress on his own computer screen, murmuring into his headset.

One man veered toward the side of the house, while the other two ran through the front yard with their heads low, ducking beside bushes near the front door. They could see through the glass outer door that the heavy inner door was wide open. The beat of muffled music could be heard from inside.

The lone figure in black ran carefully down the sloped side yard to the lower level where the pool glistened in the lights of the patio. He concealed himself behind a row of shrubbery where he could see into the recreation room. He peered into the house through a small telescoping instrument placed in front of one eye, then spoke softly into his microphone, "Looks like a teenage beer party. Charlie five."

In the front of the house the leader stood upright and removed his hood, revealing straight white blond hair and a grim expression on his rugged but youthful face. The long-sleeved nylon shirt hugged his muscled chest, and followed the taper of his torso. His black pants were slightly looser over his equally muscular legs. Several dark objects were clipped to the belt at his slim waist, the most conspicuous being a large black pistol in a holster.

He passed his rifle to his partner who remained hidden and masked, confirmed the pistol's readiness, then returned it to his belt. He adjusted the small object in his left ear, and nodded. After running his hand once through his hair, he gestured to his partner who ran, crouched, to the side of the front door, flattening himself into the shadows with one rifle in his hand and the other slung over his shoulder.

The blond man glanced alternately at the house and the small electronic display of white blinking lights he now held in his palm. Satisfied, he reattached the device to his belt opposite the pistol, moved forward, and eased himself inside the front door without a sound.

The entrance foyer stretched out in front of him; music and voices were audible from below. As he descended the stairway he paused and viewed the recreation area, where teens milled about in small groups. He then continued down the hallway, appearing nonchalant as he constantly scanned the areas around him.

He halted just before arriving at the bedroom doorway, from which he could hear men's voices. Leaning forward slightly, he could see reflections in the dresser mirror of Dr. Goodwin, Doug and Dave. With a shift of his position, he observed Vindi lying on the bed.

He stepped in front of the doorway while remaining in the hall, his right hand poised lightly over his pistol. His voice was quiet but authoritative. "I am Vindi's brother. What is wrong with Vindi?"

They gaped in surprise at the large muscular body that filled the doorway. Dr. Goodwin stepped forward. "Oh,

I'm glad you're here! We were trying to find a number to call your parents. I'm Don Goodwin. Your name is…?"

"Sven Johansson. What is going on here?" He scanned the surroundings and the three of them as he stepped into the room.

"I believe someone slipped a drug into Vindi's drink." Dr. Goodwin explained.

Sven brushed past them and leaned over Vindi, lifted her eyelids and peered into her eyes, then felt the carotid pulse at her neck.

Dr. Goodwin stood beside him, watching. "I'm a doctor, and I just checked her out. She appears fine. At this point she just needs to sleep it off."

"Where is the drink?"

"On the night stand beside you. I suspect it is either rohypnol or GHB. She drank less than half of it, so I don't think she ingested much."

"If that is all she had," Sven muttered. He picked up the drink and sniffed it, then poured a few drops onto his palm and tasted it with the tip of his tongue. "Get me a container to put this in…please." Dave nodded to his father and left the room. Sven returned his attention to Vindi.

He shook Vindi's shoulders gently and quietly called her name. She moved her head from side to side and let out a small sigh, but did not wake. Sven watched her breathe for a moment, then stood and turned. The concern on his face had been replaced by anger.

"Who did this?" He glared alternately at Doug and his father, standing half a head taller than each of them.

Doug spoke. "I'm not sure…I saw a guy bring her in here, but he claims she told him she was dizzy and he was just helping her."

"Where is he? What is his name?" At Doug's hesitation, Sven grabbed the front of his shirt. He looked down at Doug and growled the words slowly, inches from his face. "Where…is…he?"

Dr. Goodwin leapt forward, putting his hand lightly on Sven's wrist, knowing that applying more force would do nothing to break his grip. "Please…"

"No one was alone with her!" Doug said rapidly, standing his ground but holding his hands upward and palms forward in a gesture of surrender. "I followed them in here immediately, and Vindi was still awake. Ansel claimed he brought her here to lie down…so I don't know for sure whether he was the one who spiked her drink, but I threw him out, and my father has been here with her since then."

All three stood motionless for several seconds while Sven's glare bored into Doug's eyes. Neither blinked. Then Sven's facial muscles relaxed. He released his grip as Dave returned with an empty water bottle, which Sven accepted. He poured the fluid from the drink into the small opening without spilling a drop.

As he set the empty glass back onto the night stand he stealthily picked up and pocketed Vindi's driver's license, and softly said something that Doug thought sounded like "twenty-two" to no one in particular. He capped the bottle and slipped it into a mesh pocket at his left thigh, then turned back to Vindi. As he made a motion to lift her, Doug leapt forward and grabbed his arm.

"Wait a minute! We don't even know for sure who you are...or why you're even here! You're not taking her anywhere!"

"That's right," Dr. Goodwin agreed, "we haven't called anyone yet to come get her."

Sven paused. Then he stood and stepped back from the bed.

"Wake her," he demanded. At their hesitation, he repeated it impatiently, and they both understood.

Doug sat on the bed next to Vindi, and gently shook her shoulder while calling her name. She stirred several times but did not waken, and he continued with more urgency in his voice, not letting her drift back into deep sleep.

"Vindi, wake up...Vindi!"

She finally opened her eyes, looked drowsily at Doug, then gave him a silly smile.

"Vindi." Though he spoke softly, Sven's voice resonated in the room.

"Sven!" Vindi tried to sit up, then grasped her forehead and sank back onto the pillow. "Ooh, my head!"

Doug moved away, and Sven took his place, sitting on the edge of the bed, looking like a giant next to her slender frame. He held Vindi's dainty hand in his oversized one.

"Take it easy...you're going to be okay," he murmured softly. He smoothed her hair, which was tousled around her head and shoulders.

Vindi suddenly looked anxiously into Sven's face and gripped his hand tightly in both of hers. "Sven...don't leave me..." the last word faded to a whisper as she drifted back into a deep sleep.

Sven whispered something into his microphone again, as Dr. Goodwin approached him. "I was planning to call the police to file a report about this."

"That will not be necessary. I will take care of it." Sven rose and strode down the hallway to the party room, where the activities continued in a subdued manner. He scanned the area, observing teenagers playing pool, couples dancing, others talking and laughing. He crossed the room and turned off the music.

All eyes turned to him, stunned and alarmed by the imposing figure in black and the bulge of the pistol at his side. Despite his angry scowl, the girls were impressed by the youthful handsome face, pale blue eyes, disheveled blond hair and athletic physique; some of them murmured to each other.

"Pay attention!" he ordered, and all were instantly silent. "I am Vindi's brother...and what took place here tonight is...unacceptable!" he spoke slowly, enunciating the words carefully in his heavy accent. "Every one of you boys better think twice before you approach Vindi in the future. You will not see me...but...I will be watching you!" He glared at the male faces around the room as he spoke. The group remained still and silent, staring at him with emotions ranging from fear to admiration.

"Where is Ansel?" Sven glared around the room. Several fingers pointed him out, as he shrank back into the pillowed sofa. Sven pierced him with his gaze as he rapidly pulled a dark object from the left side of his belt and aimed it at Ansel. Every person in the room gasped and froze simultaneously; then gradually realized the object was not a pistol but an electronic device, apparently making a recording, with a pale blue glow emanating from the lens. He then rapidly scanned the rest of the group with the unit before anyone could react. As he returned the gadget to his belt clip Sven pointed at Ansel with his opposite index finger for several seconds, then snarled, "I will definitely be watching you!"

Sven withdrew down the hallway; almost immediately voices began to whisper, then rise in volume. They silenced again when Sven reappeared with Vindi in his arms. He proceeded up the stairway behind Dr. Goodwin; Doug and Dave followed behind.

Moments later Dr. Goodwin returned down the stairs. With Dave's assistance, he directed the girls to move upstairs to the living room to be checked out, instructing the boys to remain in the lower level.

Doug did not return downstairs, but quietly slipped into the library adjacent to the foyer and closed the door. Leaving the room darkened, he watched out the window as Sven, carrying Vindi, crossed the front lawn and disappeared into the shadows.

In the scattered glow cast by the home's decorative lighting, Doug observed a man, and then a second, follow Sven's route. They were dressed all in black and crouched forward as they ran with assault rifles carried loosely at their sides; one of them carried a rifle in each hand. A moment later one returned from the shadows, this time without the rifle or hood; he walked casually to a recent model Volvo hatchback, opened it with a remote control key, slid into the seat and drove away.

## Chapter 5

# Is it a scheme to not have a scheme?

On Monday morning Doug was waiting in the school parking lot when Vindi arrived, and approached her as she closed her car door. As he had suspected, it was the Volvo he had seen the man in black drive away from his house on Saturday.

"Vindi, how are you? Are you okay?"

"Oh, hi Doug." She smiled but took a small step backward, leaning against her car. "Ja, I am fine."

"I wanted to call you yesterday, but no one has your number." He stopped several feet in front of her, conscious of her apparent uneasiness as he advanced toward her. "I'm really, really sorry about what happened...and that it happened at my house. I can't believe anyone would do that! Do you remember anything?"

"The last thing I remember was playing pool...but Sven told me what happened. Do you know who did it?"

"Not for sure. Do you remember where you got the drink? Did someone give it to you?"

"Sven asked me the same thing. I cannot remember anything about it."

"I suspect Ansel because he was right there. He denies it, of course, and I'm sure he'll accuse me if anyone questions him, because I confronted him and interrupted his plans. I can't believe he would...that's the *lowest*...most...*despicable* thing a guy could do," he spat out the words in disgust, "...to take advantage of a girl who is defenseless. I never would have expected that from any of my friends...but obviously, I was wrong." He wanted to touch her shoulder, to emphasize his desire to protect her, but sensing her discomfort, he did not move closer. "I want you to know that no one was alone with you while you were drugged. When I saw Ansel leading you to the bedroom I was right there. You went to sleep while we were arguing."

"Then what happened?"

Doug told her about the confrontation with Ansel, his father's involvement in providing medical attention, and their effort to find her telephone number to call her parents, not mentioning the items they found in her pocket and bag.

Vindi listened with interest. "Thanks, Doug, and please thank your father for me." She took a step forward, preparing to walk toward the school.

Doug did not move out of her way. "Wait...may I ask you something?"

She paused. "Ja?"

"Ever since we met, you act like you're mad at me for something I did. Or maybe there's something you don't like about me." He studied her eyes, his expression somber.

She straightened her spine and lifted her chin as she gazed at him. "Yes, I have been avoiding you."

"Why?"

She hesitated. "When we first met...your manner..." Her eyes shifted away from his as she contemplated. "I guess it would not bother me..." She looked at the ground as she thought. "No, I think it's just that certain things about you...remind me of someone else." She lifted her face and glanced at him, then lowered her eyes. "Someone that I...had a bad experience with. I'm sorry. It's not your fault."

"Will you tell me about it?" he asked softly.

"I don't know."

"I'm really sorry."

"For what?"

"That something bad happened to you...and that I remind you of it. I don't want you to be uncomfortable with me."

She looked at him with surprise.

"What class do you have now?" he asked.

"English."

"You can skip it this once, can't you?"

She shrugged. "I suppose so."

"Can we talk now? I'd really like to know what it is about me that bothers you."

She looked thoughtful. "Well...ja, okay."

They strolled away from the school toward the athletic track, where a class was congregating at the far end. When they reached the bleachers they climbed to the third row. Doug noted that she left sufficient space for two people between them.

Vindi sat facing forward. She turned her face toward Doug but gazed into the distance in front of him as she spoke, her expression somber. "He was like you...popular, good looking...only blond." She said it with indifference, without coyness or embarrassment at flattering him. "His name was Olof. We met in the summer, at a riding camp, and then discovered we went to the same school. I was fifteen, and was used to having boyfriends, but had never been on an actual date. He was seventeen, and was a star on the football team, which is what we call soccer. He went out with a lot of different girls, and everyone liked him. I was proud that he paid attention to me at school, and one day he walked me home."

*The young Vindi and the honey-haired teen in the dark green shirt stepped onto the front porch of a narrow two-story house. Vindi unlocked the door and they slipped inside, closing it behind them.*

*Then Vindi and the boy were on the sofa. He kissed her lightly, then more passionately as he pressed himself toward her. She pulled back, pushing her hands against his chest.*

*"Don't stop me," he murmured into her ear. She continued to struggle.*

*"Stop..."*

*"Don't you love me?"*

*"Ja, but..."*

*"Then come on..."* he whispered, pushing her back against the sofa. He took a deep breath and moaned, *"I want you so much..."*

She pushed against him more forcefully, but he grabbed her wrist and continued pressing against her, kissing her neck.

*"Oh, Vindi,"* he breathed into her ear, *"if you love me you won't stop me."*

*"Stop it!"* she yelled, struggling more vigorously, hysterically writhing with her entire body under his weight.

Suddenly he was lifted off of her. His surprised face was looking up at Sven, who held him by the back of his hair, with his neck abnormally extended. Without a word, Sven thrust the heel of his large open hand into the center of the boy's face, simultaneously releasing his grip.

Olof sailed across the room with a howl of pain, rolling when he hit the floor. His nose bled profusely as he attempted to rise. Sven pulled him up by his hair, leaning over him and glaring into his eyes. *"If you ever come near her again, I will come after you and finish the job."* He dragged him to the door and flung him out with one arm. After locking the door he rushed to Vindi, who was watching through tears that flowed down her face.

Sven sat down next to her and she leaned against his chest, her shoulders shaking with sobs as he held her.

Doug's face was stony. "What a...*scumbag*," he whispered. He looked at Vindi with concern as she stared into the distance. They were both silent for a moment, then Vindi spoke softly and slowly.

"I didn't even know Sven was in the house...he was supposed to be at university. My parents were away on a trip. I was supposed to go to the neighbor's house after school, but I had a key and Olof talked me into taking him inside. I was stupid, and didn't know guys were like that. I didn't expect him to be so...if Sven had not been there..." she paused, and took a deep breath.

"Did he ever bother you after that?"

"No. I never saw him again. But I never went back to that school either."

"Why?"

Vindi hesitated, studying her hands that rested on the computer case in her lap. She then gazed into the distance in front of her. "That entire day was abnormal. After I calmed down, Sven told me he was there because...our parents...had been in an accident. He had to tell me...that they had both been killed." Her words became almost inaudible.

"Oh, no...I'm so sorry," Doug whispered.

"After that my life completely changed," she said quickly, as if trying to push away the memory of that day. "I went to live with my aunt, and went to a different school..."

Doug waited silently as she stared ahead at nothing in particular. After a few moments she took a deep breath. "I think about them a lot, and sometimes I'll be doing something that reminds me of things we did together. I have so many happy memories of them. I thought we were a perfect family."

"Is that what happened when we were riding? You were thinking about them?"

"Yes." She was composed now.

"That must have been just a couple of years ago."

"No, it was last year, right after school started, in September."

"How old are you now?"

"Seventeen. My birthday was last month."

"You mean your parents…had that happen to them…in the same month as your birthday?"

"Ja, eight days before. Obviously, it was a pretty bad birthday, you know."

"That's terrible. Was your birthday better this year?"

"Not really. I just ignored it. I really don't care too much about birthdays anymore."

They were silent for a moment, then Doug spoke softly, without emotion. "My mother died when I was eleven, about seven years ago. I know some of what you're going through, and all I can tell you is that the memories do get easier over time. In fact, I've been with just my father and brother for so many years that sometimes I have trouble remembering what it was like when she was there."

After another silence, Vindi looked at him. "Do you have any sisters?"

"No."

"Maybe that is why you pursue a lot of different girls."

*"What?"*

"Oh, I'm sorry. I didn't mean to offend you."

"What do you mean?"

"Well, since you grew up without a mother or any other female in your life…"

"You mean that I don't trust women…that I'm afraid they'll leave me like she did."

"No, I was not thinking that. It's just that I have known some guys who had that kind of situation, and they would be with one girl after another, but none for very long. I figured it was because they never experienced a relationship with the female…psyche," she struggled to find an appropriate word, "…so they related to girls superficially, and saw them as objects more than as people."

"Hmm. I don't know. I never thought about that."

"I'm sorry…I just blurted that out without thinking. I'm not trying to be judgmental or analyze you or anything."

"That's okay, I don't mind. And you have an interesting observation."

She was silent.

"Do you have any sisters?" he questioned.

"No, just Sven."

"So…if I can make an observation. You don't seem to relate to girls very well. Is that because of lack of female influence, do you think?"

She pondered for a moment. "I don't think so…it has not been that long. My mother and I were very close, and I had girlfriends when I was growing up…but my best friend was a boy."

"Oh, really?"

"Ja. And in the past year, with the changes in my life, I have spent a lot more time with boys than with any girls."

"What happened?"

She hesitated. "It...just worked out that way."

Her face became troubled, so he kept the conversation casual. "You do appear to be comfortable with boys...like when we were playing pool. You seemed so happy and natural just playing and back-talking with everyone. And sometimes the way you talk to guys...it's like you know what they're thinking."

"That is usually pretty easy," she looked at him with a sly smile.

His expression was serious. "Maybe for you. But most girls don't seem to. They like the flirting and flattery...and most of them seem to believe the lines. What I mean is..."

She snickered. "I know what you mean. Don't worry, I won't tell anyone." He laughed with her, then she became serious. "I do feel more comfortable with boys than with girls, as long as they act civilized, and control their...primitive urges."

"I can understand that." He gazed at her with a sudden insight, glimpsing for a moment the person behind the sensual beauty, who sought friendships but was forced to deal with the undesired lustful pursuit that her outward appearance generated.

Doug shifted his position, being careful not to edge closer to her. "And I remind you of Olof...and what happened with him...so you've been avoiding me."

"Ja."

"I'm really sorry that I make you think of him. I know I'm a jerk sometimes." She flashed a smile. "But I've never tried to coax a girl into doing something she didn't want to. And I would never force myself on a girl. That's *despicable*." He reached his hand out to touch her arm, then left it hanging in the air. "If anyone ever bothers you, just let me know. I'll take care of him."

"Thanks. You have done that already...two times now." Her hands remained in her lap, with her fingertips on the edge of her computer case.

"Is there anything in particular I do that bothers you?"

She thought for a moment. "No, I don't think so...it was just the memory. I can handle your lines, and your being a jerk." She smiled.

"Gee, thanks." He turned to face her and stretched out his arm to lean on the seat above him, relaxing his body. "Is your experience with Olof the reason you don't date?"

"Partly. I cannot stand the thought of a guy pushing himself against me, or breathing heavy next to my face. But I have also had a lot of changes in my life in the past year, and I feel like...I'm trying to figure out...who I am."

"Yeah, I get that." He paused. "But going out with a guy doesn't mean you have to become a couple. What about just doing something you like, just for fun?"

"I don't need a guy with me to do that."

"No, but if you were friends with a guy...and you liked being together as friends...that could make it fun, couldn't it?"

"Right, that is what girls usually think. But tell me this...how often does a guy go out with a girl because he wants to talk to her as friends?"

Now he smiled. "So it gets back to that...what guys really want."

"You tell me."

"You're looking at it from the guy's point of view. You know too much about guys."

"Perhaps."

Not yet willing to drop the subject, he continued, as if discussing the conditions of a business negotiation. "So, you might like to do something fun...with a guy who was your friend...if there were other people around and you didn't have the one-on-one issue."

She looked thoughtful, then nodded slightly. "Ja...maybe."

"Okay."

Doug checked the time on his phone. Several minutes remained until the end of the class period. Vindi looked away, which baffled him. She rested her feet on the seat in front of her and leaned forward, placing her elbows on her thighs. She cupped her chin in her hands and watched a small bird hop among the grass, as if she had forgotten that Doug was sitting next to her.

Doug could not believe it. Any other girl would be gazing into his eyes, smiling and flirting...doing anything to keep his attention on her, especially after a subtle offer of an outing with him. Annoyed, he blurted out what had been puzzling him since the party.

"I'm pretty sure that no one else saw the SWAT team that picked you up on Saturday."

Vindi sat upright, slowly turning to look at him. "What do you mean? What is a SWAT team?"

"The guys in black that were with your…brother."

"Guys in black? Sven told me a friend from work went with him to drive my car home."

"Yeah, from work." He paused. "How did he know to arrive at just that moment?"

"He said he followed the signal from my driver's license. Someone must have set it off."

Doug suspected she was referring to the vibration he had felt when he moved the tab on the back of the strange identification card. "Why do you have a driver's license like that?"

"Like what?"

Was she playing with him? "Your license is not a normal one. It doesn't have your address or any information about you…only a photo and that computer chip on the back that gives off a signal when you activate it."

"Oh." She suddenly became guarded. "Well, I guess it's because we are from overseas…I don't know any other reason for it to be different."

"What kind of work does your brother do?"

She shrugged. "He works for a security company."

"Doing what?"

"I don't know exactly. I know at university he designed some electronic gadgets, and he went through some kind of special training. But he never talks about his work with me."

"You know, there's a rumor going around that he's not your brother."

"What rumor?"

"It's being spread around by some that were at the party Saturday. They think he's your husband."

"My husband! Why would anyone say that?"

"Well...mainly because you won't go out with any of the guys. You know how we are...if a beautiful girl doesn't buy our lines there has to be a reason." His sudden grin elicited a brief smile from her. "Also, the way he came after you and carried you out of the house...and the way he threatened all the guys there."

"What? He didn't tell me that part...what did he say?" Doug told her what he had heard from his friends who had been in the sitting area when Sven confronted them.

Vindi huffed. "Ja, that sounds like him for sure."

"Well, if the guys stay away from you today, you'll know why."

"I guess so." She consulted the time on her phone. Doug noted it was not the gadget they had found in her bag, but a typical mobile unit. "We should be going."

"Yeah...oh, I almost forgot. I have your swimsuit in the car. You left it in the cabana."

"Oh, thanks. I'll get it later." They started toward the main building of the school.

"I didn't find any hidden wires in it…your swimsuit," Doug said.

She gave him a puzzled look. "What does that mean?"

"Nothing…just a joke." He then stopped and faced her. "Listen…I don't spread gossip and won't mention to anybody what we talked about. And if there's anything else you want to tell me…if I can do anything to help you…well, I'm here for you anytime."

"Okay…thanks." She looked bewildered.

Inside the school they separated as they joined the mix of students crowding the halls in a procession to their next class. Doug walked alone, deep in thought.

*How stupid am I to think she might be an undercover agent working on some secret mission at the school? And if she is, why would she admit it to me?*

*But why a SWAT team when her ID card signaled? Could it be that Sven works for a secret government agency, and thought an international enemy was kidnapping his sister—or his wife—to get at some important bigwig?*

*Or maybe he's just a Swedish engineer who looks like a lumberjack, has a secret job with a well-equipped security firm, and is protective of his sister.*

*Maybe she's a real teenager, working her way through traumatic events in her life, and honestly knows nothing about agents with rifles who escorted her home Saturday night.*

*Maybe someday she'll go out with me.*

"What do you think of Vindi?" Doug asked Quinn several days later, as they waited for the girls in the cafeteria.

"Are you kidding? She's gorgeous! I wish I had a chance with her!"

"Apart from that. Does she seem like a...regular teenager...to you?"

"What else would she be?"

"Just think about it...the way she behaves and...associates with people. Does anything seem out of place?" Doug pressed.

"She seems to have her shit together more than a lot of other people do," Quinn answered thoughtfully. "And she sure knows how to handle guys, and put us in our place...but I suppose that comes with the territory of being a gorgeous babe. Other than that, yeah, she seems like a regular teenager. You know," he snickered, "I once heard her tell someone that in Sweden she was 'nothing special...just another blonde girl.'"

"If that's the case, then I've got to go to Sweden." Doug grinned.

"I'm with you. By the way, what was that exit you two took from the party Saturday?"

"Oh, we went horseback riding."

"Did you score?"

"No." Doug shook his head.

"But at least she's not avoiding you any more, right? She's been eating lunch with us this week, and walking with you to algebra."

"Yeah, we had a talk Monday morning and worked that out. You know, I can't believe her! Sometimes we talk on the way to class, but other times she walks beside me without saying anything. I asked her why she does that and do you know what she said?"

"What?"

"She says, 'Why waste time talking about something that neither of us is interested in?'"

"Wow, I like the way that girl thinks!"

"Yeah, but she doesn't want to date because she thinks all guys scheme to go out with girls just for sex."

"And...you're saying we don't?" Quinn looked serious.

"Well, I guess it's always there, at least subconsciously. But maybe it doesn't have to be that way."

"You can say that because it's always been so easy for you...girls come after you!"

"Well, maybe...but I'd still like to think that we're not totally ruled by our sex drive."

"Yeah, let me know when you figure that one out." He grinned, but Doug did not share his amusement. "So what's your strategy now?" Quinn questioned.

"Well, she's too smart and experienced for the usual approach, so I'm going to play it passive...be a friend to her, and let her take the lead. I'm not going to ask her out or chase after her...that's what she expects from guys."

"And then eventually she'll realize that she can't resist you, and she'll come after you."

Doug smiled. "Exactly."

"Good luck with that."

His plan was in operation for less than three weeks when it was suddenly thwarted by a hoodlum on a motorcycle.

## Chapter 6

# What's a game without a little competition?

It was a Tuesday afternoon, and algebra class had barely started when it was interrupted by the loud rumble of motorcycle engines outside the windows. The teacher, Mr. Davis, paused at his desk, waiting for the racket to pass, but it continued. He strode to the window and his face hardened with disgust.

"Class," he had to raise his voice to be heard, "stay put and behave yourselves. I'll be back later. No one is to leave this room!" He hurried out.

As soon as the door closed behind him everyone rushed to the windows, where they saw a dozen or so motorcycles speeding up and down the curved street that led around the school to the parking lot at the end of the property. Most of the riders wore no helmet, and they appeared to be young men just slightly older than the students who watched their display with amusement.

Several bikers would race down the street, then return in the opposite direction, sometimes dodging other riders who approached them head-on, swerving at the last moment. They laughed raucously, as if they were putting on a display for their own enjoyment.

The students then saw Mr. Davis join the principal and a handful of other teachers who were standing along the sidewalk in front of the main entrance, where the road the bikers had commandeered curved into a circle drive. The adults passively observed the commotion, apparently not interested in confronting the unruly group.

The algebra class found the situation quite entertaining, and alternately marveled and jested about the riders and their antics. Suddenly a helmeted rider buzzed the circle at high speed, making two revolutions past the annoyed onlookers, then chopped a trail through the grass in the center of the circle, and spun to a stop.

As he leaned his heavy machine against the concrete base of the flagpole and climbed off, other members of the group rode in close formation around the drive that encircled him, gunning their engines periodically, preventing any of the observers from approaching the lone figure in the center.

The students at the window voiced their speculations.

"He must be the leader."

"He looks pretty puny to be a gang leader."

"I wonder what he's going to do."

"Mr. Davis looks really mad."

From their second floor perspective the students could see that the biker was slightly taller than average but with a slight build, and did not present an imposing figure. He remained in the grassy area and faced the building, then removed his helmet, revealing short and shaggy sandy-blond hair.

"He's cute!" one of the girls said. Others murmured their agreement, as he looked up at the building, scanning back and forth.

Suddenly Vindi shouted, "Lukas! That is Lukas!" She pounded on the window in an attempt to get his attention, continuing to call his name loudly.

"He can't hear you!" someone told her, as she tried to open a window, but it did not budge.

Vindi left the window, and ran across the room to the door. Doug overtook her and blocked the doorway before she could exit.

"You're not going out there!" he yelled over the commotion.

"Let me through!" she shouted, with increasing agitation. "It's Lukas! I know him! I used to live with him!"

"No!"

"Get...out...of...my...way!" She drew her arms back then punched him forcefully in the gut with her entire weight behind both of her fists. The impact of the blow threw him enough off balance that she was able to push her way past him, and she ran down the corridor to the stairway.

After Doug recovered from momentary breathlessness he darted after her, and arrived outside just in time to see Vindi run down the sidewalk, waving her arms and shouting. The blond biker dashed toward her, signaling the riders to let her through. They stopped abruptly, then resumed their protective motorcade after she crossed.

Vindi flew into Lukas's arms and they hugged each other tightly, oblivious to the chaos surrounding them. Then their bodies separated but their faces remained close as they shouted into each other's ears over the racket. Doug heard only fragments of their words, but enough to determine that they were both speaking in Swedish.

Within less than a minute police sirens could be heard approaching. Lukas tried to push Vindi away and approach his cycle, but she followed and hung on to him. He grasped her hands in his and they spoke rapidly, as she grew visibly more desperate.

The sirens got louder and the reflections of flashing red and blue lights could be seen advancing. Vindi finally stepped back and Lukas leapt onto his bike, gunned the engine to life, then spun around, hurling clumps of grass and dirt. The serpentine parade paused to let him pass in front of them, then followed him out the drive with engines roaring, just as a line of patrol cars arrived behind them.

As several officers hurried toward the group of teachers, Doug looked past them at Vindi. Her shoulders were shaking with sobs as she watched the bikers pass from sight. As he started toward her she suddenly became still, then turned and bolted toward the student parking lot. Surmising her intention to follow the bikers, Doug dodged the small crowd and sprinted after her across the school lawn.

He caught up with her and grabbed her shoulders, but she struggled so intensely to break free that he was forced to wrap his arms around her to hold her in place.

"Let me go!" She shook her head and twisted her body. "I have to go after him! I can't lose him again!"

"Vindi, settle down! You can't go after them!" He was eventually able to grab her wrists and control her movements, but she still fought. She looked up at him, finally recognizing who he was.

"Doug! You must help me...please! We'll take your car. You can drive me!"

"Vindi," he spoke softly this time, leaning down close to her face. "He's gone. There's no way to find him now."

She pulled back momentarily; her body stiffened, then she collapsed forward, leaned her face against him, and began to weep. Her arms went limp and Doug released her wrists, as she rested her hands on his chest. He placed his hands lightly on her back.

Between her sobs Doug heard her whisper, as if to herself. "Lukas..." She took several gasping breaths. "Don't leave me...Sven..."

Suddenly she exhaled heavily, and Doug felt her begin to slip downward. He tightened his grip, then had to bend forward to catch her before she fell to the ground. She had fainted. He adjusted his position and lifted her into his arms, then turned toward the school.

Mr. Davis and two police officers were heading toward him. They escorted him to the school's health clinic, where the nurse instructed him to place Vindi on a stretcher behind a partially open curtain. Doug told her simply that Vindi had been upset and then fainted.

The nurse performed a quick examination, then retrieved an ammonium capsule which she placed beneath Vindi's nose. After the first adequate inhalation Vindi jerked her head back and opened her eyes. She looked around her, first appearing bewildered, then frightened. Doug reached out and took her hand.

"It's okay, Vindi." She looked at him blankly, but held on tightly.

The nurse checked Vindi's blood pressure and pulse, talking to her in a calming manner throughout the procedure. She then raised the head of the stretcher, telling her that everything looked fine.

Vindi stared at her and did not speak. This prompted the nurse to speak directly to her while maintaining eye contact. She asked her several questions, but Vindi remained silent, gazing at her without recognition. Then Doug tried asking her the same questions. "What is your name? Do you know where you are? Do you know what day this is? Do you know who I am?" He received no response, merely a vacant gaze.

The nurse asked Doug to stay while she left the clinic to report to Mr. Davis and the officers who waited outside the door. They returned with her as she searched the files to call the emergency number in Vindi's health record.

Doug thought about Vindi's driver's license but decided against mentioning it. Vindi appeared to be in no danger, so there was no point in instigating a scenario like that again. Vindi's gaze scanned the room; her facial expression remained blank.

The nurse finished her telephone conversation, and Doug heard her speaking to Mr. Davis on the other side of the curtain. "Her brother is her guardian, and would like me to call an ambulance as I recommended, but he is also sending someone over to accompany her. He can't get away at the moment."

The nurse checked on Vindi again, then filled out a form on a clipboard. Eventually a paramedic team entered the clinic with their transport stretcher. As they prepared to move Vindi, Doug tried to release his hand from hers, but she grasped it even tighter and looked at him with alarm. He spoke to her gently, and tried to loosen her fingers; she began to breathe rapidly and struggled against the efforts of the paramedics.

They backed off and waited for her to calm down, then advised Doug to allow her to hold his hand as they moved her. As long as Doug kept her gaze and spoke to her softly, she allowed the team to buckle her into the stretcher without protest.

Doug walked beside her as the medics wheeled Vindi down the corridor and out the front door. As they approached the back door of the ambulance, Doug glanced at the deep ruts in the previously manicured grass where Lukas had spun out on his cycle.

He recalled how Lukas had scanned the building, prompting Vindi's recognition, and he theorized that the entire noisy stunt had been designed to get her attention. Lukas apparently had known that Vindi was in the school.

As the paramedics prepared to load the stretcher into the ambulance, a large black SUV with darkly tinted windows pulled up behind them in the circle drive. Two men dressed in black suits, white shirts and black ties emerged and walked toward them. They appeared to be in their mid-thirties, physically fit, with trim haircuts and dark sunglasses. Doug was not surprised at their appearance.

"Is this Vindi Johansson?" one of the men asked.

"Who wants to know?" the paramedic questioned.

"We are colleagues of Sven Johansson, her brother and legal guardian. He is unable to be here and would like for us to accompany her to the hospital. I have here an authorization signed by him as well as a certificate of guardianship."

The medic glanced at the papers without interest. "Well, we don't have room in the truck for you, but you can follow behind us."

"One of us will ride in the truck." The man spoke as if the matter were settled. He looked at Doug. "Who are you?"

"I'm Doug, Vindi's classmate and friend. She wants me with her and I plan to stay."

"That's fine, but you can go now."

Doug made no attempt to move. The man hesitated, then nodded slightly to his partner, who stepped forward and held Doug's free arm. The other grasped Doug's wrist, giving it a firm twist. Doug resisted at first, then relaxed his fingers, but Vindi held on tightly and cried out in pain as her arm began to rotate.

"She's not letting go, and you're hurting her!" Doug warned. The man released his grip and stepped back. Vindi calmed, but inhaled rapidly in short gasps.

"I told you, she wants me with her," Doug stated, suspecting that the men were not authorized to disregard Vindi's wishes.

The two men looked at each other again, then the confrontational one retrieved his cell phone and tapped it. As he stepped aside Doug called to him, "Tell Sven I'm Dr. Goodwin's son." When the man returned he directed the paramedics to load the stretcher, leaving Doug at Vindi's side. Through their dark sunglasses the men watched the procedure, then drove closely behind the ambulance to the hospital.

Vindi was taken to a private cubicle in the emergency room and transferred to the hospital bed, maintaining a tight grasp on Doug's hand throughout the process. Various medical gadgets and strange-looking outlets protruded from the wall above. A nurse entered and measured Vindi's vital signs, entering the results in her computer pad. She then asked Vindi the same questions as to person, place and time that the school nurse had posed. Vindi looked at her blankly and made no response.

The nurse asked Doug to leave so she could undress Vindi and place a hospital gown on her. Doug explained the situation, but tried to gently release Vindi's grip on his hand. When Vindi reacted with agitation the nurse advised him to stay where he was. "I'll inform the doctor." She exited with her clipboard.

Shortly after the nurse left the inside privacy curtain was shoved aside and Sven thrust himself into the room. Unlike his partners, he wore black trousers and a dark blue short-sleeved polo shirt with an insignia patch at the left breast. The pale complexion of his arms made him appear even more muscular than he had in the black nylon shirt. Doug did not see any weapon.

Sven eyed Doug briefly, then rushed to the opposite side of the stretcher, leaning toward Vindi and taking her other hand. He spoke to her softly but elicited no response. She gazed at him without recognition and her hand remained limp in his. "What happened to her?" His voice was sharp with concern and alarm.

Doug related the events, beginning with the noisy appearance of the bikers, as Sven kept his gaze on Vindi. When he mentioned Lukas's name Sven's head jerked up, and he drew in a quick breath. Doug paused in his narrative.

*The images in Sven's mind were those of Lukas and Vindi, both dressed in ragged, ill-fitting clothing, standing next to a mattress that lay on the floor, bare except for a worn blanket. Vindi's hair was braided behind her and her face was smudged and dirty. She glared at Sven, while Lukas eyed him warily.*

*In the next image Sven clutched Vindi's arm, ignoring her resistance as she writhed and attempted to break free. He pushed her into the passenger seat of a car and slammed the door shut.*

*He was then face to face with Lukas, grasping the front of his sweatshirt. "I am warning you...stay away from her!" Lukas's expression was passive and unafraid. The images faded.*

"Go on." Sven's voice betrayed no emotion.

As Doug finished the account of events, Sven's facial muscles twitched with controlled rage. He did not speak again but continued to stare into Vindi's eyes, which remained vacant and unresponsive.

A young male doctor wearing hospital scrubs and a white coat entered, and was given a brief synopsis of the events by Doug. Sven stood aside as the physician performed his examination of Vindi's physical and mental condition. He then spoke to both of them.

"There is no apparent neurologic deficit other than her lack of response. Her blood sugar check in the ambulance was normal. I want to perform some additional blood testing and a brain scan to confirm no underlying physical problem. Based on the history you give, I suspect this is a hysterical reaction to a psychological trauma. I'll let you know my findings." Eliciting no questions, he began to leave, then turned around. "I'm going to give her a mild sedative before we take her to CT. It should make her sleepy."

Subsequently a different nurse arrived and placed an intravenous catheter, through which she extracted blood samples, then infused a dose of medication. After a few minutes Vindi's eyes closed, she relaxed her grip on Doug's hand and drifted into a gentle sleep.

Sven motioned Doug to the opposite side of the room near the glass door, and spoke softly. "Did she say anything to you about...*Lukas?*" The name escaped his clenched teeth with a whispered growl.

Doug related Vindi's frantic appeal for him to help her follow Lukas and her words, "I can't lose him again."

"And just before she fainted she said something else," Doug recounted softly. "She had stopped struggling and was crying, and said something that sounded like, 'Lukas...don't leave me...Sven.'"

Sven looked at the floor as he pondered that. He then looked at Doug. "Are you and Vindi...going together?"

Doug jerked his head in surprise. "No, we're just friends."

"Why is she so...attached to you?"

"I guess she trusts me."

"Hmm." Sven peered into Doug's eyes, his face expressionless. He then turned his back to Vindi and lowered his voice further. Doug leaned toward him and strained to hear his accented words. "There is something else. About my work...you have seen some things..."

"You mean like those two guys at the school who look like secret agents?" Doug spoke softly.

"Yes."

"And I saw the SWAT team at my house when you came to get Vindi."

"Ja, I know."

"You do?"

"Ja. Vindi told me you asked her about it." Sven did not mention that the van driver had noted the white blip in the library when the team exited the house and grounds. "My work is...something that I cannot discuss. Vindi does not know about it, and I would like to keep it that way."

"She's not involved in any of it?"

"No."

"And she thinks you work for a security company?"

"Yes."

Doug nodded. "No problem. I won't say anything to her...or anyone else. I can keep quiet."

"Good, thanks." He turned around and looked at Vindi, raising his voice slightly. "You don't have to stay."

"I'd like to stay for a while and see how Vindi is, if that's okay with you."

"Ja, sure, that is fine. Will you wait here with her for a moment?"

"Sure."

Sven left the room, closing the glass door quietly behind him. Doug paused for a moment, then pulled the curtain aside and saw Sven walk down the corridor where the two men from the black SUV stood with their backs to the wall. Sven consulted a hand-held electronic device that looked like an oversized cell phone, then showed it to the men and appeared to give them instructions. They tapped on their own similar devices, then turned and left.

Doug continued to peer furtively through the glass, as Sven stood alone in the hallway and referred to his gadget, appearing to speak softly at times to no one.

A face suddenly appeared on the opposite side of the glass door, and Doug stepped aside to allow a young man wearing dark blue scrubs to enter the cubicle. He introduced himself, and stated he would be taking Vindi to the radiology department. Before he finished speaking Sven stood next to him, glanced suspiciously at his name tag and then his face, and insisted that he would accompany them. There was no objection. The young man pulled the curtain to one side, opened the double glass door widely, and rolled the stretcher out of the cubicle and down the hallway, with Sven following.

Doug leaned against the doorway, watching to see if the two men in black suits would return. They did not, and he eventually sat in the cubicle and occupied himself with his phone.

It seemed only a few minutes later when Vindi was rolled back into the room. The transport tech explained that they would now have to wait for the CT scan to be read by the radiologist, which could take up to an hour.

As Vindi continued to sleep, Sven and Doug waited. Doug was not surprised that Sven was no more prone to idle chatter than was Vindi. They sat in silence, as Sven studied and occasionally tapped on his electronic device, and Doug continued to fiddle with his phone.

Suddenly Sven stood and announced, "I will be back."

Immediately after he left, Doug stood and again peeked around the edge of the closed curtain; he watched Sven walk calmly down the corridor, then turn at an intersecting hallway. In the large convex mirror that hung from the ceiling, Doug saw him head toward the main entrance of the emergency room.

Doug looked at Vindi, who appeared to be in a peaceful sleep, protected by metal rails on both sides of the stretcher. He stepped out of the cubicle, closed the curtain and glass door behind him, and hurried down the hallway. Sven had disappeared through the main doorway, and Doug cautiously followed. As he peered through and then around the outer glass door, he saw Sven walk down the sidewalk, then suddenly veer toward the building and disappear around the corner.

Doug followed Sven's route until he reached the corner of the building, then paused and listened at the cluster of trees and bushes that Sven had entered. He moved forward carefully and quietly until he could see the group in a clearing near the far end of the brick wall. He froze, and remained hidden in the vegetation as he squinted between the leaves at the scene before him.

The two suited men held Lukas tightly by his arms between them, even though he stood calmly and did not resist. Lukas watched Sven's approach with no sign of fear, until Sven grabbed him by the neck, pulled him out of their grasp and pushed him against the hard brick wall of the building, almost lifting him off his feet.

Their verbal exchange was only partially audible and was apparently in Swedish, but it was fairly obvious to Doug that Sven was growling accusations as Lukas made pleas of innocence. Lukas's voice got louder and more assertive until Sven suddenly released his grip and stepped back with a stunned expression. Lukas stayed in place as Sven appeared increasingly distressed, running his hand through his white hair and pacing about as he blurted out phrases in an excited tone, while Lukas appeared to instruct him firmly but passively. Doug backed away quietly.

Doug was sitting next to Vindi when the two of them entered the cubicle, and he moved aside as Lukas approached the stretcher with a worried expression. At close range Doug could see that he looked like a teenager and nothing at all like a motorcycle gang leader. Lukas took Vindi's hand, called her name several times, then spoke softly to her in words Doug could not understand. She did not stir. He then lowered the side rail and sat beside her. He grasped her hand again, and continued to speak softly to her. Her eyes opened slowly, then widened.

"Lukas!" She sat up rapidly and drew him to her, putting her arms around his body and nestling her face in his chest. She did not cry, but breathed in and out loudly and erratically as they held each other tightly for what seemed to Doug an eternity. He waited for the couple to kiss, but they did not.

After releasing their prolonged hug, Lukas and Vindi fell into a solemn conversation in Swedish. Doug contemplated their animated expressions as Sven overtly listened to their exchange. After a time he appeared to be satisfied, and he motioned Doug to follow him out of the room. He stood at the open glass doorway, periodically glancing at the pair.

Sven gestured to his two colleagues, who were standing in the same location down the corridor as before, and they advanced.

"It looks like she will be okay," he told the men, then he looked at Doug. "The guys will take you back to the school, or wherever you want. Thanks for your help, and your concern for Vindi." He reached out and gave Doug a firm handshake.

As Doug sat in the back seat of the black SUV on his way to the school to retrieve his car, he tried to sort through the day's events. He glanced at the rear view mirror and was surprised to see his eyes narrowed in a scowl. Only then did he notice that his fists were tightly clenched and that a sharp burning sensation permeated his chest. He took a breath and exhaled forcefully as his jaw twitched and his scowl deepened.

## Chapter 7

# There's always Plan B...or C...or...

Doug did not see Vindi for the rest of the week. He again was frustrated that he had no number to call her, and no address. He thought about the records in the school nurse's office and wondered if he could find a way to sneak into the files. But if he went to Vindi's house, who would he find there? Who was this Lukas? Vindi had said she used to live with him—maybe at the university where she had lived but was not a student? Lukas looked too young for that.

Doug had given Vindi his number—why did she not call him? All he could do was wait impatiently for her to show up at school.

The following Monday Doug and Quinn sat in the outside lunch area. The weather had cooled and more of the students were sitting outdoors; the seating area was buzzing with conversations. The girls had not yet arrived, and Quinn was bemoaning his participation on the planning committee for the Winter Carnival, an event held annually in December.

"Why don't you just quit?" Doug asked.

"I would if I could, believe me. But Maggie is the chairperson. She's the one who signed me up, of course...and if I quit she'll have to do more of the work herself, and you know what that would mean. She'll cut me off, with the excuse that she's too busy, just to punish me."

"So you're stuck."

"Looks like it. She said I could get a replacement, but I've tried and can't get anyone to take it. I even asked the geeks, but they're not interested, and Vindi said—"

"You talked to Vindi?" Doug interrupted. "When?"

"Today after government."

"She was in class today?"

"Yeah. She said she has a visitor here from Sweden so she didn't want to have any after-school obligations."

"A visitor from Sweden? Did she say who it was?" Doug forced nonchalance.

"No, and I didn't ask."

Doug's facial muscles tightened. He scanned the seating area but did not see Vindi.

Quinn noticed the movement. "By the way, how's your passive approach going? Other than the fact that she fainted in your arms, that is."

"It's not going anywhere." He had not told anyone, not even Quinn, the details of the incident—all Quinn knew was that Vindi had fainted and was taken to the hospital, and that Doug had accompanied her.

"Maybe you need a more direct approach. Let her know you're interested. You know...ask her out."

"I don't know…it hasn't worked with anyone else."

"But they are not you."

"Hmf! I doubt that makes a difference."

"Whoa! It looks like Doug Goodwin has met his match! Actually concerned about getting rejected! Now you know how the rest of us have felt all these years."

"Very funny…but not helpful." Doug continued to watch the doorway as students flowed through.

"If you're looking for Vindi, she isn't coming." Ansel stepped up from behind Doug, facing him for the first time since the incident at the party.

Doug looked up and scowled at him. "No one asked you. Are you still stalking her?"

"No, I just saw her in chemistry class."

"You mean she's still talking to you?"

"Only to tell me to get lost, but I heard her tell Marie that she has a friend visiting from Sweden, and *he* is taking her to lunch on his *motorcycle*."

"So, what do you want?"

Doug and Quinn had two empty chairs between them, and Ansel took the one next to Quinn, his eyes fixed on Doug's glare. "Listen, Doug, can't we get past this? I've already lost Carleigh over it, and everybody else looks at me like I'm a pervert. You and I have been friends since grade school, and we've always been able to get past our differences."

Doug snorted. "This isn't a…baseball mitt or…a copy of a test! It's taking advantage of a girl for your own ego and pleasure. There's no defense for that!"

Ansel stood abruptly. "I told you I didn't do it!"

Doug jumped up and moved toward him, prompting Quinn to rise and try to wedge himself between them. "Take it easy," Quinn warned, glancing around the area.

Doug spoke forcefully but kept his voice low and controlled. "Anyone who drugged her would have stayed close by to benefit from the results. You and I were the only ones with her, and I know *I* didn't do it...so it's obvious to me that *you* did. If you would at least admit what you did and regret it, I could respect that. Your continued denial means nothing has changed, and you're nothing but a sleazy opportunist!"

"I don't have to take that from you!"

"No, you don't. You can get out of my sight. But you'd better stay away from Vindi, or you'll have to deal with *me*. And don't forget about the warning from her brother!"

"I'm not afraid of him."

"You should be!"

Ansel brushed his shoulder against Doug's arm as he stormed away, prompting Doug to whirl around to chase after him. Just as quickly, Quinn stepped in front of Doug, placing his hand on his shoulder. "Let him go. He's not worth it!" Doug exhaled heavily as he watched Ansel enter the building.

During the remaining weeks Doug saw Vindi in algebra class, but she usually arrived just on time after returning from lunch out somewhere. She appeared distracted, but very happy and calm. Her only interaction with Doug was a smile and greeting as they left class and went their separate ways.

Throughout the two-week vacation period Doug attempted to focus on holiday diversions with his friends and family, and arranged activities with various girls from school, but he could not get rid of the image of Vindi in Lukas's arms.

The first school day after Christmas break Doug noted that Vindi was absent from algebra class. The following day at lunch Jenna and Alisse had just arrived at his table with Carleigh when he saw Vindi enter the patio area with Marie. They were carrying their food trays, and they sat down with Kenneth, Matt and Liz. He stared at the group for a moment, then rose and approached their table.

"Hi, Vindi."

"Oh, hi, Doug."

"Could I talk with you for a moment?"

"I think you know everyone here…have you met Liz?" Vindi was purposeful in not allowing him to ignore the other students. Doug greeted each one of them, then repeated his request.

Vindi excused herself, and Doug led her to an empty table near the small trees at the edge of the patio. Doug sat with his back to the lunching students, with Vindi two seats down.

"Why are you sitting with *them*?" Doug asked abruptly.

"What is wrong with that?"

"Well...what have they ever done for you? You haven't sat at my table since you got back from the hospital. Why are you ignoring Quinn, and Jenna and Alisse?"

"Do they think I'm ignoring them?"

"Well, I'm sure they've noticed that you haven't been around."

"And...they...want me around?"

"Well, it's rude of you to not even speak to us!"

"Is this about them...or about you?"

"Okay...yes. I can't believe you're treating me this way!"

"What do you mean?"

"I thought we were friends...that you felt safe with me. After we talked...and I've been giving you your space and not pursuing you...I don't think I deserve to be ignored! And who is this guy Lukas? Why haven't you said anything about him before?"

Vindi stood up, her face reddening into a scowl, as she appeared to be searching for words.

"You...hypocrite!" Her voice became louder as her rage increased with every word. "What you're telling me is that your friendship is nothing but a *scheme*...and now you're upset that I'm not taking the bait!" Her voice drew the attention of the entire seating area, causing a hush as she glared into Doug's astonished face and shouted, "*Dra åt helvete!* Go...to...hell!"

As she stomped across the patio and into the building a male voice called out, "That's telling him!" There were outbursts of laughter, as Doug turned and stared after her, crossing his arms over his chest, enduring the ridicule he had provoked.

Doug did not look for Vindi but went directly to the algebra classroom. She subsequently entered with her usual carefree and happy demeanor, speaking with some of her classmates, but did not look in his direction. When the class was over he watched her leave and did not attempt to speak to her.

Doug skipped his last class and walked past the student parking lot to the bleachers where he and Vindi had had their previous conversation—how long ago? It seemed like ages. He sat down and thought for a while, then opened his notebook and began to write, pausing frequently to choose his words. When finished he read over what he had written.

> *"Vindi,*
>
> *I'm really, truly sorry for being such an idiot. I admit I have had some schemes concerning you, but my friendship with you is definitely not part of that. I know I'm an arrogant jerk, and I hope with your wisdom and experience with guys and our uncivilized behaviors you can forgive my stupidity and at least let me apologize to you in person. I'm at the bleachers.*
>
> *Doug"*

He walked leisurely to her car and placed the note under the windshield wiper, then returned to the same spot on the bleachers. He leaned back on the seat behind him, stretching out his arms as he contemplated the trees in the distance, and the events of the past four months since Vindi had appeared at the school.

It was some time later that students began to meander through the parking lot, climb into their cars and drive away. He watched without moving, and no one looked in his direction. Eventually he saw Vindi walking alone, swinging her arms in her boyish manner, supporting her computer pad in her curled fingers. She climbed into her car and closed the door.

The engine started and the back lights flashed as the car began to move in reverse. Then it stopped. Vindi opened her door, stepped out and retrieved the note; she then stood with the door open and the engine running.

*She's reading it now.* Her back was to him and she did not turn around, but slid back into the car. Then the engine shut off and she stepped out and closed the door.

Doug watched her approach; her expression was unrevealing. He stood and met her, and showed her to a seat as if they were at a formal dinner. He sat nearby, but not too close.

"Thanks, Vindi, for coming over to talk to me. I just want to tell you that I'm really sorry for my stupidity and egotism. I know I have no right to demand that you explain your activities to me."

Vindi gave him a slight smile. "It's okay, Doug. You are forgiven."

"Thanks. I really do want us to be friends, even if it can never be more than that."

She looked puzzled. "I do consider us friends. You have been there when I have needed help, and I appreciate that."

"I know you understand that guys can't resist pursuing a beautiful girl, and I admit I was scheming just like all the others. But if I had known there was someone else, I wouldn't have felt so…betrayed."

"What do you mean about someone else?"

"Maybe you didn't realize it, but I was with you at the hospital, and I saw how it was with you and Lukas, and figure you've been spending your time with him since then. You said you used to live with him, so I assume you two are back together again. It just took me by surprise because you never let on to anyone about him. I got upset, and I'm sorry."

Vindi smiled. "I have been spending time with Lukas, but we are not a couple. We have been friends since we were kids, and when we…got separated last year I didn't know what happened to him. I was so happy to see him again that I wanted to be with him as much as possible."

"But you lived together?"

"For a while…as friends."

Doug was not quite sure what that meant, but knew this was not the time to ask for details. He remembered Sven's obvious anger at hearing Lukas's name, and the confrontation between the two of them at the hospital. "Sven seemed quite upset that Lukas showed up here."

"Ja. That was a misunderstanding, but it has been resolved. A lot of things have been resolved."

"Oh." He remained absorbed in his own thoughts. "So…you're not dating Lukas?"

"No." Vindi smiled. "So I guess you can go back to your scheming."

"No, I wouldn't do that to you."

"Of course not!" They looked at each other, then laughed.

"Is Lukas still here?" Doug asked.

"No. Sven got him a job with his company, and he went to a training program upstate."

"He's going to work with Sven?"

"Probably not directly, but with his company."

"Doing what?"

"I don't know…whatever it is they do."

"Oh."

A few days later Doug invited Vindi to take a walk with him during their lunch period. They strolled along the sidewalks that snaked around and between the various buildings.

"Have you heard from Lukas?" Doug's voice was light and friendly.

"Ja, usually just text, but we have talked a few times online.

"How's he doing?"

"He's having a great time, and really excited about the opportunity he is getting. He says he's happier than he has ever been."

"Happier than when he lived with you?"

"Those were not such great times."

"Why?"

She shook her head. "It's not important."

"Oh, okay." It was obvious that she did not want to discuss it. Doug paused. "Listen, I want to invite you to an outing. Partly to make it up to you for being a stupid jerk, but also because I'd like to spend time with you and take you somewhere I think you'd like. There's no scheming involved," he continued quickly before she could respond. "Other people will be there and I promise I won't try to get you off alone or kiss you or anything like that, so please don't say 'no' right away."

She smiled. "Okay, I'm listening."

"It involves ice skates and snowshoes."

"Snow!" Her eyes brightened. "Where?"

"In Sequoia National Park, about three hours north of here. They have real snow for sledding and snowshoeing, and a real ice rink…not the kind they have here over the holidays. It'll be cold, too! My father and brother are going. Dave will be inviting his girlfriend, Jillian, so you two girls can share a room. We'll leave early Saturday morning and return Sunday. What do you think?"

"Oh, I really miss snow…and it's so warm here all the time."

"Here's your chance to have some real winter weather."

"Mmm…that sounds so good…" she hesitated.

"Really, you can trust me. This is not a scheme. I've learned my lesson on that one. In fact, Sven is welcome to come along, and bring a friend if he wants. You know I won't be trying anything if he's there!"

She laughed. "I'll ask him. It sounds really fun!"

"It will be, I promise."

Doug finally got Vindi's phone number and address, and followed his GPS guide to a small suburban housing development. The trail ended at a compact single story house at the end of a cul-de-sac. Planted amidst surrounding vegetation that was trimmed just enough to appear natural but not untidy, the wood paneled structure appeared to blend into the row of trees that towered behind it.

The house and lawn were separated from their neighbors by a narrow creek on one side that cut a meandering path toward the rear, and a steep downward slope on the opposite side—presenting the appearance of a cabin fortress on a small island. *How appropriate,* Doug thought.

Sven opened the door before Doug could ring the bell, and invited him inside with a friendly handshake. He wore black suit pants and a white shirt with the collar open and a black tie hanging loosely around it in a state of partial dress; his suit coat hung from his hand. Doug had never expected to see him so cheerful. *He looks like a college graduate getting ready for his first job interview.*

"Vindi should be out in a minute," Sven said. "I wish I could be going with you, and I appreciate the invitation."

"We'll have to do it again some time when you can make it. Looks like you have to wear the uniform today, eh?"

"Ja, unfortunately."

"Don't forget the dark sunglasses."

"I have them right here." Sven smiled as he revealed the inside pocket of his jacket. He then hung the jacket over the back of a stool at the counter that separated the kitchen from the living area, nodding at the thumbs up gesture Doug offered. "You have my number, ja?" Sven asked.

"Yes."

"Don't hesitate to call or text if you need me for anything."

"Sure."

"I have your number, and your father's."

"Do you want the name and number of the lodge?"

"No, that will not be necessary. I'm sure I can trust you to take good care of Vindi." Sven's eyes bored into his with a sudden glare that he held for an extra moment.

Doug was startled at the abrupt shift in Sven's demeanor. Maybe it was just his imagination, but it seemed that for a fleeting moment Sven had been a typical twenty-three-year-old who would kick back, watch a football game and down a beer with his buddies; then he had suddenly transformed into the aloof authority figure who guarded his sister with a SWAT team.

A buzzer sounded from behind the kitchen. "Excuse me," Sven said as he followed the sound.

Doug scanned the open living area, noting the clean geometric lines of the modern furnishings that at first appeared sparse, but on second look seemed to be totally functional and adequate. Outside a glass door on the opposite wall was a wooden deck which supported patio furniture that looked like it had been carved from a forest, then whittled and polished into sleek angles.

Sven reappeared carrying several white dress shirts loosely over his arm, which he apparently had just retrieved from the dryer. "You can never have too many white shirts," he said with a half-smile.

*Friendly again,* Doug observed.

Sven crossed to the far side of the room and called gently, "Vindi, you know Doug is here, ja?"

"Ja, I will be right out," a muffled voice answered.

Sven returned to where Doug stood patiently. "I have to finish packing, too. Please, make yourself at home." He waved his arm, offering him the room with polite formality, then disappeared down the nearby hall.

Doug took a few steps forward, noticing a large flat panel television atop a two-tiered glass table, and a smaller screen to the right which displayed several boxed images. As he moved closer he was surprised to see that they were various camera views outside the house. One showed the space outside the front door, now empty, while another revealed a wide-angle view of the front yard, cul-de-sac and driveway, where his father was visible in the van. There was a similar close-up view of the outside deck, and three views of what he could see were the back and side yards, surrounded by a high wooden privacy fence.

He was even more surprised by an additional monitor which stood on the opposite side of the television, displaying what appeared to be a satellite image of the house and grounds from a bird's eye view. He was stunned to see his father's van in the driveway. *This is a real time image! How does he manage that?*

"Hi Doug. I'm sorry I took so long." Vindi entered the room from behind him. He turned, then rushed to take the suitcase and parka from her hands.

"It's no problem. We're not in any hurry."

"Were you spying on the neighbors?"

"What?"

"It's the button on the left." He looked back at the monitors. "Just kidding," Vindi giggled. "Some system, ja? You would not think we were paranoid, would you?"

"Well…"

As he walked toward the front door she darted into the kitchen and began to remove items from the refrigerator and place them into a cloth bag.

"What are you doing?"

"Water for the trip, for everybody." As she started to brush past him he reached out and took the bag from her. She continued to the entrance of the hallway. "Sven, I'm going," she called quietly. Sven reappeared.

"I hope you have a great time."

"I'm sure I will. I wish you could go."

"So do I." He nodded toward Doug. "If he gives you any trouble, call me and I will send a helicopter with machine guns to hunt him down." She giggled. Sven leaned forward and gave her a light hug as he winked at Doug over her shoulder. Was he smiling? Doug could not tell.

Sven followed them out the door to the driveway. A brief commotion ensued as Sven and Vindi greeted Dave and Jillian who occupied the third seat, Doug stored Vindi's belongings in the back of the van, then Doug and Vindi discussed where they would sit. Vindi insisted that Doug sit up front to help navigate while she took the middle seat.

Dr. Goodwin had stepped out of the driver's seat and was still talking to Sven after everyone was settled. Doug recalled his father's comments when he had told him that Sven was Vindi's guardian. *Such a burden for a boy his age, to be supporting a home and his sister, and not have a father to look to.* Doug watched him place a hand on Sven's shoulder in a fatherly manner, even though that shoulder was almost at his eye level. They shook hands as they parted.

## Chapter 8

# *If I were a real cave man I would have had her by now*

Vindi's anticipation grew as the van left the California warmth and climbed into higher elevations. The landscape transformed before her eyes as bare trees in the foothills gave way to massive pines and deepening snow, giving the impression that they were traveling through time between summer and winter.

A light snow began to fall just as they pulled into the circle drive and stopped in front of the main building of the resort. Without a word Vindi jumped from the van and ran past the protective overhang of the entrance.

She stood with her arms outstretched and raised her face to the sky. The soft flakes greeted her like long-lost friends that laughed with delight as they caressed her skin, then melted into cold wet kisses. The crisp frigid air awakened her lungs with every deep, luxurious inhalation, and enveloped her body in a welcoming wintry embrace.

A warm touch on her hand brought her back to the California mountains, as she opened her eyes to see Doug's quizzical smile.

"How about coming inside before you freeze into a statue? The snow will still be here when we come back out."

He led her into the lodge, where the others were already checking in at the desk. The group then separated as they found their respective rooms to change into their winter clothing.

Jillian chattered with excitement as she unpacked, relating that she and her mother had moved from the Midwest to California the previous year. Slim and petite with straight copper red hair blunt cut at the shoulders, she appeared to be an easygoing, happy person with a humorous outlook on life.

More importantly, Vindi sensed none of the underlying antagonism with Jillian that she had experienced with some of the girls at the school; she supposed because Jillian felt no threat from her in her relationship with Dave, whom she had been dating for several months. As they chatted and changed clothes, Vindi enjoyed the expectation of a genuine female friendship.

Down the hall Doug and Dave were engaged in a more serious discussion as they unpacked in their shared room.

"What's our signal going to be if one of us gets lucky?" Dave asked.

"We don't need a signal, because it won't be me. Just put the privacy card on the door."

"Okay, that'll work."

"Are you and Jillian at that level?"

"It hasn't happened yet, but you never know."

"Are you prepared?"

"Of course. Dad and I had 'the talk' a while back. You know, the 'protection is your own responsibility' lesson. But he just recently gave me the scientific stuff."

"Have you read it?"

"Yeah. Does it work?"

"Oh, yeah." As Doug removed his jeans he pulled two foil squares from the pocket and dropped them on the bed.

"I thought you weren't expecting anything to happen."

"Well, you never know," Doug smiled. "Always be prepared."

The group met in the lobby, then rented snowshoes and set off on a short trail to get their legs acclimated. They arrived at the small outpost at the ice skating rink, where they had a light hot lunch.

Dr. Goodwin skated for a brief period, then watched from the cafe window as the teens expended their energy on the ice. When they had finally had enough, they took off their skates and played in the snow—throwing snowballs, making snow people and forts, and chasing after one another. Jillian and the boys appeared to share Vindi's determination to squeeze an entire winter's fun into one afternoon, as they cast aside their teenage sophistication and played like children.

After a rest and hot chocolate the group snowshoed back to the main lodge, where they changed clothing and met at the restaurant for dinner. It was the busy season, but many of the hotel guests participated in evening activities at the various outposts, so they had no problem getting a table.

The group chatted and laughed about the day's proceedings, as the teens chided each other for cheating in the snow battles. The topic then switched to school events, current and past. This prompted Doug and Dave to begin telling stories about each other's humorous childhood incidents, with their father adding supplemental information at just the right moments to upset their rivalries and cause them to laugh at themselves.

Doug observed Vindi during the reminisces, concerned that the discussion would generate troubled memories for her. He was pleased to see that she appeared comfortable and happy, as she caught his eye and smiled.

After the meal Doug and Vindi made their way to the high-ceilinged main lounge where an immense log fire crackled in a stone fireplace that covered the entire wall, and reflected in the adjacent wall of glass that overlooked a hill of snow. The scattered groupings of sofas, love seats and chairs were sparsely occupied at this hour, and they settled down on a curved sofa covered with soft upholstery and plush pillows. Dave and Jillian had disappeared, and Dr.

Goodwin was conversing with other adults in the small club room adjacent to the restaurant.

"This day has been so fantastic," Vindi sighed with contentment. She slipped off her shoes and curled her legs under her. "I didn't even know that California had snow...and I didn't realize I had missed it so much."

"I'm glad you had a good time." Doug rested his elbow on the back of the sofa as he turned to face her. "At the end of the semester we'll have our annual senior trip, where we go skiing at Big Bear. It's not as cold as it is here, but I'm sure you'll enjoy it."

"It sounds great!" She looked into his eyes. "Thanks for bringing me here."

He gazed back at her. "Thanks for coming, and for giving me a chance to redeem myself and show you I'm not a total jerk."

She smiled. "Well, the night isn't over yet."

"Thanks for the confidence." Doug chuckled, then became serious again, as he maintained eye contact. "Really, sometimes I don't know what comes over me. These feelings and urges...they just happen in a flash and overpower my brain...like a compulsion."

"It must be your hormones responding to your natural instincts."

"What do you know about that?"

"Evolutionary theory...survival of the fittest," she said matter-of-factly.

"Oh, you mean where animals and humans have a natural instinct to survive and reproduce in order to pass on their genes...and those who are the most successful have their traits carried on in the gene pool, which causes the species to evolve and change over millions of years."

"Yes, that is it. You sound like you are reciting it from the textbook."

"We covered it in biology last month, so it's still fresh in my mind. But it's about changes that happened millions of years ago...I never thought about it relating to me."

"Well, it does...it relates to all of us. You still have the same instincts that evolved in cave men to help them survive and reproduce. They keep popping up to influence your behavior."

"The behavior you're referring to would be planning and scheming to get sex."

"Ja."

"So you admit that it's a natural instinct for guys to do that, and yet you don't like it when it happens."

"Hmm, you're right...I did get mad at you for that, didn't I?" She smiled. "I guess that is because a girl's view of sex is different from a guy's."

"That's for sure. You make us work for sex like it's a prize. Don't girls have the same instincts to spread their genes?"

"Yes, but our instincts promote different behaviors. Did your biology course cover evolutionary psychology?"

"No, I haven't heard about that."

"It relates current human behavior to our evolutionary instincts, and gives a good explanation for why males and females view sex differently."

"So, let me in on the secret of the female sex drive." Doug spoke softly and dramatically as he leaned forward with interest.

"Good evening. Can I get you anything?" A young attractive waitress had suddenly appeared. She was wearing black pants that hugged her round hips and matched her short black hair; in between a white polo shirt was stretched to the limit across her large breasts.

Doug's eyes widened as he scanned her up and down rapidly; he then turned to Vindi. "Do you want anything?"

"How about some hot chocolate?" She placed her fingers over her mouth, suppressing a giggle.

"Make that two," Doug instructed. The waitress gave Vindi a quick smile as she walked away.

Vindi's amusement burst forth. "Did you see what you just did?" She laughed.

Doug looked confused. "What's so funny? What did I do?"

"It was so perfect!" Eventually her laughter calmed, but she continued to chuckle between words. "The way you looked her over...it was a perfect illustration...of what we are talking about. A guy's instincts motivate him to want to have sex with an attractive woman whenever he can." She became more serious, but continued to smile at his puzzlement. "That is a good strategy for guys to pass on their genes, because they can theoretically make a baby every time they have sex."

"I wasn't thinking about having sex with her."

She giggled again. "Maybe not consciously, but it was your unconscious instinct that stimulated your interest in her appearance. That's the way instincts work…we are usually not aware of them."

He smiled in defeat. "Okay, I see your point…and I agree that guys will get sex whenever they can. Now tell me what motivates girls to have sex."

"I'm sure you already know, but here is the theory." Vindi shifted her position on the sofa. "Girls do have a prize to give, because a guy has millions of sperm, but a girl has only one egg at a time. A guy can have sex and then just walk away, but if the egg is fertilized the girl has to grow the thing inside her for nine months, then take care of a helpless infant and keep it alive. So her instincts tell her not to have sex with just anybody who comes along, but to shop around for a good partner."

"Okay, like in the animal world," Doug suggested, "where the males fight over females, and the winner gets to mate with her, because he proved he is stronger. Or like male birds having bright colors so the females will choose them. I suppose with humans that's like a guy being handsome, so he can give a woman healthy children…big and strong, so he can fight lions and bring home food…"

"Drive a cool car, which proves he has money in the cave bank," she added.

"Right."

"Those are all things that work for you."

"Well, thanks for noticing." He peered into her eyes. "So, tell me…why don't they work on you?"

"Who said they don't? I am here, ja?" She flashed a coy smile.

"You mean…there's a chance…"

"There you go, scheming again."

"Well…"

She leaned toward him and spoke seriously. "I recognize that I'm attracted to your good looks, and muscular body, and evidence of success. And if I didn't know these were my instincts I might think it meant that I was in love with you, and that you should be in love with me. That's the other motivation that girls have for sex. Caring…love…the feeling that a guy will make a commitment to them and be in love with them only."

"You're right…I do know about that one. We *all* know about that one."

"You sound like it annoys you."

"Well, sure it does. Girls will act interested in me, then when I get interested they start wanting me to be exclusive with them…it happens practically every time. Then they get mad that I don't want to get tied down."

"Girls cannot help that…it is their natural instinct."

"Why?"

"It's the egg again. A girl cannot just have sex and walk away like a guy can. In cave man times while the baby was growing inside her and after it was born, she needed help from the guy to keep her and it alive."

"Oh, I get it. So cave women who had sex freely and didn't insist that the guy hang around to help didn't pass on their free-spirit genes, because their babies didn't survive. But those who insisted that a man make a commitment, like bringing her food and not taking food to other women, would have passed on their 'wanting a commitment' genes.

"That's right…and multiply that over thousands of years, and here we are with the same instinctual urges, whether we know it or not."

"Yeah, that definitely fits. But now that we have birth control, girls could loosen up a little."

"Well, they have, but our instincts don't evolve that fast, so girls still have a desire for their partner to be committed to them. We are still guided by our cave woman brains, you know, just as you guys still have a cave man inside you."

Doug thought for a moment. "Nature is a cruel jokester. A guy's instinct is to have sex with any girl, and to keep looking around for other opportunities. The girl's instinct is to *not* let the guy have sex with her unless he stays with her and ignores the other girls. No wonder they call it a war between the sexes."

The waitress arrived with mugs on a tray, and Doug presented an obvious display of disinterest in her as he signed the receipt.

"Did you see that?" he asked after she had left. "I can control my instincts."

"Congratulations. You actually have an advanced human brain."

"What do you mean?"

"Just because your instincts are motivating you to do something doesn't mean that you have to follow them. Your instincts come from your primitive brain. You also have a section in your brain that is more advanced. It can analyze your motivations and choose whether to follow them or not." She narrowed her eyes and peered at him. "You must *own* your instincts."

"How do I do that?"

"That means you *understand* them, *control* them, and do not let them control you. It *is* possible, you know."

"Hmm. Why don't you show me how that works by controlling *your* instincts that tell you not to have sex with me?"

"Oh, that is very funny." He winked at her across their mugs as they sipped their cocoa.

"So, here's a question," Doug offered as he set his mug on the table in front of him. "How do men and women ever get together?"

She laughed.

"Why is that so funny?"

"It's funny that you have to ask that. Obviously, you have always had girls interested in you without having to work at it."

"That's what Quinn says."

"You're an alpha male. You have the characteristics that females look for in a partner, so they come after you. They each want you exclusively, but your instincts are to spread your genes with as many of them as possible, as often as you can."

"Wow, you really know me."

She chuckled. "You are in the textbook. But tell me this...why do you think Quinn is with Maggie, and Dave with Jillian?" She took a long drink of her cocoa and watched him as he thought.

"Well, I could say because they like them, but to be honest, I'd have to say that they are giving the girls what they want...an exclusive relationship...so they can get what they want, which is sex. But that makes it sound like that's the only thing that guys care about...that it's all about the sex."

She chuckled. "That is the whole point. Nature has designed males and females to seek each other in order to reproduce, even though we are not consciously aware of it. All we know is that we find someone we are attracted to and enjoy being with. If there were no male or female sex drive, girls would probably be happier hanging out with girls, and boys with boys, because our interests are so different...don't you agree?"

"Hmm, if there were no sex involved, would I want to hang around with girls?" Doug scanned the massive rafters the supported the wooden ceiling as he pondered his question. "Wow, I see your point. It would be like before puberty, when I thought girls were a nuisance." He paused in thought again. "But if we didn't have the whole reproductive process, we probably wouldn't have the differences that drive each other crazy."

She laughed. "That makes sense!"

"So we're stuck with our differences that create conflicts, and draw us to each other at the same time," Doug surmised. "Girls want to be in love, and guys want sex."

"That's right. But consider this: there is also an instinct that causes males to 'fall in love,'" she made quotation marks with her fingers, "because it gives their offspring a better chance of survival. So watch out...it might even happen to you someday."

"It probably will, but not for a long time. My alpha male instincts are still going strong." Doug smiled seductively. "No pressure, but since you're attracted to me, why not follow *that* instinct and sample the goods?" He opened his arms and puffed his chest as he spoke.

Vindi's lips curved into an amused smile. "Thanks. But I'm not looking for a protector or provider right now, so I think I can resist your charms a bit longer."

He snapped his fingers. "Rejected again! You really know how to trample on my feelings!"

"Oh, ja, I am so worried about that!"

Doug became serious. "So, where did you learn all this stuff?"

"When I was at university in Sweden, some of the guys would talk about their anthropology classes. I read some of the chapters, and we would discuss them."

"How did you happen to be there?"

She hesitated. "Well, Sven was a student there...it was his last semester. I...had nowhere else to go, so he sort of smuggled me into his dorm."

"How long were you there?"

"About three months."

"Was it an all-male dorm?"

"Ja."

"Hmm. I guess you learned a lot about guys while you were there."

Vindi's lips formed a half smile. "You could say that. I felt like that woman…what was her name?…who studied the apes."

"Oh, right." Doug nodded. "I'm sure it was just like being in a jungle."

Vindi chuckled, then changed the subject. "Speaking of university…what are your plans for college?"

"Well, I'll have all my high school credits after this semester, so next semester I'm going to take a foreign exchange class where I'll be going to Europe for three months. I still have to decide where I'm going to college after that."

"You mean you won't be at school any more after this semester?"

"That's right."

"That is just three weeks away!"

"I know. Will you miss me?"

"Hmm…maybe."

He shook his head. "You just can't give a guy a break, can you?"

"Well, no," she smiled. "I guess it's my instinct."

"Right."

"Are you going to miss the class ski trip?"

"Oh, no, I wouldn't miss it for anything. I'll be heading out the following week."

"Will you be going to Sweden?"

"No, just England, France, and Germany. I'll let you show me around Sweden some other time."

"Oh, no! Is he boring you with his grandiose plans?" Dave interjected as he approached with Jillian at his side. "Looks like we got here just in time!" Laughing, they plopped down on the small love seat across from the sofa.

"Don't laugh," Doug said in a low, sinister voice. "Vindi has been telling me the secrets of female desires."

"Oh, no, Vindi, not that!" Jillian gasped. "You'll be kicked out of the club!"

"You'll have to fill me in on that later," Dave said with interest.

"Trust me, you don't want to know," Doug advised.

Vindi laughed. "Ja, that is for sure."

"So, what's the plan for tomorrow?" Dave asked.

They discussed their options for their final day in the snow, then chatted until they began to feel sleepy.

The four of them walked to the girls' room, and as they neared the door Dave and Jillian stopped in the vacant hallway and engaged in a prolonged kiss. Vindi opened the door and stepped inside. Standing in the doorway, Doug folded his hands in front of him and flashed a sly smile. "Don't worry. I'm going to keep my promise."

"You have been the ideal gentleman." She took his hands in hers. "And this has been a fun day." She then stepped forward and raised her face, waiting for him to kiss her. Remembering her traumatic experience with Olof, Doug kissed her gently, taking care not to press toward her, and he backed off when she pulled away.

"Goodnight," she whispered. "See you tomorrow."

Doug heard the door close behind him as he started down the hall. Dave and Jillian were still wrapped in an embrace, and ignored him as he walked past them. He rubbed his chin and pursed his lips in thought. *I wonder what time that waitress gets off work.*

## Chapter 9

# A kiss should be a beginning, not an end

Vindi rejoined Doug's group at lunch most days, when the two of them were not taking a walk on the school grounds. They frequently discussed topics covered in Doug's biology class that morning.

Alisse and Jenna did not try to hide their displeasure at their loss of Doug's attention. They were even more disturbed when the group began to talk about the upcoming ski trip and Vindi was consulted by the boys as the local expert on skiing and snow.

The days passed quickly, and soon their final exams were completed and the semester was over. Almost every member of the senior class and several chaperones boarded a bus early Saturday morning and traveled to Big Bear for the annual overnight outing.

While many of the students headed for the snowboarding playground, Vindi joined Doug, Quinn and others for skiing. They separated early on as they chose terrains of varying difficulty, but kept in touch with their cell phones.

Toward the early afternoon, text messages circulated among the group suggesting an early return to the lodge for a soak in the outdoor hot tub before dressing for the semiformal class dinner and dance party.

The first to arrive to the large in-ground whirlpool were Doug, Jared, and Alisse. Quinn, Maggie, Carleigh, and Jenna arrived shortly afterward. As they relaxed in the hot water surrounded by steam that rose from the surface, Jenna suddenly exclaimed, "Well, it looks like Vindi is having her own party!"

The others followed her gaze to a second floor window in the adjacent wing of the hotel. The cascading snowy hair was unmistakable against the patio door, where a body clad in one of the lodge's white terry robes was backed against the glass, apparently kissing someone whose form was not distinguishable.

As the others laughed, Doug leapt out of the water and rushed to the entrance at the end of the building. Whoever was with Vindi was obviously forcing her against the glass and pressing up against her…something he knew she would not be doing willingly.

As Quinn and Jared dashed to follow Doug, the bodies in the window shifted and Carleigh gasped, "That's Ansel!"

Doug ran up the stairway and arrived at the room to find the door locked. He backed up, then planted a firm kick next to the locking mechanism with his bare foot, as he had done many times to a board in karate class. The door moved slightly. After a second, then third kick the wooden door frame split and the door flew open.

Ansel did not turn around, but was now pressing Vindi against the wall as she struggled against him. Doug raced over, and finding Ansel's hair too short to grab, placed his hand around the front of his neck and jerked him backward forcefully, grabbing his wrist with the other hand. He then released his neck and, by manipulating his arm, spun him around and forced him to flip over and land squarely on his back. Ansel let out a loud *OOF!* and then moaned, unable to move.

Jared and Quinn had entered the room behind Doug, and observed the action. They immediately checked on Ansel, bending over him and finding that he was out of breath but otherwise did not appear injured.

"We'll take care of him," Jared said gruffly.

Ansel was heavy and limp as they pulled him up between them, but he opened his eyes and his face twisted into a snarl. "Doug, you're a fool...playing into her game! She's nothing but a slut and a tease!"

"That's enough!" Quinn growled, as they dragged him out the broken door.

Doug ignored Ansel and rushed to Vindi, who was slumped down against the wall in the corner. She was not crying, but was breathing in gasps with a glazed look in her eyes. Doug noted that her blank gaze was similar to the one she had exhibited after the trauma of seeing Lukas ride away.

"Hysterical reaction," the doctor had said. He squatted down in front of her, placing a hand on her shoulder.

"Vindi, look at me! It's Doug! You're safe…everything is fine. Look at me!"

Her glance came and went as he continued his attempts to rouse her. He lifted her chin and stared into her eyes, keeping his face close to hers to block out their surroundings. Finally he detected a glimmer of awareness.

"Look at me, Vindi! Stay with me! Everything is fine. You're safe now. Look at my eyes!"

"Doug…"

"Yes, it's me. Everything is okay." He slowly stood up, grasping her arms and pulling her up with him, continuing to examine her face. "Come on, stay with me."

As she stood up she glanced around fearfully, then gazed at Doug, her expression gradually changing into one of recognition. Tears escaped her eyes, rolling down her cheeks, and she leaned forward and lowered her face into his chest. He held her tightly, talking to her gently as she wept. She gradually calmed, but continued to tremble between spasmodic breaths.

The damaged door was open, allowing cold air to enter from the hallway, and Doug shivered with a sudden chill. He ignored it, but Vindi pushed away and touched her hand to his naked chest, finding it still damp from the tub and cold to the touch.

"You're freezing!" she exclaimed. "You need to put something on!"

"I'm okay," he protested, but Vindi had already rushed to the closet and returned with a plush terry cloth robe which she helped him into. Doug then moved to close the door of the room as securely as he could, while Vindi pulled the bedspread off one of the beds and tried to wrap it around him. "I'm okay, Vindi, really. What about you? You're not wearing anything more than I am!" He suddenly noticed her bikini under the open robe that she wore. He closed her robe and tightened the sash securely, then took the bedspread from her hands and wrapped it around her. He guided her to the edge of the bed and sat next to her, placing his hands over the spread that covered her arms. He could feel her body quivering. "Are you okay?"

"Yes. I'm just shaky." She stared past him across the room. "I want to go home. I want to call Sven...he will come get me."

"If that's what you want...I'll find a way to take you home if you want me to." Doug spoke softly and put his arms around her, resting his hands lightly on her back. "You know, you don't have to leave and miss the snow and skiing tomorrow. You're safe now. I'll stay with you and keep you safe, and I'll make sure you won't be seeing...*him*...again."

She leaned toward him, pulled her arms out of the bedspread and wrapped them around his body, pressing her face against the soft fabric that covered his chest. He hugged her protectively, and stroked her hair.

They sat silently except for Vindi's occasional deep breath followed by a slight shudder. Gradually her body became calm and her breathing even. She loosened her grip and sat up. His hand remained on her back.

"I'm okay," she said.

"Do you still want to go home?"

"No. I'm not going to let him ruin the weekend."

"Do you want to call Sven?"

"No. He would probably just overreact."

*That's for sure.* "Good. I'm glad you're staying. I guess we'll skip the hot tub. Are you ready to get dressed for dinner?"

"No, I don't want to see anyone tonight. I think I'll just get room service."

"You don't have to do that. I know…I'll take you to this cute little pizza place just down the mountain. You'll like it."

"You don't have to miss the dinner for me. I'll be fine."

"No, I'm not going to leave you by yourself. I've been to these kinds of dinners and dances enough times…it's no big deal. And we can spend the day together tomorrow, if you want to."

"I would like that."

He leaned forward and gave her a light brotherly kiss on the top of her forehead, which did not appear to bother her.

"Will you stay here while I get dressed?"

"I'm not going anywhere."

She rose, dropped the spread behind her, gathered several items from her suitcase, then went into the bathroom.

There was a knock on the door, causing it to slide open, the broken latch providing no resistance. Mr. Davis was one of the chaperones on the trip, and had been informed about the incident by Jared and Quinn. After hearing Doug's account of the event he called the lodge manager and arranged for a meeting with the security officers. Upon learning there were no available rooms, he made the decision to trade rooms with Vindi and her roommate.

Vindi emerged from the bathroom, dressed in formfitting stretch slacks and a lightweight pale blue sweater just as Kristal, her roommate, returned from skiing. The four of them transferred the girls' belongings to Mr. Davis's room down the hall, after which Kristal immediately went into the bathroom to shower.

Vindi held Doug's hand as Mr. Davis explained that Ansel would most likely be expelled from school, and that statements would have to be filed with the lodge security and local law enforcement. It would be up to Vindi whether to press legal charges.

An hour later the reports had been made and Doug finally had his opportunity to get out of the bathrobe and into some clothes. Vindi accompanied him to his room, and waited while he showered and dressed. Quinn was there, wearing an elegant suit and tie, and kept Vindi company with light conversation about winter Olympic events.

Doug insisted that Vindi bring her parka, hat and gloves. A brief taxi ride brought them to the cozy pizzeria. It was bustling and noisy, but they found a corner where they were able to ignore the crowd. Vindi kept her hand in his until their food arrived. She was controlled and serene, quieter and more serious than usual.

"Thanks for saving me…again," Vindi said calmly.

"You don't have to thank me. What happened…or do you not want to talk about it?"

"He said he had to talk to me about something, then he pushed his way in and grabbed me. He smelled like he had been drinking beer."

"I'm really sorry."

"It looked like you flipped him. How did you do that?"

"Jujitsu. It's a martial art that uses body mechanics and the physics of motion. You should learn some defensive moves. You don't have to be strong for them to be effective, and you can use them on people who are bigger than you are."

"That sounds like a good idea. I think I'll look into it." She paused. "So…you're leaving on Monday?"

"Yes, to the campus, then we leave on Thursday to Europe."

"When will you return?"

"In May. I plan to come to prom and graduation."

"I will miss you."

"That's good to hear." *What timing! I might actually have a chance with her now, and here I am leaving the country for three months! Who knows what might happen if I didn't go on this trip?* He felt they had established a connection, and could almost see himself having an exclusive relationship with her.

As they finished their meal and he paid the bill, he checked the time. "Looks like it's time for your surprise."

"What?" She looked at him quizzically, her eyes glistening in the reflected candlelight.

He led her out the front door and down the walk along the side of the restaurant. On a snowy path just behind the back parking lot stood a sturdy black horse harnessed to an open-air sleigh.

"A sleigh ride!" Vindi hurried forward. She greeted the driver, then they climbed in and placed a heavy blanket over their laps. Doug adjusted her hat over her ears, tucking her hair behind her shoulders.

It was a clear, cold night, and after leaving the lights of the town area the sky became black, with bright specks of light scattered throughout the entire canopy. There was no sound except the muffled scrunches of the horse's steps and the swoosh of the sled runners on the packed snow.

Vindi gazed around her in all directions. A moment later she lowered her face and leaned against Doug's soft jacket. It took a few seconds before he realized that she was crying silently. Remembering her reaction when horseback riding, he did not say anything, but put his arms around her and lightly smoothed the wisps of hair that fluttered around her shoulders.

When she regained control she said, "I'm sorry."

"You don't have to apologize. Were you thinking about Sweden?"

"Ja...about how my life changed when my parents...everything was so...oh...I'm just being selfish and feeling sorry for myself." She wiped her eyes with her glove.

"I hope this ride isn't making you sad."

"Oh, no, it's wonderful! Thank you so much!" She looked up at him, and he leaned his face down and touched his lips lightly to hers. She returned the kiss without hesitation, touching his face and neck, then sliding her hand to his chest. The remainder of the scenery passed by unnoticed as they continued to embrace, until they eventually felt the sleigh come to a gentle stop.

They were at the back of the lodge, with silent woods on one side and an expanse of smooth moonlit snow stretching toward the building on the other. Vindi chatted with the driver as she petted and murmured to the horse. Doug waited, then finally beckoned her to the path toward the building's back entrance.

As their footsteps crunched on the snow-covered sidewalk, they could see the second floor windows brightly lit where the senior class students were finishing their dinner and starting the dance. They barely glanced at the curious faces looking down at them as they walked arm in arm toward the doorway, stepping carefully on the slippery surface.

"Now I want to do what we do in Sweden after a sleigh ride!" Vindi said with excitement when they reached the dry steps.

"And what might that be?" Doug asked hopefully.

"Drink hot cocoa and sit in front of a warm fire!"

"Oh, of course. Well, let's do it!"

With hot cocoa in hand, they could hear music from the dance above as they passed by the staircase. They discovered that seats near the fireplace were taken, so Doug led her to an alcove that provided only a fragmented view of the crackling fire, but was dim and private.

"Do you want to go upstairs to the dance?" Doug asked.

"No, not really." He was satisfied with that answer. They removed their coats and sat on the firm sofa, sipping their cocoa. When Vindi put down her mug, Doug moved closer and took her hand as he leaned forward to kiss her.

"What are you doing?" She placed her hands on his chest and he backed away as she pushed against him.

"Continuing where we left off."

"No. I don't want to do that now."

"Do you want to go somewhere more private?"

"No!" she huffed.

"You didn't stop me before!"

"I know, but this is different!"

"How different?"

"You can't figure it out? We had on coats...and were in a sleigh...I felt safe."

"And now you don't?"

"No! You are doing just what others do...pushing me...and breathing on me!" She stood and walked a few paces away from him.

He rose and followed her. "I don't get it! First you're hot, and then you turn cold!"

"I thought we were friends!" She spun around and faced him.

"What, like the way you and Lukas are friends? Obviously, I don't excite you as much as he does!" He glared down at her.

"What is your obsession with Lukas?"

"You're hiding something about him. Tell me the truth!"

"Go away and leave me alone!" She turned and stood with her back to him.

"Fine. Keep your secret. What do I care?" He walked away, then stomped noisily up the wooden stairway.

Vindi remained motionless with her arms crossed, fuming with anger. After a few moments she heard the unmistakable sound of billiard balls clicking against one another. She peered beyond the alcove area and saw a dim paneled room that was vacant except for Matt and Kenneth, who were playing pool under a focused overhead light. She walked toward them.

## Chapter 10

# A monkey in a tuxedo is still a monkey

"Hi, Vindi," Matt said. "We didn't hear anything."

"Is there anything we can do for you?" Kenneth asked.

"No, thanks anyway. Wait…yes! You can let me play pool with you!"

"I've heard you're really good."

"Sometimes. Are you afraid?" She smiled.

"Of you? Huh! Never!" Matt puffed out his chest.

She looked more closely at him. He was not wearing his glasses, and he had a new, more stylish haircut. Both he and Kenneth were dressed quite fashionably.

"Did you get contacts?" she asked.

"Yes…and how about our fancy duds?"

"You guys look great! Why are you not at the dance?"

"Oh, no one wants to dance with us. I'm sure we'll have more fun here. Even with our new look, we know...we just don't fit in."

"Who does?" Vindi shrugged.

Kenneth racked the balls for a new game, and the boys insisted that Vindi break. She made four successful shots, then missed. As Matt took a turn, Vindi inquired, "Do you guys ever ask anyone out?"

"No."

"Why not? Are you interested in anyone?"

"How about you?" Kenneth suggested.

"No, I'm not interested in dating, but there are many other girls who are."

Kenneth took a turn after Matt, the two boys playing as a team against Vindi. After he finished he stated abruptly, "Matt has liked Alisse since grade school."

"Be quiet!" Matt was obviously embarrassed. "I know...it's totally unrealistic."

"Maybe, maybe not," Vindi said thoughtfully, "but why would you want to date someone who does not share your interests?"

"I don't know why, but I've always been attracted to her. She doesn't even know I'm alive! Do you think my new look might help?"

"I don't know, Matt, but you're smart and interesting. You don't have to change yourself for anyone."

"Maybe a little change won't hurt," Kenneth observed.

Vindi sank two more balls on her turn, then the boys scolded her for purposely missing the next shot.

"What about Marie and Liz?" Vindi asked.

"Oh, they're just friends."

"You have never asked them out? Why?"

"The usual…fear of rejection," Kenneth replied, and Matt nodded his agreement.

"Girls feel that too, you know."

"They do?"

"Of course! But even if you get rejected, you will at least know you made an effort. Take a chance!"

The game ended when Kenneth sank the eight ball prematurely.

"We should go to the dance," Vindi decided. "You guys look too good for me to have you all to myself!" They hesitated, but followed her upstairs.

Loud music was playing, and a few of the teens were dancing freestyle in small groups. Vindi and the boys picked up soft drinks, then joined Marie, Liz and a few other girls at their half-empty table. She directed Matt and Kenneth to sit on opposite sides of the table next to the girls, while she took a seat next to Matt.

"Wow, I thought the boys looked good, but you girls look amazing!" Vindi smiled at each one in turn, unconcerned that her own casual attire was totally out of place. Matt and Kenneth voiced their agreement as they surveyed the sophisticated and attractive hairstyles, cosmetics and cocktail dresses the girls displayed.

Suddenly Jared plopped down next to Vindi, and leaned in close to speak into her ear over the noise. "Are you okay?"

"Ja, I'm fine…thanks."

"What happened with you and Doug?"

"Nothing to talk about."

"He's such a jerk! How about a dance?" She agreed, and they moved to the dance floor. She caught a glimpse of Doug dancing with Jenna, his casual slacks and sweater contrasting with her elegant dress, jewelry and stylish hairdo. He did not look at Vindi.

Doug's disinterest was noted by the other boys in the room, who saw the potential opportunity and hovered around Vindi during and between the subsequent dance numbers. She shared her attention among them, and avoided pairing off with any particular one.

When the music slowed several boys asked Vindi to dance, but she declined and returned to the table where the others had remained seated the entire time.

"Come here, Matt," she beckoned, and after some flustered hesitation, he allowed her to lead him to the dance floor. As Vindi's rejected partners gradually stopped staring and filtered away, Matt's unease faded. It became evident that he was quite a good dancer, and he began to enjoy the moment.

After they returned to the table Jared, Chad, and Adrian took the empty chairs near Vindi. Not to be left out, Alisse, Carleigh and a few others pulled chairs up and joined them. Across the room Doug and Jenna were left sitting with Quinn and Maggie.

The DJ announced a "Dance through the History of Rock and Roll," and started a lively tune from the fifties era. Matt jumped up and reached for Vindi's hand. "Let me show you how to shag!"

"How to what?" She followed him to the dance floor.

"My parents are in a dance association, and I've been doing this since I was a kid!"

Vindi faltered as he attempted to teach her the basic step. Suddenly Alisse stepped in. "I'll show you how to do it!"

Vindi backed off and watched with amazement as Matt and Alisse danced synchronously to the lively rhythm— stepping, passing and twirling. The other students gathered around them, clapping and cheering them on, and applauded when the number ended.

"How do you know how to shag?" Matt asked Alisse.

"My father is in a club, and he makes me dance with him all the time," she laughed. "You're really good!"

When the next song from the sixties began, Vindi persuaded everyone at her table to form a freestyle group on the dance floor. When Chad, Jared and others tried to get her to split off with them, she refused. Instead, she moved about the floor, bringing other dancers into the cluster.

Eventually a large circle was formed that incorporated practically everyone on the dance floor. Not yet satisfied, Vindi approached students who remained at the tables and invited them to join the group.

Doug watched Vindi's efforts, and without waiting to see whether she would approach his table he stood up. "Let's get in on that!" He led the others to the circle, which expanded to make room for them.

Noticing the activity, the DJ transitioned the music without interruption to keep the action moving. Individuals and couples began to take turns stepping into the middle to show off their moves, as the dancers that formed the ring laughed and applauded.

It became a magical moment, as the group of students—most of whom had been classmates since grade school—felt their teenage anxieties and perceived isolation melt away in an air of joyful familiarity and acceptance of one another. Doug found himself cheering for former friends he had not paid attention to in years, even though they still shared his classrooms every day.

Matt and Kenneth took the center together and performed an intricate robot dance, eliciting applause and genuine respect from the crowd. Alisse then pulled Matt back in; their moves and spins to the seventies disco beat made them look like professional dancers, to the delight of their astonished classmates.

Todd led Vindi to the center to join them. As he twirled and spun her the group began to chant, "Go Todd, go Todd!"

The crowd continued to call the dancers by name as they moved in and out of the center. Several times boys pulled Vindi in to dance with them at their turn, and she happily followed their lead.

Liz hesitated at her turn, as the excited group chanted, "Go Liz, go Liz!" Kenneth led her to the center and stood behind her, holding her hands as he directed her through robot moves synchronized to a techno beat. Overcoming her embarrassment, she laughed as the crowd cheered.

Marie was next, and moved forward awkwardly to chants of "Ma-rie, Ma-rie!" She smiled shyly, but stood clapping her hands to the beat, obviously reluctant to attempt any dance moves. Seeing her discomfort, Doug dashed to her and guided her gently through several turns as if he were waltzing with a princess, keeping his step in rhythm with the pounding pulse of the music.

She beamed and blushed as she gazed at him in awe, and he returned to his place in the circle amidst an approving applause, surprised by the reaction his deed had elicited. He sensed a sudden awareness of the respect his classmates felt for him, and realized that every person in the room was as much a friend to him as they had ever been—it was he who had created a barrier that they could not cross.

He had little time to ponder his thoughts, as Quinn took a turn and motioned Doug into the center with him to perform the "monkey man" dance they had invented in the sixth grade. The group laughed and cheered at their antics, as they laughed at themselves.

Next Maggie brought Jenna in with her, and they danced around each other, mostly wiggling their hips and bumping them together in rhythm to the music. As Maggie returned to her place, Jenna pulled Doug in to dance with her, as if she were jealous of his attention to Marie and intended to reaffirm her position with him.

A dynamic rap number came up next, and several students took turns at performing various hip-hop and breaking moves, to the delight of the energetic crowd. Adrian brought Vindi in, and she laughed as she tried to mimic his moves while the group began to chant, "Vin-di, Vin-di."

As they continued, the music morphed into a punk beat and the dancers in the center began to jump up and down with their arms in the air; others began to join them. The circle gradually lost its shape as the teens jumped about erratically, clapping their hands high over their heads and cheering with uninhibited euphoria.

The DJ activated a strobe light and played short bursts of various soundtracks in rapid sequence, with a gradual increase in volume that seemed to echo the energy of the crowd. When the set finally concluded there was a prolonged cheer of elation followed by happy exhaustion.

The lights dimmed and a slow song began quietly, as many of the students picked up drinks and sat or stood in clusters, conversing with a newfound fellowship and ease. Vindi accepted an invitation to dance with Todd. As they moved about the floor she observed with pleasure the relaxed contentment of her classmates, and smiled when she saw Kenneth and Liz holding hands as they talked. She bumped into the couple behind her, and her eyes widened in surprise when she turned around to see Matt wink at her over Alisse's shoulder, as he guided her confidently across the dance floor.

Two days after the ski trip Vindi received a text from Doug. It surprised her at first, but then she remembered that she had given him her number when they went to Sequoia.

"*Here I am apologizing again. U must get tired of hearing this but I really am sorry. It seems I'm not as civilized as I thought I was. It's probably good that I'm leaving. BTW what u did at the dance was really cool. Hope to see u at prom.*"

She replied: "*I hope u have a good trip.*"

She did not see or hear from him again until four months later, when he walked into the hotel ballroom with Jenna at his side.

The senior prom was a formal affair; the boys wore tuxedos while the girls displayed elegant colorful dresses of all styles and lengths. Vindi's dress was a subtle swirl of pale blues with embroidery at the bodice and halter neckline and a long, draping skirt. Her hair was lifted at the crown and cascaded in soft curls that created a shimmering halo, with wispy swirls fluttering around her face.

The mood was electric as couples alternately danced and mingled, testing their elegance and sophistication in anticipation of an auspicious future. The magic from the dance at Big Bear still lingered, and no one in the class was outcast on this occasion, as evidenced by the spectacle of

Matt and Alisse waltzing gracefully to their requested number.

There was a small commotion at the ballroom entrance, and from across the room Vindi could see that Doug and Jenna had arrived. Doug looked fantastic in his black tux, and it surprised Vindi that she was so attracted to his handsome image. His tan had faded, causing his black hair to present an even more conspicuous contrast to the shades of blond to which she was accustomed. She observed his movements and laughter as he greeted his friends and answered their queries about his European excursion.

"Vindi…would you like to dance?"

She looked at her escort. "Ja, I would love to."

When the crowd around Doug finally dispersed he scanned the room, looking for Vindi. He saw the sparkling white hair first, then the pale curve of her upper back as her partner led her in a slow dance.

Doug's head jerked and he inhaled sharply when the couple turned and he caught sight of her dance partner. *It's Lukas!* His stomach tightened and his heart thumped against his ribs.

As he continued his blatant observation, he eventually recognized that it was not Lukas. This guy had a more athletic physique, and his hair was more brown than blond. He was better looking than Lukas, too, with the seductive look of a soap-opera actor. He appeared to be a few years older than the teenagers—probably a college student. As they danced he held Vindi gingerly, as if she might break.

Doug crossed the room and was waiting when the dance ended.

"Hi, Vindi."

"Hi, Doug. It's great to see you. You look great!"

"Thanks. You look...amazing." He looked at her escort. "Hi, I'm Doug."

"Hello, Doug. Ian." They shook hands. "Nice to meet you."

"Likewise. How do you know Vindi?"

"I am teaching her jujitsu."

"Oh, really?" *Hmm, British accent. Where did she find him?*

"Yes, and she is a great student." Ian smiled at Vindi. "A fast learner, with great technique."

Doug narrowed his eyes at Ian, wondering if he was insinuating something besides martial arts.

"It was your idea," Vindi said, "and a good one."

"Great!" Doug replied with forced enthusiasm. A momentary image flashed through his brain of Ian sparring with Vindi in a jujitsu hold, their bodies pressed against each other. He then put himself in the image in Ian's place. After the slightest pause, he looked at Vindi. "Can we talk for a moment?"

"Ja, sure." She excused herself and he led her to the outdoor balcony of the ballroom. As they walked he leaned close to her ear.

"What's going on around here? Jenna told me about Matt and Alisse, and Chad and Carleigh, but...Jared with Marie?"

"Ja," she smiled. "A few things have changed since you have been gone."

"Incredible!" He shook his head. "I'm sure you had something to do with that." The music and laughter became muffled as the door closed behind them.

"Actually, I think you did," she said quietly. They walked to the railing. The wisps of her hair swirled in the soft evening breeze as they glanced at the ocean below.

Doug looked at her. "Where does Ian teach martial arts? I haven't seen him before."

"Oh, he doesn't teach anywhere. He's giving me private lessons."

"Oh, really? Has he taught you enough yet to fend off his advances?"

Vindi chuckled. "Not yet, but not to worry. He works with Sven, so you know what that means."

Doug huffed. "Yeah. He won't be getting fresh with you...unless you want him to." He shook his head and thumped the railing with his fist. "Damn! There I go again, questioning your relationship with another guy. I have no right to do that!"

"It's part of being an alpha male. As the textbook says, you are...compelled to compete." The accented words rolled off her tongue as she looked into his face and smiled.

"Yeah, maybe." The electric torches that decorated the outside of the building cast a soft glow and revealed sparkles of tiny sequins on her dress; he contemplated the reflections in her pale eyes. "Are you still mad at me for what happened at Big Bear?" he asked somberly.

"No, it's okay."

"No, it's not okay. I don't do that." He shook his head and scowled.

"Do what?"

"Put pressure on a girl. There's no excuse for what I did, and I'm really sorry."

"You didn't put pressure on me. You were just..."

"Being a jerk."

"Well, yes, that is true." Her lips curved upward as she cocked her head slightly and gazed at him.

"I felt bad about it the whole time I was in Europe."

"Oh, ja, I am sure that is all you were thinking about."

He chuckled at her amused expression. "All right. I guess I forgot who I'm talking to. Maybe that was an exaggeration. I did think about you, though." He met her gaze. "How have you been?"

"Very good. Having fun. Is everything okay with you?"

"Oh, *there* you are, Doug," Jenna announced crisply as she approached from the doorway. "Hi, Vindi." She glanced at her sideways, with a bored expression.

"Hello, Jenna. That is a beautiful dress."

"Thanks." She took Doug's arm. "Let's go inside. The wind is messing up my hair."

Doug frowned, not moving. "Well, that's awfully rude. We happen to be talking."

"Well, can't we talk inside?"

"You go inside. I'll be in when Vindi and I are finished."

"Well!" She turned abruptly with a swish of her red gown and marched into the ballroom.

"I'm going to be in trouble for that one," Doug sighed.

"Well, I'm sure you can handle it, now that you understand women so well." Vindi had turned to face the ocean, her hands resting on the balcony railing. She looked at him and smiled.

"What?" He then realized she was referring to their conversation at Sequoia. "Oh, yeah, right. That's not much help."

Vindi scanned the ocean that melted into blackness before them. Doug gazed at her as puffs of the night breeze played with wisps of her hair that danced around her face. *You don't have to stay with Ian tonight. Let's take off and go somewhere.*

The unspoken words floated through Doug's mind, followed by images of Vindi holding her gown up as she ran barefoot in the surf below. He followed, his tux trousers rolled to his knees, his bare feet sculpting fleeting footprints in the wet sand. They laughed as he caught her. Their kiss was long and passionate.

*She'd never go for it. What about Jenna...and Ian? Maybe she is dating him. This isn't some Hollywood movie. What happens after the kiss? We live happily ever after? Hardly.*

He saw the kiss again in his mind. Suddenly she pulled away, turned and walked into the darkness. He stood alone with his arms out. Empty.

"I should get back to Ian." Vindi's words brought Doug back to reality. "It has been really good seeing you again." Her eyes lingered on his.

"You too."

She turned and stepped lightly toward the door. He followed, noticing that her former boyish movements had given way to a feminine grace. Doug contemplated the sway of her hip, the creamy smoothness of her shoulders and neck, her lithe body gliding in the dim light. She looked so fragile, so vulnerable...so untouchable.

He reached forward and opened the door, then entered the ballroom behind her. She did not look back as she walked toward Ian, who was chatting with several students. Doug scanned the room, looking for Jenna.

For the next two weeks Doug reacquainted himself with several of the girls from school, but spent most of his time with Jenna or Quinn. He did not see Vindi again until the graduation ceremony.

He arrived late and took his place in the long line of flowing gowns and cardboard caps. Behind him was Matthew Howe, who had stood next to him in alphabetical line-ups—and had been ignored by him—for the past eight years. Next in line was Vindi, and this time it was Matt who stood with his back to Doug and chatted with the most beautiful girl in the class.

In addition to his new haircut and contacts, Matt displayed an air of confidence Doug had never seen before;

and even Jenna had placed her stamp of approval on the stylish clothing Alisse now picked out for him.

The music began, and Doug had no opportunity to talk to Vindi as the procession of students filed into the auditorium and took their seats. When the ceremony ended and the new graduates scattered to find their families, she disappeared among the chaos.

He waited for his father and brother to make their way through the crowd, and they followed the flow to the grassy expanse outside the auditorium where the former classmates, families and teachers gathered in clusters, taking photographs and saying their goodbyes.

It was impossible to miss seeing Sven, who stood a head taller than almost everyone. He was wearing khaki slacks and a yellow polo shirt; his white blond hair ruffled in the light breeze.

*Looks like a surfer today,* Doug mused.

The girls in the class took notice. Doug observed groups of them greet Vindi enthusiastically, then turn aside and flirt blatantly with Sven, who appeared to be enjoying the attention and taking none of it seriously. Doug saw him laugh frequently—again the typical twenty-three-year-old.

While the girls thronged around Sven the boys avoided him, remaining outside the cluster as they talked with Vindi and had photos taken of themselves with her. Doug thought he would wait until the crowd cleared before approaching her, but his father and brother headed toward the disordered assembly, so he accompanied them.

As his father spoke with Sven, the girls turned their attention to Doug, questioning him about his recent activities and cutting short his answers with additional questions. When he saw his father place a hand on Sven's shoulder as they shook hands, signaling the close of their discussion, Doug extricated himself from the chattering girls and approached Sven with slight apprehension. He was not sure what Vindi had told him about the Big Bear excursion.

He was surprised when Sven greeted him warmly with a smile and firm handshake. This time Sven placed his hand on Doug's shoulder.

"I have not had a chance to thank you for what you did for Vindi at Big Bear." Sven's gaze was suddenly somber. "I am glad you were there, and able to manage that...*skitstövel.*" Sven growled the word, making its meaning obvious.

*Oh, that.* Doug returned his gaze, equally serious. "No thanks necessary. I'm glad I was there at the right time."

"And that you know how to kick a door in."

They chatted briefly, this time as almost equals, but with a hint of fatherly authority from Sven. As Doug said goodbye and turned away, the clumps of people shifted again, like a living organism taking a breath. He made his way to Vindi, which prompted the boys around her to back away, while the girls returned to Sven's sphere.

Dr. Goodwin congratulated Vindi with a hug, then insisted on taking a photo of Doug and Vindi together in their caps and gowns. Vindi gave Dave a brief hug, then gave Doug a more prolonged one.

She backed away slightly and looked up at him, and he had a fleeting thought that she wanted him to kiss her. Instead she said simply, "Goodbye, Doug. I hope you have a good summer." Her attention was then distracted by the approach of Kenneth and Liz, and Doug and his family moved on through the gatherings.

*Chapter 11*

# A bee has to fly to the flowers that have nectar, doesn't he?

Doug enrolled in summer session at a nearby campus, where his attention was divided between his studies and dating various girls who had stayed for the summer. He became familiar with the high-spirited social sisters who occupied the largest and most elite house in Sorority Row. This prompted him to join a fraternity during the brief summer rush, after which he moved in with his fellow brothers in their all-male residence on the campus perimeter.

He was pleased to find that many college girls were amenable to short-term and intermittent encounters, giving him the freedom he enjoyed in dating. The downside was a higher level of competition from other male students who were equally interested, and whom the girls apparently found as attractive and alluring as he felt himself to be. "Too many alpha males," Vindi would say.

*Ah, Vindi. Should I call her? What would I say? If I got her to go out with me, then what? I guess Quinn was right—she beat me at my game.* Doug returned his gaze to the page in his textbook and read the same paragraph again.

*Still, I know where she lives...we're practically neighbors. I'll see her again some day.*

As the mass of students arrived on campus for the fall semester, the fraternity brothers and their friends prepared for the annual pre-football season party at the house. After discussing drinks and food the conversation inevitably turned to girls.

Tyler, a second-string football player with a stocky build and short black hair, began to boast about the girl he would bring to the party. Doug had just met him, and found him to be a braggart and somewhat of a bully; he began to tune him out until he caught the phrase, "gorgeous Swedish babe." Tyler would not give her name or answer any of his questions, but laughed raucously.

"You'll have to wait and see, Duggie-boy. She's got the cutest little accent, especially when we're in the sack!" Doug scowled at his leering grin.

On Saturday Doug leaned against the kitchen doorway of the frat house, trying to conceal the fact that he was monitoring the front door for Tyler to enter with his girlfriend. He was pleased that he had finally gotten Trish, whom he had pursued all summer, to be his date for the party, and he did not want to lose his chance with her. Yet he could not shake his apprehension that Vindi would show up with Tyler.

Was his concern for her an instinctual protectiveness that carried over from the events in high school, or was he troubled that Tyler might have a relationship with her that he was never able to achieve? He really was not sure.

His heart pounded when Vindi entered the building, followed by Tyler. She was radiant, as always, and her appearance attracted the attention of everyone in the large open room. Though he did not put his arm around her or touch her, Tyler moved around with her, introducing her to his friends and the frat brothers. From what Doug could see, he was making a good pretense at being a polite gentleman.

As Tyler headed to the adjacent kitchen entrance to obtain drinks, Doug made an excuse to Trish and bolted to Vindi's side.

"Vindi! What are you doing here?"

"Oh, hi Doug." She greeted him without surprise, as if it were the most natural thing in the world for her to make a stunning entrance into his fraternity house. "I heard there was a party here." She smiled as if she had made a joke.

"How do you know Tyler?" Doug ignored her attempt at humor.

"Oh, he's in one of my classes."

"Where? Here?"

"Ja, I just started class this week."

"I didn't know you were coming here!"

"Well, here I am!"

"Are you dating him?"

"No. He just is here, with about a hundred other people."

"You mean you didn't come with him?"

"No. He asked me to, but I told him 'no.' He was outside when I arrived and he came in behind me," she explained without concern.

"Listen…do you know what he's telling people about you? He's saying you two have a relationship…and he's very crude about it."

Vindi rolled her eyes. "Tomma tunnor skramlar mest."

"What?"

"Oh, that is a Swedish saying. It means, 'empty barrels make the most noise.'"

"Yeah, it fits. But you'd better be careful…"

Tyler returned with two drinks and handed one to Vindi as he scowled at Doug. "Hey, Goodwin, Trish is looking for you and she's hoppin' mad."

"Sorry, I need to go," Doug told Vindi, ignoring Tyler. As he headed toward the kitchen Tyler walked beside him and leaned toward his ear.

"So, what do you think about the babe? Tasty, eh?"

"You're a *slimeball!*" Doug bumped against his shoulder as he cut in front of him, causing Tyler's drink to slosh out of the plastic cup he held.

"*Scuzzbag!*" Tyler then turned his attention back to Vindi, who had already abandoned, untouched, the drink he had given her.

When Doug got to the kitchen he found that Tyler had lied. Trish was chatting with two of her sorority sisters—something about clothing.

It was difficult for anyone to describe the incident that occurred a short time later. The boys had taken notice of Vindi and vied for her attention, but she was friendly to all, in her usual fashion, not committing her time to any one person or place. Tyler was always nearby, trying to give the impression that Vindi was his date for the evening.

One of the boys in the living room area remembered seeing Tyler and Vindi near the hallway, and thought he saw her push him away, then turn and walk away from him toward the center of the room. Tyler jumped after her and grabbed her arm; he might have put his other arm around her from behind. Suddenly Tyler's body appeared to roll over Vindi, and he landed flat on his back on the floor with a crashing thud.

"I told you to stop it!" Vindi yelled, looking down at him. Tyler was breathless, unable to move.

Most of the onlookers were too stunned to act, and stood gaping at the scene. Doug and Trish were in a cluster of partygoers in the opposite corner of the room, and the noise of Tyler's fall caught their attention. Doug saw Vindi standing over him and immediately deduced what had happened. While some of the boys rushed to check on Tyler, he instead darted after Vindi, who was heading out the door.

"Vindi!" he followed her out, then leapt in front of her, attempting to look into her eyes. "Are you all right?"

"Yes!" She did not look up.

"Look at me," Doug demanded softly. He stopped her on the front lawn and held one hand gently on her shoulder;

with the other he lifted her chin and scanned her face and eyes. "What did he do? Did he hurt you?"

Her lips were tight with anger. "No…he didn't have a chance!" Her face was a scowl and her eyes dry; she avoided his gaze. She took a deep breath and her shoulders twitched in an involuntary shudder.

Doug tried to hug her but she placed her hands on his chest and pushed as she stepped backward away from him. "Why do boys have to be such…Neanderthals!" She glared at him.

He looked grim. "No evolved brain, I guess."

A few students approached and asked what had happened. Vindi gave them no attention as she stood with her arms crossed, scowling at the ground in front of her. Her rapid breathing gradually slowed as Doug studied her face with concern. He glanced up and saw Trish standing on the front veranda of the frat house, watching him.

"I'm going home. I have had enough of partying." Vindi's voice was flat.

"Look at me." He touched her shoulder and she looked up at him, her face still in a frown. "Are you sure you're okay?"

"Ja."

"How did you get here?"

"I walked."

"From where?"

"Thirteenth street."

"You're not walking across campus by yourself at this hour!" He knew he should offer to walk her home, but was certain that if he left now his chances with Trish would be over for good. He felt like a louse, but knew nothing would happen between him and Vindi that night. He paused, debating what to do.

"I will walk you home, Vindi." The voice spoke with an accent, as a darkly handsome student with a slight build and straight black hair approached her, ignoring Doug.

Vindi looked up at the exotic Latino and attempted a smile. "Okay, Alejandro...thanks." She glanced briefly at Doug. "I'll be okay, Doug...goodbye." She walked away from him briskly, as if she could read his mind and knew he did not want to waste his time with her.

Doug winced as if he had been kicked in the gut, but said nothing. He watched Alejandro speak animatedly to Vindi as the pair strolled across the lawn. He then turned and strode toward the frat house. Trish was gone from the veranda, and he hurried to the door.

Doug did not see Vindi the following week, and as he walked across the school grounds in the bright sunshine he realized he had not even taken the time to ask her what classes she was taking, or what her plans were—he had been too distracted with Trish. True to form, Vindi had not disclosed where she actually lived; there was an entire row of apartment complexes on thirteenth street across from the school.

*I screwed up again! It seems like every time I'm with her I make things worse. So here she is on my campus and I can't even call her because I'm such a disgusting jerk!* He crossed the busy intersection with the walk signal and continued past the off-campus bookstore.

*There are plenty of other guys who will be after her...like that Alejandro. They'll be all over her...and they'll be bigger jerks than I am. Like Tyler. Maybe I should call her.*

He entered the martial arts facility, or dojo, where he practiced several mornings a week. As he passed the training room his musings were abruptly interrupted when he caught sight of a snowy blonde head in front of the mirrored wall.

It was Vindi, dressed in the traditional white cotton uniform, or *gi*, tied with the orange belt of a midlevel student. Her hair was plaited on each side of her head, then made two braided loops in the back. She was speaking with the instructor, whom they called Sensei. Several boys hovered around, eying her with interest, but dared not interrupt.

Sensei enforced strict rules of respectful conduct in the dojo, some of which comprised traditional Japanese etiquette for the martial arts. He was in his late thirties, with a solid build that matched his military background. He had traveled and read extensively, and was well versed in both Western and Eastern philosophy, as well as various branches of science. He made himself available as a mentor and counselor to his students and was viewed by many of them as a father figure, especially those who were away from home for the first time.

Doug hastily changed into his gi in the locker room, eager to join the group. It was a jujitsu class that encompassed all ranks, where participants initially trained with random partners, then subsequently paired off with those of similar rank. There were two other girls and five boys in the class on this particular day, which was usual for a morning session.

When Doug returned he was relieved to note that Vindi was still talking to Sensei, and none of the boys had been able to approach her. Once the class began Sensei did not allow discussions about anything other than the techniques being practiced.

Sensei introduced Vindi, after which the students formed two lines in order of their belt colors. They counted in Japanese along with the leader during the warm-up exercises.

With his advanced level black belt, Doug occupied the left end of the front row, while Vindi placed in the center behind him. Although he knew he was supposed to focus on the movements and clear his mind of external thoughts, on this particular day he followed the motions mechanically, his brain focused on how to get paired off with her in the next segment—certain that every other male in the room was involved in the same thought process. This was no time to play a passive game, worry about rejection or feel guilty about his recent dismissive treatment of her.

The warm-up period ended with breakfalls; Sensei then called for paired training. Doug moved to Vindi, but the young-looking blue-belted student next to her was already asking her to partner with him. Doug interrupted politely, unabashedly using his rank to his advantage as he assumed the legitimate role of instructor, questioning Vindi about the breakfall they had just performed. As the discussion continued, blue-belt recognized the tactic and sought another partner.

The pairs began with simple grabs and escapes, then moved to more complex techniques. As they conferred about the next maneuver, Doug broke Sensei's rule by suddenly leaning forward and murmuring softly, "How about lunch after class?" Vindi nodded. Doug had trouble hiding his smile as he fulfilled his fantasy of sparring with her.

As a practical matter, Vindi had been trained to respond to grabs more than punches. She responded to Doug's grabbing attacks with wrist locks, then subsequently performed body drops and hip throws, which she performed smoothly and skillfully, propelling his weight over her with ease. She finished with either arm locks or simulated head kicks.

She then attacked Doug with punches. He blocked these, then followed with hip throws and arm locks. When he threw her she floated gracefully over his body, landing with perfect breakfalls. Doug was deliberate in keeping his attention focused on the moves, suppressing the images his testosterone-filled brain was trying to formulate.

"Show me what happened with Tyler," Doug urged.

"Oh, he was trying to get me to go with him to his friend's room…supposedly to show me some stupid thing. I said no, and he grabbed my arm, and started to pull me down the hall."

"Like this?" He placed his right hand around her left arm as if to guide her in a forward direction.

"Ja...so I escaped." She jerked her arm upward rapidly, breaking his grip, then turned around abruptly. "Then when I started to walk away he came after me and grabbed my other arm really hard. I could tell he was mad."

As she moved forward, Doug moved behind her and gripped her right arm. She suddenly stopped, jerked her elbow backward into his ribs—not using her full force—and at the same time bent her knees to lower her shoulder beneath his right arm, grabbing it with her left hand. She then straightened her legs and leaned forward, rolling his body over her shoulder in such a smooth and rapid move that it was all he could do to slap his arms on the mat to break his fall.

He looked up at her with a shocked expression, then smiled. "Impressive!"

"Thanks." She grinned, as she gave him a hand up.

"Tyler never had a chance with that one! You know he broke a rib when he landed."

"No, I didn't hear about that!"

"Yeah...serves him right. I don't know what he told the football coach, but I'm sure his overinflated ego was hurt even more than his ribs!" Doug chuckled.

Sensei had been moving about the room observing the pupils' performances, and called for regrouping by rank. Blue-belt rushed toward Vindi, as Doug joined Marco, the other black-belt student. They sparred with advanced throws and blocks, demonstrating techniques at Sensei's prompting when he approached to observe them.

After the cool-down and change of clothing, Doug waited outside the dojo for Vindi, suspecting that the other boys who were standing around chatting had the same idea. She emerged with her hair out of the braids and floating around her shoulders, emitting golden yellow sparkles of sunlight. He saw that his assumption was correct, as they gathered around her.

As she had done in high school, Vindi met each admirer cordially, learning names and smiling, as Doug remained in the background observing the interaction. There was no rock-paper-scissors this time when they made their invitations; Doug stood like a proud conqueror when Vindi told the boys she already had plans, and approached him with a smile.

Their lunchtime stretched on for several hours, as they related their activities since Doug had left high school in January. They talked as they walked from the restaurant to a remote section of the campus, where a thin ring of trees surrounded and overlooked a small pond. Doug led her through the vegetation to a shaded bench. The leaves above them fluttered in the breeze; rays of misty sunlight sliced through to the water's edge, where an extended family of ducks drew zigzag lines across the tranquil surface.

"Oh, it's so peaceful," Vindi sighed. "I didn't know this place was here!"

"I don't think many people know about it, or care. I've always come here by myself before, when I needed some quiet time to think."

"Thanks for bringing me," she said solemnly, as if he had entrusted her with a confidential invitation to his own private hideaway.

"It'll be our secret," he whispered melodramatically, with amusement.

Vindi had not heard anything about Doug's semester in Europe, and she listened with interest to his experiences and insights. Doug asked in general how her summer had been, mindful not to question her about dating, or relationships with boys. She did not approach the subject, just as she did not ask about—nor did he discuss—aspects of his social life. Neither one mentioned Lukas.

They fell into a habit of having lunch together several times a week after morning jujitsu classes, frequently followed by extended conversations at the duck pond. He had forgotten how enjoyable it was to talk to her. They discussed their classes and schedules, and the courses of future study that interested each of them.

"How long have you been doing jujitsu?" Vindi asked him one day as she tossed pieces of bread into the water's edge.

Doug watched the ducks chase after the bread as he spoke. "I started with karate when I was eight. It was the 'in' thing to do at the time, and my parents took Dave and me regularly. I really enjoyed it, and as I got to the higher levels I switched to jujitsu and liked that even better."

"Did you ever play other sports, like baseball or football?"

"Not football, but I did play baseball in an after-school league for a few years."

"Did you ever play on a team at the school?"

"No, by the time I got to that point I decided it took too much time away from other things I wanted to do."

"Like what?"

He looked at her with a sheepish grin. "Like being available for the girls who were chasing after me. You know, following my instincts with my primitive brain."

"When was that, when you were ten?"

He chuckled. "Not quite...a few years later."

"So why did you continue with the martial arts?"

He became serious. "After my mother...was gone...my father insisted that we keep going regularly, I guess to give us something to focus on. It became a time of togetherness for the three of us. I participated in competitions for a while, and the physical challenge and philosophical aspect of martial arts really helped me get through those tough times."

"Is that why you still do it?"

"I haven't really thought about it...I guess that's part of it. I know it helps keep me balanced."

"It's useful, too," she pointed out.

"I guess we both know that."


"I see you've been hooking up with Vindi after mixed class," Marco remarked one afternoon as they spotted each other while working out in the gym. "She's a babe! Is she as good as she looks?"

"It's not like that." Doug huffed with the weight of the barbell as he lay on his back performing chest presses.

"What? You mean she doesn't put out?" Marco stood at his head, and as Doug achieved muscle fatigue, he reached forward and helped guide the bar to its stand.

"Not since I've known her...back in high school," Doug panted. He rose, wiped off the bench, and they switched positions.

"So, what's the deal?" Marco began his presses.

"I really like talking to her. We go to lunch after class...and we've gone cycling and hiking a few times on the weekend. She's fun to be with...loves the outdoors and going to new places. I like to find different places to take her."

"And then what happens?"

He shrugged. "I get a kiss at the door, and that's it."

Marco finished his set, with Doug's assistance. "You haven't put her to the test?" he panted.

Doug picked up a dumbbell and positioned himself on the end of a nearby bench for bicep curls. "Hmf! Not lately! I've tried that before...and I know it doesn't work." He spoke in rhythm with his arm flexes. "She has her reasons...I don't want to put pressure on her...and get her mad at me...again. She knows I'm available...anytime she wants it."

"So, you don't take her out at night?" Marco sat on an adjacent bench and started his curls.

"No...I usually hook up with Kayla...or Leslie...or one of the others. Dealing with their social activities...and mood swings...is enough of a challenge. I don't need to add Vindi...to the mix."

"Yeah...and why bother...if you're not going to score anyway."

Doug paused, breathing heavily. "Well...I don't think I'm that shallow!"

"Yeah, right." Marco continued flexing, ignoring Doug's indignation. "And Vindi doesn't ask...what you do at night?"

"No."

"Do you think she knows...you hook up with other girls?"

"Oh. She knows." Doug began curls with his other arm.

"So, you figure...she doesn't want to infringe...on your freedom."

"Probably."

Marco finished his set, then rested, panting lightly. "Or maybe...she doesn't want to go out with you." He inhaled and exhaled heavily. "Don't you ever wonder what she's doing at night...while you're having your fun? She might be dating other guys."

"Oh, great." Doug looked at him as he paused again. "Thanks for that thought!"

## Chapter 12

# *Did the planet shift its orbit…or is it just me?*

On the Sunday before Christmas break Doug took Vindi on a cycling trip in the central valley foothills. They paused for a rest at a picnic table, surrounded by tall trees that whispered in the crisp winter breeze. Munching on trail mix, they absorbed the silent energy of the vibrant forest of red and gold leaves.

"Are you doing anything special for Christmas?" Doug asked.

"Well, Sven has to be out of town for work during the week of Christmas, so he's taking me to Hawaii for three days before that."

"Really? Why a trip to Hawaii?"

"We have not been able to spend much time together in the past year, so he thought a little trip would be a good opportunity for us…and he wants to do something special for me. He thinks I'll enjoy Hawaii. I have heard it's beautiful."

"I'm sure you'll love it. But what will you do for Christmas?"

She shrugged. "I'll be busy enough."

"How about joining the Goodwin family for Christmas dinner?"

"Oh, I would not want to intrude on your family celebration."

"No intrusion. Dave will have Jillian there, and my father loves to cook for guests. It gets lonely sometimes with just the three of us, especially on holidays."

"Well…if you want me to come."

"I definitely want you to come. In fact, come over in the afternoon and we'll go horseback riding."

"That sounds good!"

The following week students left the campus as their classes ended. Vindi finished on Wednesday and headed home, but Doug had to attend a mandatory session on Friday morning.

His encounter with Kayla on Wednesday night turned sour when he declined to accompany her to spend the holiday with her family, and she walked out in a huff. A similar scene occurred the following evening with Leslie, who also wanted to take him home with her.

By Friday he felt relieved to be getting away from women and back to his home of bachelors. As he walked to the parking garage he received a text from Jenna: *"Im home, when can we gt tgthr?"*

He replied: *"Tnite. I'll be ovr at 6."*

A few days later he was surprised to receive a text from Vindi: *"Hawaii is beyootifull!!!"*

He smiled and replied: *"Have a great time."*

The following day his text signal woke him just before two in the morning. It was from Vindi, who most likely had forgotten about the two-hour time difference: *"My first luau. Roast pig everywhere. Ulph!"*

He texted back: *"Don't forget to eat some spam."*

He then received a photo of Vindi smiling in front of a magnificent sunset. *Well, now we're getting somewhere! She finally realizes that she wants me! This next semester may be very different...if I don't do something stupid to screw it up!*

Vindi arrived in the early afternoon on Christmas Day. Doug helped her carry in several large cloth bags from her car. After greeting Dave and Jillian, she found Dr. Goodwin in the kitchen.

"Vindi...hello! Merry Christmas!"

"Hi, Dr. G. God Jul! That's Merry Christmas in Swedish."

"Guud zhu!" he repeated.

"Thank you so much for letting me come. I hope you don't mind...I brought some traditional Swedish Christmas dishes."

"Oh, that's great!" He watched with interest as she began to unpack items from the bags.

"This is rice porridge, which is a dessert. And this is a version of glögg, a drink for after dinner. If you let me know when the meal is ready to serve, I'll start heating them so they will be ready afterward." She pulled out a tray, then a copper pot, lid and ladle from another bag, followed by a metal stand.

"Is that a fondue pot?" Doug asked.

"Something like that, but it's a glögg pot, actually. You put the flame under it here, and it keeps the glögg warm."

"What's in the glögg?" Doug pursed his lips as he tried to pronounce the word the way Vindi did.

"The original is made with wine, but I made a nonalcoholic version with black currant and raspberry juices. It's made with spices."

"Oh, that sounds good. When did you prepare these?" Dr. G asked.

"I made the rice porridge this morning, but I did the glögg last week so it could rest and mix well. It's better that way." Vindi continued unpacking glass mugs with copper bottoms and handles, which she placed next to the pot. "What can I do to help you?" she asked.

"Not a thing!" Dr. G replied. "You kids go have fun now. Dinner won't be ready for several more hours." He shooed them out of the kitchen.

Doug and Vindi went directly to the stable, this time cinching saddles onto Sugar and Vader. Doug observed her with concern, but Vindi appeared to have no painful memories this time as they raced across the meadow. They explored the full length of the trails, speaking only when Doug, who rode behind, gave her directions at forks in the path.

They emerged from the shady stillness at the far end of the clearing, rejoining the bright sunlight that bathed the blanket of grass that spread before them in a warm glow. Vindi stopped and raised her face toward the sun as Doug halted Vader beside her.

"Mmm...I can't imagine growing up here where it is so warm and sunny every day!" Doug smiled, observing her joy and contentment. She brought her head down and opened her eyes, scanning the hill of green. "I want to sit in the grass!"

He laughed. "I'll show you the best spot!" He led her to the top of a gentle slope where they dismounted. He walked in a small circle, as if searching for a specific location, then plopped down and stretched out on his back with his hands behind his head. Vindi lay down beside him, leaving a space between them. Her hair created a swirling crown around her head, and she closed her eyes, extended her arms beside her, took a deep breath and exhaled with a sigh.

"Mmm, it's so warm and soft," she whispered. "I feel like I'm falling into a pillow, and I can feel the earth's energy radiating up into my body. Can you feel that?"

Doug spread his arms along the ground and breathed deeply, concentrating on letting the weight of his body sink into the ground below him. "Yeah, you're right...that's amazing. And with the heat of the sun on top..."

"It's like being in a cocoon of radiant energy."

"Hmm…" Doug murmured sleepily. They remained silent for a time.

Eventually Vindi spoke, without changing her position or opening her eyes. "Why did you look for this particular place?"

"Oh, I used to lie in this exact spot when I was a kid, when I needed to think about things."

"What kind of things?"

"Oh, kid stuff. Except after my mother died…oh, I'm sorry! I didn't mean to bring that up."

"It's okay…I'm all right. You can talk about it if you want to."

"Not really. I was just remembering that I would come here sometimes at night and gaze at the stars. And I would imagine that I could feel the earth pushing me through space as it orbited around the sun…and my life was so small and insignificant compared to that."

Vindi paused. "Mmm…I can feel that." Another silence ensued. The air was still and occasional bird chatter was audible in the distance. "Does your father ever date anyone?" she asked suddenly.

"Sometimes." Doug kept his eyes closed as he spoke. "He has never brought anyone to the house because he didn't want to intrude on our space…and I guess he still feels it's not appropriate even though we're older now. The other reason I think is because he hasn't found anyone he cares about that much. I think he still misses my mother."

"Oh, that is sad." Vindi sighed softly, then rolled toward him onto her stomach; when she got herself situated her arm was brushing lightly against his, which she appeared not to notice. He did not move, but looked up at her face, aware that this was the first time she had closed the distance between them. "Do you think you have been closer to your father and brother since your mother is gone?" she asked, fingering the grass in front of her.

"I know I have. Dad changed his work schedule so he could spend more time with us. And I guess we appreciate each other more, since we know what it's like to lose someone."

"How do you think you would feel if your father wanted to marry someone?"

Doug shifted onto his side to face her, his arm bent at the elbow, supporting his head with his hand. "I think I would like it if he found someone that made him happy...especially after Dave goes to college."

"You don't think it would make you jealous?"

"Maybe, a little. But I think anyone he would like that much, I would like too. And I don't want him to be alone." His voice lowered to a whisper. "I wouldn't want to be alone." He leaned his head forward and began to kiss her. She responded with more intensity than usual, and did not pull away when he expected her to. He placed his hand on her back and scooted closer to her, prolonging the kiss.

Suddenly she began to giggle.

The horses had been wandering nearby, and Sugar had approached Vindi and was nuzzling her hair and gently pushing against the side of her head. The kiss was interrupted as Vindi raised her head; then she sat up and stroked the animal's jowl.

Doug rolled onto his back. *Now I'm thwarted by a horse!* He crossed his arms and looked at the sky, but his attention was drawn to Vindi's laughter as she caressed Sugar, and he could not help but smile. "She likes you."

"Oh, she's a sweetie!"

Doug sat up and looked for Vader. "We'd better get back to the house and see what's going on."

The dinner was in its final stages, so Doug showed Vindi to the downstairs guest bedroom and bath, where she could shower and change clothing.

"If it bothers you to use this room, there's another guest room upstairs you can use. Or you can use my room and I'll use this one."

"Why should this room bother me?"

"It's the one Ansel brought you to when you were drugged," Doug answered softly. He scanned her eyes with concern.

"I don't remember any of that. This room is fine. Don't worry about me."

Doug's room was further down the hall, behind the billiard room and kitchen. It was a spacious downstairs master bedroom, with a large private bathroom. Glass doors to the patio area offered an alluring view of the sunlit crystal water of the pool.

They met upstairs, where Vindi prepared the items she had brought and left them to warm up, as the table was set and filled with numerous foods, some of which she had never seen.

"Is your Christmas celebration in Sweden similar to ours?" Dave asked as they began the meal.

Doug glanced at Vindi. "I don't know if that's a good subject to discuss."

"It's okay." She smiled at Dave. "We actually start our Christmas celebration on December thirteen, which is the winter solstice, and we barely see the sun. It is called Santa Lucia's day. Most towns have a singing procession where a young girl wears a white dress with a red sash, and a crown of lingonberry branches on her head with candles burning on top of it. Of course, these days they usually use electric candles.

"Then the next big event is Christmas Eve when we have our julbord. Have you heard of a smörgåsbord?"

"Oh yeah, that's a buffet table full of all kinds of food that you pick and choose."

"That's right," Vindi nodded. "It was invented in Sweden. The julbord is the Christmas version of that."

"What kind of food do you serve on it?" Dr. G asked.

"Traditionally it's divided into three courses. First is cold seafood like herring, salmon and eel...then cold cuts like the Christmas ham, turkey, roast beef with cheese and bread...then hot dishes like Swedish meatballs, red cabbage, boiled potatoes, sausage, lutfisk."

"Wow, that sounds amazing!"

"What is lutfisk?"

"Oh, that is a whitefish that is soaked in lye."

"Oh, really…hmm." Dr. G commented.

"Do you have Santa Claus in Sweden?" Jillian inquired.

"Sort of. We have a tomte, who is a gnome that looks sort of like Santa Claus with a red hat and white beard. The story is that he would live under the floorboards of the house or barn, and look after the family and the livestock. Some families have someone dress up like a tomte and bring the presents in a sack over his shoulder, then give them out.

"But before Tomte comes, we have another tradition that you will not believe. Every year on Christmas Eve we stop everything at three o'clock in the afternoon to watch the Donald Duck Christmas special! It is called 'Kalle Anka och hans vänner önskar God Jul,' which means 'Donald Duck and his friends wish you a Merry Christmas.'"

"Oh no we missed it!" Doug jested. "Maybe we can find it online."

"No thanks," Vindi smiled sweetly. "I have seen it enough times."

When the meal concluded, Dr. G and Vindi prepared their desserts as the others cleared the table. Vindi spooned the rice porridge into bowls, which Doug distributed around the table to accompany the servings of pumpkin and pecan pies.

"This is really good! What is it?" Jillian asked.

"It's rice porridge, called risgrynsgröt…it's made with rice and milk, with cinnamon sugar and butter."

"Ooh! Is there supposed to be something hard in it?" Doug sputtered.

"Oh! That's an almond!" Vindi began to laugh hysterically, and was momentarily unable to speak. When she recovered she explained her amusement. "I forgot to tell you that we put one almond in it, and whoever gets it is supposed to get married within the next year!"

Now the laughter spread throughout the table at the trick she had played on them, and the absurdity of the suggestion; then at Doug, who grabbed his throat as if choking.

"It still counts, even if you spit it back out!" Vindi warned, with a giggle.

"Who dished out the porridge?" Dave asked.

"I did," Vindi admitted, "but Doug brought the bowls to the table."

"So, you served it to yourself!"

"Must have been subconscious," Dr. G concluded with a smile.

The table was cleared again, the kitchen and dishes cleaned up and leftovers put away. Vindi announced it was time for glögg, and had Doug carry the tray holding the copper pot and mugs to the table.

"There aren't any hidden almonds or threats of marriage in here, are there?" Doug peered at the pot suspiciously.

"No, don't worry!" Vindi laughed. She asked Doug to ladle the hot drink into the serving mugs while she prepared small bowls of almonds and raisins for each person to place a few into his or her cup. The five of them carried their warm treats to the living room and nestled into the plush furniture that created a grouping next to the colorfully trimmed Christmas tree. Melodic seasonal music played softly in the background, as it had throughout the dinner.

Vindi sat down next to Doug, placed her mug on the coffee table, then immediately jumped up and went to the kitchen, returning with one of her cloth bags. From it she extracted wrapped gifts and distributed them to each person in the room, generating protests from all directions.

"Oh, you shouldn't have done that!"

"This isn't necessary!"

She did not reply, but sat down and smiled with anticipation for the gifts to be opened. Dr. G went first, discovering a small plump wooden horse that was painted brightly red with yellow, green and blue trim.

"That is a Dala horse," Vindi advised. "It comes from a place in Sweden called Dalarna, and is a traditional symbol at Christmas. It represents the hand carved gifts that were made in the past during the long winters."

"Thank you! It's lovely…and so unique."

She informed Dave and Jillian that their gifts were identical, so they opened them simultaneously, each finding a small four-legged animal made of straw, wrapped with red ribbons. Long sweeping braided horns looped around their heads.

"That's the julbock…the Christmas goat made of straw. We put it under the Christmas tree to symbolize the last crop harvested. People also use straw ornaments on the tree."

"Thanks, Vindi."

"It's so cute!"

Doug opened his gift to find a fat multicolored candle, which he examined with curiosity, then placed on the coffee table in front of him.

"Candles are usual Christmas gifts," Vindi explained, "especially homemade ones. People would use their leftover stumps of different colors to make one candle, so it would come out looking kind of like that. I didn't have any leftovers, so I just got different colored waxes to make it look traditional."

"You made this?" he asked with surprise. She nodded. "When?"

"Last week."

"Thanks, it's great." *I wonder when we'll be able to use it for a romantic evening.*

Doug rose and approached the Christmas tree, then crawled under it and picked up a lone gift that appeared professionally wrapped. "What's this? It looks like Tomte forgot something!" He handed it to Vindi. "This is for you, from me."

"Oh!" She looked at him with surprise, then reached out and accepted the package. She stared at it as he returned to his place beside her. She carefully removed the ribbon and paper, then opened the box and gasped to find a necklace on a silver chain. The pendant was a sterling silver six-sided snowflake dotted with small diamond accents.

"Oh, it's so beautiful," she whispered. She showed it to the others, then looked at Doug. "Thank you...I love it."

"Put it on," he said quietly.

Vindi removed the chain from the cardboard slots with some difficulty, then fumbled with the small ring clasp. Doug had fastened a few necklaces in the past, and was confident in his ability.

"Here, let me help you." She handed him the chain and watched as he opened the tiny clasp. He held it up as she gazed at him expectantly. "Turn around," he instructed gently. She turned her back to him. "Now lift your hair."

She slid both hands up the back of her head, lifting her hair loosely, with her elbows extended on each side.

"Hold it with one hand...no, your left hand...lift it higher." She moved to comply with each command. Was it possible that she had never received a necklace as a gift before? Doug detected a light scent of cologne and felt a sudden urge to kiss the back of her neck; his father's presence was sufficient to aid in suppressing it. Vindi turned her head and looked at him quizzically, as if she could read his mind.

He reached over her left shoulder, guided the chain around her neck and closed the clasp. Vindi fingered the pendant, and turned toward him as she dropped her hair. "Thank you." She gave him a shy, childish smile.

"You're welcome." *I wish we were alone so I could kiss her right now. The way that pendant sparkles against her skin...I wonder why I've never seen her wear jewelry.*

"Oh! I almost forgot! There is one more thing!" Vindi reached into the bag from which she had retrieved the gifts, and handed a music disc to Doug. "This is some traditional

Christmas music from Sweden. I thought you might like to hear it."

Doug inserted the disc into the player and switched the music sources. The song began softly, then an ethereal melody gradually rose in volume. A faraway soprano voice began to sing words that were strange and beautiful to the listeners' ears.

Doug turned off the lamps. The group sat silently, sipping glögg, mesmerized by the delicate music that floated around and between the pinpoints of light on the Christmas tree. Doug smiled at Vindi, feeling completely at ease and content in the moment. She appeared equally relaxed; her face radiant and tranquil.

Suddenly she blinked her eyes several times and her expression became distressed. She turned her face away, then rose and quietly left the room.

"Dammit!" Doug exclaimed, as he raced to the disc player. "I was afraid this was going to happen!" He switched the music input back to the radio channel's selection of holiday songs.

"What's the matter?" His father rose from his seat.

"She got upset…I think she's having memories of her parents."

"Oh, the poor thing. It's very common to experience painful memories on holidays. We shouldn't have been questioning her the way we did. Why didn't she say something?"

"That's the way she is. She doesn't want anyone to know about her problems."

Doug searched for Vindi, discovering that she had slipped down the back stairway. He found her standing next to the pool, and placed his hand lightly on her shoulder. She turned and leaned her face and arms against his chest. She did not cry, but stood silently as he circled his arms around her. "I'm sorry," she whispered.

"Don't apologize. I know part of what you're going through...but I can't imagine what it would be like to lose both your parents. I can't believe you made it through the whole day as well as you did."

"I was okay...but the music got me. You should listen to it later...I think you will like it."

"I do like it...it's beautiful."

She sighed, then pulled away from him. "I guess I should go."

"No, don't go yet. It's early....unless you really want to be alone right now."

"No, not really."

"Let's sit for a while."

"Okay." They crossed the patio and sat on the swing. The sky was dark outside the soft glow of the outdoor lights, the air still and silent.

Doug placed his arm around Vindi and she rested her head on his shoulder. Neither spoke. The only sound was the soft creaking of the swing as it rocked.

Doug's relaxation began to fade as he felt the warmth of her body against his, but his brain was vigilant. *I'm not going to screw it up this time! Play it cool!*

Vindi lifted her face to his, and they shared a prolonged kiss. She touched his neck, then slid her hand down to his chest; he noticed that she left it there, as if prepared to push him away if necessary. He recalled that she had always done that when they kissed. He was careful not to give her any cause for anxiety, and when she backed away he did the same. She lay back on his shoulder with a sigh, keeping her hand in place.

Doug felt a sudden rush of sadness. Was he sensing her grief? Here she was on Christmas Day with no one to go home to, missing her parents who were gone, and needing someone she could trust, but the only person she could turn to was scheming for an opportunity to satisfy his own pleasure. What a friend he was!

"Is there anything I can do for you?" he whispered.

"I don't think so."

They rocked and the swing creaked. The air around them seemed to grow heavier along with their moods.

"Do you think a game of pool would cheer you up?"

"I don't know...maybe," she responded without enthusiasm.

"How about I ask Dave and Jillian to join us?"

"Okay."

After the first round of plays Vindi appeared no less melancholy, and she took Doug aside. "It's no help...I need to leave."

He lifted her chin and peered into her eyes. "Are you okay?"

"Ja. Really, I just want to be alone now."

"I understand."

"I'll get my things later, if that is all right."

"Sure, that's fine."

She forced a smile as she said goodbye to Dave and Jillian.

Dr. Goodwin was puttering in the kitchen upstairs, and looked concerned as Vindi thanked him and gave him a hug. He followed her to the door, motioning Doug to remain behind. They stepped out to the porch and talked quietly, then Doug saw him give her a gentle fatherly hug.

Dr. G reentered the house and nodded to Doug. He hurried outside, where Vindi was walking to her car. "Is everything okay?"

"Ja." She smiled weakly. "Your father is very kind and caring."

"I'm sorry this had to happen…"

"I too, but it's okay." She stopped at her car door and turned toward him. "I had a really great day…thanks so much for inviting me. It gave me something to think about and plan for all week."

Doug stood in front of her and took her hands in his, then placed her palms on his chest. He slid his hands gently up her arms and let them rest lightly on her shoulders. He then leaned forward just enough to brush his lips against hers, and kissed her tenderly with sincere affection. He pulled back before she did and studied her face, trying to see the person behind the pale blue eyes as he stroked her hair. "Do you want me to call you tomorrow?"

"Ja, sure."

"Remember, I'm here for you if you need anything."

"Thanks." He watched her slide into her car and drive off, and was suddenly surprised when a thought popped into his mind. *I just kissed her and I wasn't even thinking about sex!*

## Chapter 13

# Roller coaster

The next morning Doug called Vindi—a text just did not seem appropriate.

"Thanks, Doug, but I would really rather be by myself today."

"What if I bring your stuff over?"

"No, not now."

"I'm concerned about you being alone." Doug could hear the sadness in her voice.

"I'm okay…honestly. I'll call you if I need anything."

Doug brooded throughout the day, and declined Jenna's invitation that afternoon. He let Vader lead him through the trails, stopping him momentarily on the pathway where he had found Vindi crying the first time they had ridden together—was it really more than a year ago?

As he continued riding, the shadows that permeated the pathway chilled his skin. He peered through the heavy stillness, his chest rising sluggishly with every breath of stagnant air. Vader stepped slowly, echoing Doug's inertia with the plodding scrunch of his hooves on dead leaves.

When it seemed that the damp melancholy of the labyrinth would never end, the horse and rider emerged into the blinding sunlight that bathed the meadow.

The warm rays of the sun reminded Doug of Vindi's sunlit hair. He kept Vader at a slow walk as he circled the patch of green grass where they had lain side by side just yesterday. There was no trace of their bodies, only the green cushion that twitched here and there in the breeze.

He brushed Vader mechanically, and only after returning the stallion to his stall did he notice the dancing light and shadows in the cool stable. He tried to envision Vindi standing there the first time she had smiled at him, but she did not appear.

That evening after dinner he sat by the pool with his arm stretched over the back of the swing, but the seat beside him was cold and empty.

The following day he called her again, and was pleased that her voice once again possessed its usual brightness.

"You sound better."

"Oh, ja! Lukas is here! He surprised me early this morning!"

"Oh."

"Maybe the three of us can get together sometime this weekend."

"No, I don't see that happening. I guess I'll see you at school sometime. I hope you have a good visit."

"Okay, thanks!"

Doug ended the call, and thought for a moment. He then brought up Jenna's number and tapped it with his thumb.

A few days later Doug received a call from Quinn, who was attending college at his father's alma mater in the Northeast. "Do you have plans for New Year's Eve?"

"No. Jenna has to make a family trip with her parents."

"Good. I just got in from visiting my folks at the Springs, and there's going to be a bash at the lake, with live music and fireworks. You and me...lake house...boat...chicks looking for a party...need I say more?"

"No, it sounds great! I need to get out of this place."

They caught up on each other's activities as they drove to the small lake that was shaped like a wide pea pod; the house owned by Quinn's parents sat near the center on the eastern side. It was almost noon when they arrived; they carried the cooler of just-purchased picnic items to the dock.

The winter sun was bright and the air a comfortable cool. A few engines buzzed in the distance as the boys uncovered the thirty-foot open-deck power boat, filled the motor with fuel and set out. They crossed the lake at full speed, then played at cutting tight circles and sharp angles, creating choppy waves and plumes of rainbow-filled sprays of crystal droplets.

Eventually Quinn guided the craft to a small alcove near the lake's narrow end where the water was calm and the surrounding vegetation rustled softly in the light breeze. He dropped the anchor onto the shallow sandy bottom. They stretched out on the aft bench of the boat and retrieved sandwiches and sodas from the cooler.

"Aah, the Sack," Quinn murmured. "What better place to lunch."

"Oh, yeah," Doug agreed. "The Sacrifice of the Virgins…such memories." He smiled at the name they had given the alcove, as he pictured a large tractor tire inner tube floating on the still water next to the boat and a second one twenty feet away, each hiding the heads of an adolescent boy and girl within its circle as they giggled, kissed and experimented under the water. "Too bad we were the virgins."

They both laughed.

"Yeah, we didn't always score, but it was always fun trying," Quinn added.

"That's for sure. Which reminds me," Doug said nonchalantly, "I haven't told you yet about Vindi."

"*The* Vindi?"

"Yep. She showed up at my campus last fall."

They laughed as Doug described her handling of Tyler at the party. He then spoke with indifference as he covered the highlights of their lunches, weekend day trips, and her Christmas visit. When he finished, Quinn nodded his head and smiled.

"So. You and Vindi. You're my hero, man."

"What do you mean?"

"If any girl would slip through your fingers, I figured she would be the one. But you did it, don't you see? Your passive strategy worked! She felt no pressure from you, and now she's eating out of your hand! You...da...man!" He raised his hand and slapped Doug's palm as he held it out.

Doug chuckled. "Yeah, only one problem. I'm still not getting any from her."

"Well, there you go! You have proven that you can have a relationship with a girl without sex! Doesn't that make you proud?"

"No."

"Why not?"

"Because I still want to have sex with her! The only reason I don't is because she won't let me."

Quinn shook his head and waved his hand. "You're hopeless!"

Doug leaned forward, then spoke softly. "There's something else." Quinn waited. "There's this Swedish guy from her past that keeps showing up. Lukas. She used to live with him...as 'friends.'" He made quotation marks with his fingers. "She's with him now." Doug stared at the cooler as boat motors hummed in the distance.

Quinn spoke solemnly. "Friends with benefits, huh." He paused. "She's playing you, man."

Doug leaned back on his seat, stretched his arms out over the warm fiberglass surface of the boat, looked at Quinn and smiled. "So, what do you recommend, Doc?"

Quinn grabbed a soda from the cooler, popped it open, leaned back and took a long gulp. "New strategy. It's obvious. You're in it this far...you've got her interest. You keep playing her game but you start turning the screws little by little. Turn on the charm…then the coaxing…then a little desperation if it gets that far. It may take time, but it has always worked for me."

Doug grinned at him. "I knew you'd be good for something someday."

Quinn held his soda can between his two hands as if praying, and bowed forward briefly with a smile. "Lowly student pleased to be of service to the master."

The rumble of an engine approached rapidly, and they looked up to see the pointed front of a speed boat heading toward them on a collision course. They were on their feet instantly, as the boat suddenly swerved, generating a large spray that rained down on them. The boat circled around and sped past them in the opposite direction, as the occupants— three girls in shorts and bikini tops—laughed and waved, their hair fluttering behind them.

"Ooh, they're looking for trouble!"

"They just found it! Break's over. Time to get back to the battlefield!"

When he returned to campus Doug was pleased that neither Kayla nor Leslie held a grudge against him, and he made plans with both of them. He did not make it to the dojo on Monday, but attended on Wednesday. Vindi was there, and flashed him a shy smile as they lined up on the mat.

*Damn! She acts like nothing happened!* His mind raced as he performed the warm-up exercises. Suddenly Quinn's advice, which had sounded so wise and clever while on the lake, was not very useful. *I've never pushed myself on a girl before, and I'm not going to do it now.*

As Sensei called for mixed pairs, Doug glanced at Vindi. She was looking at him, and he could see trust and expectation in her eyes. As the blue-belt at her side turned to partner with her Doug gestured for her to accept, then turned to the purple-belt next to him. *Especially after what she went through with Olof, and Ansel. I can't do that to her.*

Purple-belt challenged him with punches; Doug responded automatically with blocks, as his contemplation continued. *What about Lukas?* Doug reacted to the next punch with a hip throw, which he performed more forcefully than necessary; Purple hit the mat hard. "Sorry," Doug said as he gave him a hand up.

Doug attacked Purple with light punches. *The best thing to do is to just back off and get away from her for a while.* He slapped his arms back to break his fall as he hit the mat from Purple's throw. *I've got to get her out of my head!* He made another punch, then flew over Purple's shoulder onto his back again.

Sensei called for regrouping by rank; Doug and Marco found each other. "Are you still doing competition?" Doug asked him.

"Yes."

"Good. Show me what you've got." Without further warning, Doug attacked him with more force than appropriate for training. Marco reacted with equal speed and power. Doug hit the mat hard, but with sufficient breakfall, then sprang up and immediately attacked again. Marco responded to Doug's aggression with controlled defensive moves, ending with a shoulder throw.

Doug landed hard again, then rolled and attacked Marco from the side. Marco went down, pulling Doug along with him.

"Goodwin! Llenza!" As Sensei approached, Doug and Marco scrambled up and stood side by side, panting. "Save it for sport class!" Sensei stopped in front of them. "You can do fifty to cool down, then go." They bowed politely, and he turned his attention to another pair of students.

Doug huffed through his push-ups rapidly, and had his belt off already when Marco entered the dressing room.

"Bad weekend, huh?" Marco asked.

Doug grunted as he jerked off his cotton jacket and threw it on the floor beside him.

Marco grabbed Doug's arm firmly just above the elbow. "If you want to feel some pain, come to sport class tonight. I'll make you forget about her." He grinned.

Doug glared at him. "Thanks. I might do that."

Marco turned and crossed to his locker as Doug let his pants drop and stepped into the shower.

Doug waited for Vindi outside the dojo. He could not think any more, and stood with his arms crossed, staring at nothing.

"What was that all about?"

He turned to find Vindi beside him, and let his arms drop. "Nothing…just fooling around."

"Oh."

Doug took a deep breath. "I can't make it for lunch," he lied. "I have to finish a paper."

"Oh, okay…but may I ask you something?"

"Sure."

"Can we go to Sequoia this weekend?"

He stared at her, dumbfounded. Had she no clue what a punch in the gut she had given him last week? "You mean…to spend the night?"

"Ja…separate rooms, of course."

"Of course." He was totally confused, yet from somewhere in his mind there flashed a spark that an opportunity was presenting itself. "Do you trust me?" He scowled.

"Hmm…not completely…but I think I can handle you." She smiled mischievously, ignoring his ill humor.

Her smile ignited the spark, and it flamed in his brain. Did she have any idea what she was doing to him?

"Sure, we can go, if that's what you want." His voice and face softened. He then noticed that she was wearing the snowflake necklace he had given her. The tiny diamonds glittered in the sunlight as if laughing at his hesitation, and he was tempted to accompany her to lunch—or follow her anywhere—but instead he turned and walked away, trying to sort out the chaos in his head.

Doug had been unable to formulate any logical conclusions by Saturday, but had pushed aside his thoughts of Lukas and anticipated what the day—and night—would bring. They arrived in the early afternoon and snowshoed to the ice rink.

Vindi had seemed happier than usual at lunch on Thursday, and her cheerful mood was even more evident as they skated. Doug noticed that she touched him more than she ever had previously—holding his hand or his arm, and brushing against him as they made circles together. He decided to stop analyzing, and allowed himself to get caught up in her enjoyment of the moment, and they laughed and chased, spun and played in the chilly winter brilliance.

They paused for soft drinks at the cafe, lingering in their relaxed exhaustion as they watched the skaters outside the window.

Vindi pointed. "Look, how beautiful it is that the skaters' reflections move around with them."

"Where?" Doug slid closer, placing one arm around the back of her chair as he wrapped his other hand around hers.

She turned and flashed him a smile. "Can you see it now?"

"Oh, yes, I can see much better now." He felt her lean into his shoulder.

"I like this time of day, when the sun makes everything look yellow. You can see it in the ice."

"Mmm, yellow ice…beautiful," he murmured next to her ear, then drew back and scanned her face. "Not as beautiful as what's in here."

"Oh, be careful…you might melt the ice! I think I might faint!" She fanned herself with her hand as she giggled.

"Hey, that's one of my best lines! It's not nice to shoot me down like that."

"Oh, I'm sorry. Try another one."

"No. You don't deserve it." He faked a pout as he looked away.

She touched her fingers to his chin, turned his face toward her, and peered solemnly into his eyes. "You know," she said gently, "in this lighting your eyes look like black pearls with sparkling diamonds in the center." As he gazed back at her she put her hand over her mouth to suppress a smirk.

"You're wicked. You know, that don't you?" She giggled as he faked indignity. "I can't believe you used a line like that on me. I'm not that easy!" He turned his face away again, raising his nose into the air.

"Oh, well, then my plan is spoiled. We might as well go home."

He looked back at her and leaned into the back of his chair. "All right, you win. Do with me what you must. I can't fight it any longer." They laughed.

Doug sat up and looked out the window. "We'd better get back outside if I'm going to have time to throw snowballs at you."

"You would like that, ja?"

"I've been dreaming about it all week!"

"Actually, I would rather go back to the lodge and have an early dinner."

"Are you coming on to me again?"

She gave him a sly smile. "You will just have to wait and see."

"All right, then let's go!"

After they showered and changed, they texted each other and met in the hallway outside their adjoining rooms. Vindi was wearing a soft lavender sweater with a scooped neckline, where the snowflake pendant lured his eye as it winked at him.

"It has been fun having a day of winter again." Vindi took his hand and moved in close, raising her face for a kiss. Surprised, he kissed her as her other palm touched his cheek for a brief moment; she then pulled away and led him to the elevator.

*Oh, yeah, she's hot for me,* he mused as they strolled hand in hand to the dining room. *My passive strategy finally worked! She wants me, and obviously has plans for tonight. All I have to do is sit back and let it happen. Wait till I tell Quinn!*

After they ordered, Vindi moved from her seat across the table and took the chair beside him. She leaned against his arm as she showed him her cell phone photos and videos from her Hawaiian excursion. When the food arrived she returned to her seat, and they chatted throughout the meal.

The wisps of hair around Vindi's shoulders glistened in the scattered overhead lighting, as the snowflake above her breasts twinkled in the table's candlelight. They seemed to reflect her happiness and hint at a promise that the evening would fulfill. Doug relaxed into his chair, feeling her radiant energy absorb into his being as he savored the anticipation.

When the waiter returned for the dessert order Vindi suggested, "Why don't we take some hot chocolate to the room?"

Doug's eyes widened. "Well, you're just full of surprises, aren't you?"

Her only response was a coy smile.

They carried large mugs of hot cocoa to Vindi's room and lit the gas-fueled fireplace. Doug tossed the sofa pillows onto the floor and they sat among them while the blue and yellow flame danced quietly between the crevices of the imitation log.

The hot, sweet liquid enhanced Doug's tranquility as it warmed his chest. He set his mug on the floor behind him and leaned against the sofa, waiting for her to make the next move.

Vindi sipped her cocoa, then set her mug on the end table. Her eyes probed his as she announced quietly, "I want to tell you about Lukas."

## Chapter 14

# Enlightenment

*CRASH!*

Doug's serenity was shattered like a baseball hitting a pane of glass, sending stabbing shards through his stomach and chest. Blood pulsed throughout his body, transforming his warm calmness into a pounding burn. He took a breath, then exhaled slowly. Externally, his face barely flinched as he waited for her to continue.

"I met him when I was seven," she began. "I was walking to school, and something hit me on the head…"

*A young girl with white blonde curls peered into tree branches above her. She saw a boy of similar age looking down at her with a smirk as he dropped pieces of bark.*

*"Stop that!" she demanded. He laughed impishly and continued his prank. "I said, stop that!"*

*"You can't make me!"*

*She dropped her book bag and scrambled up the tree, ignoring her dress and stockings that scraped against the rough surface of the limbs. When she got to his level he sat motionless, his face without expression, as he peered at her. He was a distance away from the trunk on a limb that she deduced would not hold the weight of both of them.*

*She paused and looked at him. His face was smudged with dirt and his clothing ill-fitting and disheveled. He was thin, with sandy blond hair that was shaggy and uncombed. She lost her anger. "Hi. I'm Vindi. What is your name?"*

*"Lukas."*

*"Why are you dropping things on me?"*

*"Just for fun."*

*"Don't you go to school?"*

*"Sometimes."*

*"Do you want to be friends?"*

*"Okay."*

*"I'm going to school. Do you want to come with me?"*

*"Okay."*

"He was in a grade above me, so I didn't see him at school," Vindi continued, "but he usually walked with me to school and would wait to walk home with me when I got out. He hung around outside my house but would not come in. We sat in the tree together a lot, and talked about all kinds of things...mostly silly childish ideas and fantasies. I would sneak food to him after our dinner...it seemed he never got enough to eat. If he had a home, he didn't want to go there, and he never talked about it.

"Sometimes we would go to the park and push each other on the swings or play on the slide and climbing bars. Sometimes we just sat on the bench and talked.

"This went on through grade school, and even though my girlfriends didn't want him around, I started to feel like he was my best friend. My parents didn't know about him but Sven started noticing, and told me to stay away from him, but I didn't listen.

"After I changed to secondary school I didn't see him there, but he would meet me at the park. Then he suddenly stopped showing up. I still went there every day waiting for him, and finally one day he came and told me that Sven had ordered him to stay away from me. I only saw him a few times after that." She paused and took a deep breath. "Then the thing with Olof happened, and my parents...were gone..." Her voice wavered, and Doug took her hand.

She controlled herself, and went on. "Sven was at university, so I was sent to my aunt's house, and I went to a different school. She didn't really want me there, but she liked the money the government sent her every month. She didn't spend any of it on me, though. She just made me do all the housework and cooking for her.

"I hated it there...at the school and at my aunt's house. One night I went to the bus station and called Sven. I told him I was not going back...that I was going to run away. He borrowed a car and came right away."

*A sad-looking adolescent with shoulder-length white blonde hair sat on a bench in a bus station, clutching a small bag in her lap. A handful of people were scattered about the room.*

*Sven burst through the door, scanned the room, then rushed to her.*

*"Sven!" She jumped up and tried to hug him. "You came for me! Thank you!"*

*He gently pushed her away, holding her shoulders. "Not here." He glanced around, as he led her to the door. As they exited a brisk wind caught them, and Vindi's hair blew wildly about her face. Sven took off his brown knit cap and placed it on Vindi's head, smoothing her hair under it, while his straight white hair fluttered in the turbulent breeze. They continued walking, and he led her to a nondescript compact car. He guided her into the passenger seat, then squeezed into the small driver's seat and drove off.*

*A short time later they sat across from each other in a small cafe, where she eagerly ate hot soup that contained large chunks of potatoes.*

*"I understand what you're telling me, Vindi, but you have to face reality. I cannot do anything about the situation right now. This is a really tough and important time for me, and I can't afford to be distracted. After next semester I'll graduate, and then things will be different, but right now I need you to get through this, and manage to survive without me."*

*Vindi nodded without looking up. "I'm sorry, Sven. I will not bother you again."*

226

*"I have a training session over the holidays, so I won't be able to see you then either."*

*"Okay."*

*"Promise me that you will not do anything stupid, like running away."*

*"I promise," she murmured.*

*They returned to the house. Sven walked her to the front door, then leaned over to give her a hug. She pressed her face against his chest and hugged him tightly, and did not release her grip until he gently pulled her arms away. He slid into the vehicle and drove away. She stood motionless and watched the car disappear around a corner, as tears streamed down her face.*

*"Sven...don't leave me..." Her whisper was lost in the wind.*

Vindi's voice was without emotion as she continued her story. "I kept going to school, but I was depressed and didn't talk to anyone. I didn't feel like fixing my hair and just left it in braids. Then I started growing and my clothes got too tight, but my aunt would not buy me anything else so I had to wear my jacket all the time; then it even got too small for me. My classmates made fun of me and I had no friends...I was an outcast." She looked solemn for a moment, then suddenly her expression brightened and her eyes lit up.

"Then one day a wonderful thing happened...I saw Lukas at the school! All the classes were gathered in the gymnasium for some kind of presentation...I don't remember what. These boys were underneath the bleachers where I was sitting, and I saw him with them…"

*Vindi's hair was plaited around her ears and her braids hung to her shoulders. Her face was scrubbed but her clothing was worn and barely covered her lanky frame; her wrists protruded from her jacket sleeves. Her skirt was pleated with ample fabric to cover her hips, but the hemline approached her mid-thigh and the stockings under it were frayed and stretched. She wore no shoes—rubber boots with buckles on the sides covered her feet.*

*She sat slightly apart from well-dressed classmates who filled the tiered benches, gazing forward and politely listening to a speaker.*

*Vindi heard whispering below her and looked down to see several boys under the bleachers. They were disheveled and rough looking, in stark contrast to the students above them. A tousled mass of sandy blond hair caught her eye, and when the boy turned his head she gasped to see Lukas.*

*He was too far below her to hear her whisper, so she curled small wads of paper from the handout she had been given and dropped them down onto the group one by one, smiling to herself as she remembered how they had first met. Her missiles missed their mark and Lukas did not look up, but one of his companions eyed her and made a threatening face.*

*When the assembly was over, the students moved quietly out the large double doors, then proceeded in various* directions to their respective classrooms. *Vindi strained to peer over shoulders all around her, but could not find Lukas. She turned down a hallway as she followed the flowing crowd. Suddenly a hand came out of nowhere and grabbed her, pulling her into a corner under a stairway. It was the boy who had looked up at her, and he was angry.*

*"So, you're the creep who thinks she's so funny!" He grasped the front of her jacket and pushed her against the wall.*

*"Let go of me!" She struggled. "Where is Lukas? I want to see Lukas!"*

*"You want to see Lukas? What will you give me?" He pressed toward her, trying to clutch her wrist in his free hand.*

*"Lukas!" she yelled, as she tried in vain to push the boy away.*

*The boy unexpectedly pulled away from her, and she saw Lukas thrust him forcefully toward the nearby wall. He hit with a thud, but seemed to bounce off the hard surface as he leapt toward Lukas and stood with his fists out, ready to strike. Lukas, who was taller, met his challenge by glaring down at him, fists clenched at his sides.*

*"Leave her alone!" Lukas took a step forward. "She's with me!" The boy backed away.*

*Lukas turned back to Vindi, and approached her with an expression of concern on his face. He was the boy she remembered—taller, but still thin, and still shabbily dressed. He wore a loose military-looking coat over his t-shirt and trousers.*

*Vindi rushed forward and wrapped her arms around him. They hugged each other tightly, hidden from the students who tramped up the stairway or made their way down the corridor. Vindi began to cry silently, then wept with an eruption of despair.*

*"Vindi...what is it? What happened to you?" Lukas asked, but she continued to sob.*

*Lukas opened a door under the stairwell and led her through a dimly lit storage area—around boxes and dusty equipment—and then through another door. They were outside in a gravel-covered loading bay which was secluded from outside view by rising slopes on each side. A makeshift bench—consisting of a long board lying on top of large overturned buckets—rested against the brick wall of the building.*

*As they sat on the bench and talked Lukas kept one hand on her shoulder, hugging her each time the tears returned. She finally calmed, and they conversed solemnly. Eventually they heard a buzzer sound, and made their way upstairs to Vindi's locker, where she retrieved some books and the knit cap Sven had given her. They exited the front door of the school, and walked to one of the buses lined up in a row, where Vindi paused, shivering in the frigid breeze. Lukas took off his coat and helped her place her arms into the oversized sleeves, then pulled her cap down over her ears.*

*"Will I see you tomorrow?" She kept her eyes fixed on his.*

*"Ja, and every day after that," he assured her. She smiled, then turned and boarded the bus.*

"I did see him practically every day after that, even though I would not skip class as much as he wanted me to. I nagged at him to study and pass his courses, and he did enough to get by…just to please me, I think."

"Then something happened…" she paused, sipped her cocoa, then drew her legs up and tucked them under her. Doug still held her hand, and followed the flicker in her eyes as she gazed at the flaming artificial log.

"It was just before the Christmas holiday. My aunt had a boyfriend who started living with us, and he would always look at me in a creepy way. When I had to be there I stayed in my room, except when I was cooking or doing chores in the rest of the house.

"One day when I came home from school…he had been drinking…I don't know where she was…"

*Vindi entered the house, set down her books and went to the kitchen. She removed Lukas's coat and placed it over a chair, then placed Sven's cap on top of it. She began running water into the sink to wash a stack of soiled dishes piled on the counter. She wore a sweater that was too short for her arms, and tight across her developing chest. Her skirt was short and her stockings ripped, exposing a segment of bare flesh at her thighs when she leaned forward over the sink. She still wore the sloppy snow boots.*

*As she worked, a figure appeared in the doorway from the hall, scanning her up and down. He was a mid-sized man, dressed in sweat pants and a wrinkled t-shirt, looking as if he had just gotten out of bed.*

*The man crossed the room without a word and grabbed her from behind, putting his arm around her waist. "Stop it!" she yelled, as she spun around and pushed him away. She ran toward the door, but he caught her arm and pulled her back into the kitchen.*

*He was slightly taller than she, with a stocky build. She struggled against him desperately, but he was eventually able to grab both of her wrists; he then pushed her against the wall opposite the sink. He pressed his body against hers and his face against her neck, as he panted heavily with alcohol-tainted breath.*

*Vindi fought hysterically, but could not loosen his grip. He then let one of her hands go and put his hand on her waist, trying to slide it under her sweater. Her free hand was helpless against his bulk. She tried to kick and, unintentionally, her thigh hammered the soft flesh of his groin.*

*He released her with a yelp, then fell backward to his knees in agony in the center of the kitchen floor. In a frenzied rage, Vindi ran to the sink and began to throw the dirty dishes at him one by one. Plates, mugs, food scraps and liquids flew at him as he rocked in pain. She then grabbed pots and pans from the open cabinet, hurling them with the intensity of her anger.*

*Not yet satisfied, she ran to the small dining table, picked up one of the heavy wooden chairs and threw it at him, knocking him over. He wailed loudly in pain as she threw a second chair; she then grabbed her coat and hat and bolted out the door into the snow.*

"Ow, be careful!" Vindi exclaimed. Doug realized that he was squeezing her hand tightly, and he loosened his grip. He scowled with a worried concern, as he brushed his other hand against her face.

"Oh, Vindi," he murmured. "I'm so sorry...if I had known...it wasn't just Olof..."

"Shh," she whispered. Her eyes were dry and solemn. She took both of his hands in hers, as she continued talking.

"Lukas had taken me once to the place where he went after school, but he made me stay outside while he went in to get some food. It was a bar, and he said a rough crowd went there. I eventually found the place. It was almost dark but still early and there were not many people there yet. I saw Lukas inside at the pool table, and tapped on the window..."

*Vindi crouched in the darkness behind the bar and peered through the bottom of the window pane. She could see Lukas inside leaning over the dimly lit pool table with a cue stick. He was alone. She tapped lightly against the glass, then more firmly. He turned and saw her. His expression remained neutral as he glanced around the bar. He left the window, and a moment later came out the back door and rushed over, squatting down in front of her.*

*"Vindi! What's going on?"*

*"Lukas, I need you!"* She grasped the front of his sweater, and he placed his hands on her shoulders. *"I'm not going back there!"*

*"Tell me what happened!"*

She spoke in short bursts. He scowled with anger and made a move to rise, but she held on to him.

*"Where is he?"* he growled.

*"No...no, Lukas! Don't leave me! I don't care about him! I just need you to help me...I don't know where to go."* Her eyes filled with tears, and he hugged her tightly as she collapsed into his arms and wept.

After Vindi became calm, Lukas said softly, *"Wait here, I'll be right back."* He went inside, and a moment later returned with something in his hands. It was a pair of pants. *"Here, put these on."* She stood up and placed a hand on his shoulder as he knelt down and helped her take each foot out of her boot, through the pant leg, then back into the boot. She pulled the pants over her skirt and sweater, under her coat. They were loose and baggy, but stayed in place.

Lukas pulled down the folded brim of her cap and tucked her braids up under it as smoothly as he could. He shifted her oversized coat to cover her neck as much as possible. He studied her appearance, then brushed away a patch of snow from the ground and scraped some soil from the surface with his hand. He smudged the dirt around her face and chin.

*"It will have to do."* He gazed at her solemnly. *"Listen...you have to pretend to be a boy. That's the only*

*way you will be safe in here. If you have to speak, use a low voice. Be serious...don't smile or laugh. And don't swing your hips when you walk."*

*She nodded, and they went inside. She glanced around the room. A few small wooden tables with empty chairs were scattered in the center. At the far end two men sat at a paneled bar with their backs to them; one turned and looked at them with disinterest, then went back to his drink.*

*Lukas led Vindi casually around the pool table, then unlocked a small door at the building's end and directed her inside. He turned on a light, which was a single hanging bulb, revealing what appeared to be a large storage closet. Tools, cleaning equipment and miscellaneous items were stacked in the corner and along the opposite wall. Just inside the door a sloping wooden ladder led to an attic above; on the floor beneath it was a small bare mattress covered with a worn blanket.*

*Lukas closed the door. "This is where I live...you can stay here for now. You can use the mattress. I'll make a bed for me upstairs."*

*"How long have you lived here?" Vindi's eyes were sorrowful as she thought of the hardships Lukas must have faced throughout his life.*

*"A while." His voice held no emotion. "Alef owns the place, and lets me stay here in exchange for doing cleaning and repairs. I work behind the bar when it gets busy, to help pay for my food. I'll tell him you're my cousin, and that you need to stay for a few days. Just lay low and keep quiet and he should not mind."*

*"Okay...thanks, Lukas."*

*"What do you have on under the coat?" She removed her coat, revealing the tight sweater that displayed her shapely chest.*

*"That will not work." He rummaged in a box, and retrieved several shirts and sweaters. "Put on as many of these as you need to get rid of the girl look." He left the room, closing the door behind him.*

*Within a few minutes Vindi peeked around the door and he returned and checked her appearance. She wore a bulky sweater covered by a large flannel shirt that was partially tucked into the pants; these were tied with a cord she had found in the box. The long shirt sleeves were rolled at the cuffs but still covered part of her hands, and the collar was buttoned closely at the neck. She presented the appearance of a young male street urchin. Lukas nodded his head. "Not bad."*

*They exited the closet, and he began to show her how to play pool. A short time later a couple of rough-looking older boys entered the bar and approached the table, greeting Lukas as they selected pool cues. Lukas introduced Vindi as his cousin, Vincent. They appeared to accept the disguise without a second look, and began to play.*

Vindi paused, and Doug's lips curled into a smirk. "So you really did live in a pool hall."

She smiled. "Ja, I did. I played pool a lot with Lukas and his friends...there was not much else to do. I kept quiet and they did not question who I was, and after a while I became friends with them. I think Alef suspected that I was not a boy, but he didn't say anything, especially after I started doing some cooking for him in the kitchen behind the bar, and the customers started ordering more food and drinks."

"Did you go back to school?"

"Oh, ja. I walked to school, and kept my clothes in a shed behind an empty house that was on the way there. I would change on my way to school, where I was a geek girl that everyone ignored, then I would change back into a boy on the way home."

"Wow." Doug recalled images of Vindi playing pool with the boys at his house—how she had laughed and bantered with them so naturally. His vision then shifted to the bar where Vindi, dressed as a ragamuffin boy, was surrounded by uncouth ruffians. "You must have heard some pretty nasty language from those guys, especially relating to girls."

"Ja, I did, even though Lukas tried to control them."

"No wonder you know what boys are thinking about." Vindi's lips curled in a partial smile, as Doug shifted uncomfortably. "Did your aunt ever look for you?"

"No. I was sure she didn't care where I was as long as she got the checks from the government. She was probably glad I was gone."

"How long did you stay there?"

"Until spring...about five months. Sven called the house now and then to talk to me, and either no one answered or my aunt would tell him that I was not there at the time. He eventually got worried and went there to look for me..."

Chapter 15

# Cold shower

Sven was confronting his aunt, his face reddened with anger. "What do you mean she has not been here since before Christmas? Where is she? Why didn't you let me know?"

"How can I help it if she wanted to run away with a boy?"

"What boy?"

She shook her head and threw her arms out dramatically. "Some young boy came by and took all her clothes and stuff! I don't know who he was!"

"Did anyone at the school ever call you?"

"No!"

Sven stomped out of the house, slid into his car and slammed the door shut. The vehicle leapt forward as the back tires spit loose gravel from the pavement. He sped to the school and rushed into the administrative office.

A secretary listened to his frenzied accusations, then calmly searched her computer records. "Vindi Johansson has not missed a day of school since Christmas break," she *told him calmly. "She has had no disciplinary actions against her. There has been no reason to notify anyone."*

*"Is she here today?"*

*"There is no indication that she did not arrive."*

*He stood motionless, assimilating the information. "Thank you," he finally said, then walked calmly out of the office. He returned to his car, drove down the entrance street to the school, then turned around, confirming that the entire building was within his view. He shut off the engine and waited.*

*School buses soon began to arrive, and parked in a row in front of the school, requiring Sven to adjust his vehicle's position in order to maintain a view of the school's entrance. Shortly thereafter, students began to flow out of the building; he scanned them attentively. Some boarded the buses, others began walking in all directions away from the school.*

*As he surveyed the activity, Sven saw a lone figure walking across the lawn behind the school, away from the rest of the students. She had long blonde braids, which were customary. He did not recognize the oversized jacket; her skirt, stockings and clog shoes were shabby and commonplace.*

*He slowly drove forward, scrutinizing her until he was certain that it was Vindi. He followed her stealthily, winding around streets and neighborhoods to keep up with her as she cut across lawns and vacant lots.*

*He then saw her slip into a run-down shed behind a house that appeared unoccupied, with an untidy lawn and broken front window. He kept it in his sight as he circled around a small pond to get closer. Suddenly he saw what appeared to be a young boy wearing loose-fitting pants, a shapeless military jacket and brimmed beret-type cap step out of the shed and walk calmly across the grass away from him.*

*His heart pounded as he accelerated around the next block to reach the driveway of the house. By the time he got there the boy was in the distance. Sven ran to the shed.*

*The door was unlocked and there was no one inside. It was musty and damp, with a few rusty tools scattered about. In the center of the floor there was a large burlap bag; inside he found several articles of clothing, including the skirt and jacket he had seen Vindi wearing. The bag also contained a small paper sack which held a hairbrush, comb, small mirror, and several plain hair clips.*

*In a second large bag he found a pair of boys' pants, and several worn shirts and frayed sweaters. From the bottom of the sack he pulled out the brown knit cap that he had placed on Vindi's head the last time he had seen her.*

*He thought for a moment, then dashed back outside and scanned for the boy he had seen, who was still visible in the distance. He ran back to his car and sped away, veering onto a main road which took him in the same direction. He eventually saw the boy enter a door at the back of a building, and he made several turns on side roads to reach the front of the structure. His eyes narrowed and the muscles in his face tightened into a scowl when he saw that it was a rundown bar.*

*Sven rushed inside and looked around. The boy was not in sight, but several youths were playing pool. He immediately recognized Lukas, and bolted across the room, grabbing the front of his sweatshirt and throwing him against the wall with such impetus that the pool cue he was holding went flying. The other boys stood motionless and silent in stunned alarm, not daring to intervene.*

*"Where is she?" Sven snarled into Lukas's face. "I told you to stay away from her!" He pulled him away from the wall, turned and threw him forcefully against the window, which shuddered at the impact. Sven rushed forward, this time clasping Lukas's neck with his oversized hand, pressing him against the glass with the strength of his rage.*

*"Sven, stop it! Stop it!" Vindi's distressed voice came from behind him, and he paused. "Let him go!" she demanded, trying vainly to pull Sven's powerful arm away from Lukas's neck.*

*Sven released his grip, turned and looked at Vindi. It was the boy he had seen walking; her face was smudged with dirt. He glared at her shabby clothing, then at her innocent gaze. He grabbed the hat and pulled it off her head, allowing the braids to fall onto her back.*

*Lukas's companions gasped with shock. Lukas stood quietly as Sven grasped Vindi's arm with gentle force, and led her out the front door of the bar.*

*They stood beside the car. Sven crossed his arms and scowled, as Vindi defended her actions, omitting any mention of the attack in the kitchen of her aunt's house.*

*"I know I promised, and I'm sorry, Sven, but I just could not stay there! But I have been going to school...and...I'm surviving, like you told me."*

*"Where do you live?"*

*"Here. I help Alef with the cooking and cleaning. Nobody bothers me...that's why I dress like a boy."*

*Sven snorted. "Like a derelict! And Lukas?"*

*"He lives here too...with me." She stood tall and looked up at him with defiance. "He's always here when I need him."*

*Sven flinched, as if he had been slapped. "Well, this is going to end now. You're coming with me!"*

*"No! I'm fine here. I want to stay! I'm doing fine in school!"*

*"This is not a discussion. I am your brother and your guardian, and you will do as I say!" He made a move to open the car door.*

*"No, wait! I have to get my things. Please...let me say goodbye to Lukas. Please!"*

*Sven stopped and looked at her face. Traces of tears made lines in the smudged dirt of her disguise.*

*"Okay...but if you make this difficult, I'll have to hurt him," he said dispassionately.*

*They went inside, and Vindi motioned Lukas to their closet-room. Sven followed them in, gaping in disgust at the miserable accommodations. He eyed the mattress on the floor and scowled at both of them. Vindi glared back in anger, while Lukas gazed at him passively.*

*"Where are your clothes?" Sven asked.*

243

*"They are not here. They are in the shed."*

*"You mean that is all you have?"*

*"Ja." Vindi picked up her school books, which Sven took from her hands, then collected a few other items. She turned to Lukas. "Lukas...thank you for everything..." She attempted to hug him but Sven pulled her away.*

*"That's enough," he said gruffly. She allowed him to lead her outside, with Lukas following. As they approached the car, she began to struggle and cry.*

*"No! Sven! Let me go! This is not fair!"*

*He held on tightly, forcefully placing her into the car, tossing the books into the back seat. He leaned close to her ear. "Stay put if you don't want him to get hurt! And clean your face!" She calmed, glaring darkly at him as he slammed the door.*

*He turned around and grabbed Lukas's sweatshirt again. "I'm warning you...stay away from her! Don't even TRY to come after her!" He pushed him away, slid into the car and drove off.*

*Vindi watched out the back window as the image of Lukas disappeared when they turned a corner. Streams of tears flowed down her face.*

Vindi shifted her position, releasing Doug's hands. She picked up her mug and sipped her cocoa. "That was the last time I saw him...until he showed up at the school...on a motorcycle..." She chuckled and flashed a brief half-smile.

"Was he there looking for you?" Doug asked.

"Ja. He told me he had been monitoring the Internet, and someone mentioned my name."

"How did he get here from Sweden? And with a gang of bikers?"

"He was never worried about rules. And he thought the biker part was fun." She shook her head. "He has always been a rebel."

"Why didn't he take you with him that day?"

"He said he was afraid he could not protect me from the other guys...he was going to get away and come to my house later...but I could not bear to have him leave, and I...well, I guess you know the rest."

"What made Sven finally accept Lukas?" Doug recalled the confrontation he had witnessed at the hospital.

"When I was at the hospital, Lukas told him about my aunt's boyfriend attacking me...that it was the reason I left her house and we started living together. Sven was upset that he didn't know about it. He was partly mad at himself, because he had basically told me not to bother him.

"I told him I didn't call him because I knew he could not do anything except put me in a foster home or something, and I didn't want that. So I didn't blame him for not being there...but he still blames himself. And he realized that Lukas was protecting me, even though he didn't have much else to offer at the time."

"So he didn't know any of that until Lukas came here?"

"No. He was mad at me for running away and living with Lukas. He thought Lukas was taking advantage of me, but he never confronted me about it. The whole time I was at university with him he just acted like I was a naughty little sister, and he was my prison guard. He made sure I finished my school work, plus more."

"Is that where you went after he took you away from Lukas?"

"Ja. He only had about three months left before graduation, so he thought he could sneak me into his dormitory room for that period of time."

"And it worked?"

"Oh, there was not any problem with the school…they didn't know the difference. But I really tormented him."

"What do you mean?"

*The image returned of Sven and Vindi in the car. She sobbed uncontrollably with her face in her hands, using the wadded up tail of the flannel shirt she wore to wipe her eyes. Eventually she quieted and the sobs became sniffles.*

*"It's about time," Sven said with annoyance. "You look like a disgrace!" She made no reply. He made a brief call on his cell phone. Vindi stared blankly at the road ahead throughout the remainder of the trip.*

*When they arrived at the university, Sven pulled up to a large campus building. "Stay here," he commanded. He left her in the car and went inside.*

*Within a few moments he returned, accompanied by a smiling, well-dressed girl with short light brown hair. He brought her to the car, and opened Vindi's door.*

*"Vindi, this is Tonni. Tonni, this is…my rebellious sister, Vindi."*

*Tonni looked at her in surprise, then smiled. "Hi, Vindi." Although only a few years older, she spoke to her as if she were addressing a five-year-old.*

*"Tonni is taking you shopping for some clothes," Sven instructed. "You will NOT give her any trouble." He handed Tonni a credit card and they spoke briefly.*

*"Oh, wow." Tonni gaped at Vindi's attire when she stepped out of the car. Vindi maintained a blank stare into the distance. "I have an idea," Tonni said brightly. "We will go to my room and find you something to wear for our shopping trip. You can take a shower, too, if you want."*

*Vindi stood motionless, prompting Sven to move toward her, but Tonni put her hand out to stop him. "It's okay, Sven, we just need a bit of girl time."*

*"Don't forget," Sven murmured softly. "I know where he is."*

*Vindi looked at Tonni, who smiled. "Do you like this shirt? I have another one like it in yellow that would look great on you." She began to walk toward the building. Vindi watched her for a moment, then hurried to catch up.*

*"Bye, Sven," Tonni waved.*

*"Call me if she gives you trouble." He returned to his car.*

*Several hours later, while studying at the desk in his dorm room, Sven received a text from Tonni: "we r at union hall." He rose immediately and left the room.*

*He did not see Tonni when he entered the recreational area of the student union building, but his attention was drawn to cheers and laughter coming from a group of boys at the pool table. As he approached them he observed the round hip of a shapely blonde girl he had not seen before, leaning over the table making a shot. There was another cheer as she stood and shook her snowy hair that danced in waves around her shoulders and back. He pushed his way around the table to get a look at her face.*

*He stared in shock at the image of Vindi he had never seen before. A lightweight sweater and formfitting slacks displayed the filled-out curves that had been hidden by the baggy clothing of her boy disguise. The smudged face had been replaced by one of natural beauty and radiant innocence that appeared totally out of place as she studied her game, ignoring the boisterous males that surrounded her.*

*Despite the enthusiasm of her spectators, Vindi's expression was flat and unsmiling, and when she saw Sven it evolved into hostility and defiance as she met his glare. She ignored his sudden expression of anger and returned her attention to the balls on the table, preparing her next shot.*

*Sven barged through the small crowd, eliciting startled protests.*

*"Hey! Watch out!"*

*"No cutting in!"*

*"Take a number!"*

*As the challengers looked up and became aware of Sven's overpowering size, they backed off without another word.*

Sven placed his large hand around Vindi's upper arm, gently but firmly forcing her to stand motionless beside him. She turned her face away from him and stared at her cue tip with a blank expression as she twirled the stick with her fingers.

"Listen up, you apes! This happens to be my LITTLE SISTER, who is SIXTEEN years old! SIXTEEN...get it? Do not get any ideas about trying...ANYTHING..." he scanned the group, staring threats into the eyes of each one of them, "or you will have me to deal with!"

As the boys scattered, Sven grabbed the cue stick from Vindi's hand and hurled it onto the table. "What do you think you're doing?"

"Just trying to have some fun!"

"And what is the idea, looking like that?"

"What am I SUPPOSED to look like?"

He exhaled with a grunt. "Where is Tonni?"

"I don't know. She went somewhere with some girls...said she would be back."

"Hmf! We're going!"

"But it's early! Can't I even finish my game?"

"Do...not...defy...me!" He led her away from the pool table toward the doorway.

The images changed, and Vindi was sitting at Sven's desk in the cramped dorm room, referring to a textbook as she wrote. Sven interrupted her and handed her additional books and assignments. His face was stern and she scowled at him.

*The next image was one of Vindi lounging on the sofa of the dormitory living room, reading a textbook. Her back was resting against the upholstered arm, her legs stretched out on the seat cushions. A young blond man approached, lifted her legs and sat down, preparing to place her feet on his lap, but she pulled her legs back and curled them under her. He looked at the book she was reading, and they began an earnest discussion.*

*A second young man entered, pulled up a low stool and sat in front of Vindi, interrupting the exchange. She smiled with amusement as the pair vied for her attention.*

*A third youth came up from behind the sofa and leaned over it, handing Vindi a drink in a glass. She accepted it with thanks, setting it on the table beside her. He maintained his position, resting on his elbows against the back cushion, inserting himself into the conversation.*

*The other boys protested, and they began to argue. Vindi leapt up and moved away from all of them, with her book in her hand. "All right, enough! You can stay and have a civilized discussion, or you can go away and leave me alone! And back off and give me some space!"*

*They quieted and backed away, and she returned to her seat on the sofa, directing them to sit in the chairs which completed the furniture grouping. They complied, and eventually a friendly exchange ensued.*

*Suddenly Sven entered; finding Vindi laughing and talking with the boys, he erupted in anger and drove them away. He gruffly reprimanded Vindi, who scowled sullenly at him.*

"It was really kind of amusing," Vindi smiled slyly. "Instead of being one of the guys like before, suddenly they were using their lines on me! It was quite educational, comparing how they treated me to the crude things the boys in the pool hall would say to each other about girls."

"Yeah, I'll bet," Doug murmured.

"Sven was going crazy threatening them to back off, but I became friends with a lot of the boys. They never got aggressive with me...they were just doing their natural guy thing. I kept them under control, but sometimes when Sven was around I played along just to harass him."

"What do you mean?"

"Oh, I would giggle and flirt with them when he was watching."

"Why?"

"Because I was mad at him for taking me away from Lukas, and for thinking I was a...loose woman."

"How do you know he thought that?"

"He never said anything, but it was pretty obvious. I can't blame him for that...Lukas and I were living together. He only saw the one mattress and didn't know Lukas was sleeping upstairs in the attic."

"And you didn't explain it to him?"

"No, why should I?" Her face took on a stubborn scowl. "I was mad at him." Immediately her expression softened. "I know. I was...how you say?...a brat."

"Are you saying that you and Lukas were never...intimate?"

Vindi gave him the kind of smile a kindergarten teacher would give one of her inquisitive pupils. "Listen. Sven is my brother, who is always in control. I have known Lukas for so long that he is like a brother to me...only one who has needed my help sometimes, so in a way I feel closer to him than I do to Sven. But I would not kiss Lukas any more than I would kiss Sven."

"And he never tried to kiss you?"

"No...I always thought he felt the same way."

Doug paused in thought. "Wait a minute...you've just told me everything that happened after Olof."

"Ja."

"So you've never been intimate...with any guy?"

"No."

Doug exhaled deeply as he moved away from her, leaning his back against the sofa and folding his arms across his chest. After a thoughtful moment he asked, "Does Sven know that now?"

"Ja. After he talked to Lukas at the hospital, he and I talked...about everything. He had been hurting too, about our parents...and was trying to protect me. We cried together..." Her eyes became moist; Doug reached out and took her hand in his. She blinked back the tears and took a deep breath. "We finally got over being angry with each other, and now we are closer than we have ever been." She wiped her eyes, and her expression became one of calm happiness.

Doug held her hand tightly. "You mean until then you two were still mad at each other?"

"Yes."

"How did you manage that while you were living together, and you were going to high school?"

She shrugged. "We shared the same house, but I didn't see him much. I guess he figured there was no point in trying to control me, so he mostly left me on my own."

"So you were basically living by yourself?"

"Ja, mostly."

Doug's expression became troubled. "I had no idea you were going through all that...you never showed any of it. And everything you've been through...you were experienced with guys, but not in the way that everyone thought. Everybody misjudged you...including your brother."

"I know...it doesn't matter."

"And I've been just as bad as the rest of them...or worse."

"No. You have been a good friend." Vindi moved closer, locking his eyes with her gaze. "I have had a lot of boys as friends, but ever since Olof...and the other time...I have never wanted any boy to kiss me or even get close to me...except for you." She leaned forward to kiss him. The touch of her lips was a gentle caress, and he accepted it passively as his arms wrapped loosely around her shoulders.

To Doug's surprise, she prolonged the kiss. When he expected her to pull away she touched his face and neck, resting her other hand on his chest, as her warmth pressed into him. She slid her hand to the back of his head, pulling him to her.

Doug inhaled deeply to feed his racing heart, feeling the heat of desire spread throughout his body. Suddenly he broke away and pressed his cheek against hers. "What are you doing?" he breathed.

"I'm kissing you," she whispered.

"I know that, but...you're not stopping."

"No." Her lips were next to his ear as she feathered his hair between her fingers. "I want us to be...more than friends tonight." She turned her face and began to kiss him again.

He froze, opened his eyes and pushed her away. "Oh, no. This is not happening!" He twisted away from her, then stood and stomped across the room.

"What?" She jumped up and followed him. "Doug, what is wrong? I don't want anything from you...I'm just talking about tonight. I'm not expecting anything else!"

"Oh...wonderful. That's just great!" He turned around and glared at her. "You think you've got it all figured out!" His fists were clenched and his face stony as he opened the door between their adjoining rooms. "I'll see you tomorrow!" He stepped through the doorway, slammed the door behind him and clicked the deadbolt.

Doug paced back and forth in his room, exhaling forcefully as he scowled at the floor, his fists still clenched. Suddenly he stopped, glanced around the room, then dashed out the door into the hallway.

Vindi walked toward the fireplace. A light blue glow danced across her bewildered face as she stared at the flame. She then crossed the room, slid open the glass door and stepped outside onto the balcony. With arms crossed tightly against her chest she lifted her face and stared at the sky. A tear slid slowly down her cheek, reflecting scattered light from the stars that ignored her pain as they winked at each other through the cold blackness of the night.

Doug huffed rhythmically in short gasps. His sweater made an irregular lump on the floor of the lodge's small exercise room as he lay on his back on the weight bench, performing rapid chest presses against the mechanical arm that alternately creaked and whispered above him. The stack of rectangular weights raised and lowered in synchronization with his breathing, and the sweat beaded on his face and moistened his t-shirt as he winced with the strain of each thrust.

The next morning Doug received a text from Vindi: "*R u up?*"
"*Y.*"
"*Bfast?*"
"*Gmme 10.*"
He had already been up and dressed, and in less than ten minutes he knocked on the door between their rooms. She opened the door and examined his face, her expression uncertain. "Good morning. Are you okay?" she asked.

He had barely slept, and could feel the fatigue throughout his body. "Yes…but…I'd like to just get some breakfast and then leave."

"What is wrong?"

"I don't want to talk about anything right now." He did not look at her, but stared across the room.

Her voice was a combination of concern and irritation. "If that's what you want."

"I'll check out while you pack." He turned and left.

After a wordless breakfast, they started the trip home.

Vindi finally broke the silence. "Doug, please, tell me why you're so upset! I only told you those things last night because I thought you wanted to know about Lukas. I was not trying to put any pressure on you!"

"I really don't want to talk about it now." He kept his gaze on the road ahead.

"You are being very rude."

He did not respond.

When they returned to town he carried her belongings into her apartment, then turned and left without a word.

As Doug walked to his car he tapped his cell phone and waited for a response. "Hi, Trish. I got back early. Are you doing anything? Okay, I'll be over."

*Chapter 16*

# Territory

Vindi did not hear from Doug, and he did not show up at the martial arts mixed class when she went on their usual Monday, Wednesday and Thursday. On Friday, Alejandro approached her as they left their shared anthropology class. As he had done almost every week since the beginning of the semester, he invited her to go out.

"Vindi, there will be some hot music at the salsa club tonight. You should be there with me!"

She smiled, preparing to give her customary refusal, then hesitated. "Ja, okay."

"Chevre! I will pick you up at six thirty, we will get something to eat, then top it off with hot salsa!"

He arrived at her apartment door precisely on time, sporting a button-front shirt with a subtle tropical print. She wore a bright red sleeveless dress with a low-cut neckline and a ruffle on the hem at the mid thigh, newly purchased on her impromptu shopping trip that afternoon. Her hair was pulled up on the sides, and floated around her shoulders when she moved.

"Very nice," Alejandro murmured as he looked her over. He led her outside to a large sedan occupied by three dark-haired people. "I hope you don't mind sitting in the back."

"No, that is fine."

"This is my cousin, Jorge, his girlfriend, Sonia, and my cousin, Ileana." Each one smiled with the introduction.

The small group was boisterous and high-spirited at the off-campus Mexican restaurant, where they ate tacos, burritos and fajitas.

"Is this what you eat at home?" she asked her companions.

"Oh, no!" Alejandro replied. "We are from Puerto Rico. Our food is much better!"

"Si, like bistec encebollado…arroz con gandules…"

"Mofongo…tostones…"

"Amarillos…"

"Pasteles…"

"We will have you over some time for dinner, so you can try them," Alejandro promised.

"That sounds good!"

The salsa club was actually a private residence with a large room that had been cleared for dancing. Most of the guests appeared to know each other, and their group was greeted heartily with handshakes, hugs, and cheek-to-cheek kisses. Vindi was introduced to so many people that their names were a blur. After watching a few dances, she was eager to give it a try. Alejandro was patient in teaching her the simple steps of merengue, then the more complicated ones of salsa.

As the room filled there was a frequent exchange of partners between and even during dances. Lively and attractive, Ileana was a skilled dancer and had her choice of partners. Alejandro refused to allow the eager males to cut in; he kept Vindi to himself.

When they rested and mingled among the crowd, Alejandro introduced Vindi to her first *Cuba libre*, a rum and cola mixture over ice.

"It means, 'free Cuba,'" he explained. "It is a popular drink on my island. Of course, we drink a lot of rum because we make it there out of sugar cane."

"I like it!"

As the evening progressed the combination of rum, energetic Latin music, and being whirled on the dance floor by Alejandro made Vindi's head spin, and she could not stop laughing.

Much later they hugged their goodbyes and Alejandro escorted her to the car. She felt as if she were floating, without a single thought or concern in her head. Ileana stayed behind, and Vindi and Alejandro occupied the back seat as Jorge drove with Sonia beside him.

When Alejandro began kissing her she was too relaxed and uninhibited to resist, and responded passionately. The embrace was interrupted, though, when her body slackened and she nestled her head on his shoulder and fell asleep.

Vindi roused when they arrived at her apartment. Alejandro guided her upstairs, opened the door with her key and led her inside.

She leaned against his shoulder, then turned and hugged him. "Mmm, I had such a great time! I want to dance some more!"

He laughed gently. "I think you have had all the dancing you need for one night."

"Oh! I don't have any music! I must download some salsa music! Where is my computer?" As she moved away she stumbled; Alejandro caught her, then steered her down the hallway to the bedroom.

"Where are we going?"

"I am putting you to bed."

"Mmm…that is nice."

He pulled the covers aside and helped her lie down, then removed her shoes and tucked the blanket around her. She fell asleep immediately. He kissed her lightly on the cheek.

"Dulce sueño, Chulita," he whispered, then caressed her face. He turned out the light and then left the apartment, leaving the key on the counter and securing the locked door behind him.

It was almost noon when Vindi awakened. She was puzzled to discover that she was wearing her dress in bed.

"Ow!" She sat up and grabbed her head, which was pounding. Her stomach was queasy, and her entire body ached. "Oh, I'm sick!"

She showered, then put on her cotton pajama pants and a t-shirt. She went to the kitchen but felt too ill to eat or drink anything; instead, she collapsed on the sofa and slept.

After a time her phone, which had been left on the counter, chirped with an incoming text message. She opened her eyes with the second signal, but did not move. Shortly thereafter the doorbell rang, and she sat up slowly, holding her head. There was a loud rapping at the door. Finally she rose and dragged herself across the room to open it.

"Ai, Chulita, you look like you feel terrible...but never more beautiful!" A smiling Alejandro entered the room, guiding her with one arm back to the sofa. "Now, you sit here and we will make it all better." He placed a narrow vase containing a single red rose bud on the end table next to her. "This is to lift your spirits. And now, for your head and stomach." He removed a container from a small brown paper bag and mixed its contents with a glass of water, moving quickly to the kitchen and back.

"Wow, you're smooth," Vindi murmured to herself.

"Here, drink up. You will feel better, I promise. Drink it very fast." She complied, then slumped back onto the sofa. Her feeling of inertia was overwhelming as she watched him bustle about the room. He placed a music disc into the player and adjusted the volume, then sat next to her.

"No dancing today," he said softly. "This music will relax your pounding head." The melodious harmony of a Latin trio sounded far away.

"How did you know I would be feeling so bad?"

He smiled. "I should not have let you drink so many Cuba libres. They sneak up on you."

"You mean…I'm feeling this bad…from *drinking*?"

"Si, mi amor. So, you are having your first hangover."

"Ohh…it's terrible! I'm never going to drink again!"

He laughed. "That is what everybody says."

Vindi turned her head slowly and looked at him. "How did I get into bed last night?"

"I put you there."

"Oh, I'm so stupid." She rubbed her face with her hands and pushed her hair back.

He took her hand in his, and looked at her solemnly. "You have no need to worry. You are the same girl today that you were yesterday."

"But you could have taken advantage…"

"Some muchachos might, but I would not. My pleasure comes from giving pleasure to my partner, and you have to be awake for that!" He kissed the back of her hand.

"Thanks, Alejandro." *Wow, this guy is super smooth!*

"Now, you lie down and rest." He stood and helped her get situated. "If you like, I will come by later and bring you something to eat…or we can go out."

"No, thanks. I just want to suffer alone."

"As you wish. Call me if you want anything, Chulita." He kissed her on the cheek, then left.

*He has obviously done this a few times before*, Vindi concluded as she drifted off to sleep.

As Vindi steered her bicycle across the vacant campus on Sunday, she heard the chirp of an incoming text on the phone in the pocket of her shorts. Her skin tingled in the crisp midmorning air, and lingering dewdrops winked at her as she entered the bike path that snaked around the off-campus community. Her head was clear today, but her leg muscles objected to the forced labor, not wanting to awaken from their comfortable lethargy.

A repeat alert signaled, followed by a second new text. Vindi ignored them as she increased her speed, her heart thumping a crescendo rhythm as it pumped new vitality throughout her body. The chin strap of her helmet strained against the turbulence of the passing breeze, while loose strands of hair danced in the sunlight around the single braid that fluttered on her neck and upper spine.

She fought to keep her speed on the upward slopes and allowed invigorating accelerations on the downward sides as she circled the sleepy neighborhoods. The final challenge was the long sloped dam over the reservoir, where she geared down and pumped vigorously despite slowing to a near stop as she reached the top. As she rode down the opposite side her racing heart struggled to overcome the starvation of her muscles, and when she reached level ground at the bottom she stopped at the widened rest area that overlooked the large lake that was just beginning to awaken for the day.

Sun rays filtered through the morning mist that rose from the still water and evaporated, allowing the mirror image of the pale blue sky to gradually come into focus.

Vindi stared out over the lake. Her breaths were rapid and deep as she stood straddling her bicycle on legs that trembled with exhaustion.

A new text chirp sounded in her pocket, and she reached for her phone and studied the screen. It was the third message from Alejandro. She typed her reply: *"All is good. I'm biking. Don't come over tday. See u in class tmrw."*

She pocketed the phone, then took a drink of water. As she reattached the water bottle to the bar a ring tone sounded. She checked the screen again; Alejandro was calling. She did not answer, but slid the phone back into her pocket and continued her journey.

The path ended on the opposite side of campus, leading into one of the main entrance roads near the stadium. At the empty intersection she turned to the right into the bike lane to head back to her apartment. Suddenly she stopped, paused in thought, then made a U-turn and rode leisurely down the long straight roadway in the opposite direction.

As she traveled the flat surface, she did not take notice of her surroundings until she saw the rectangular buildings in front of her grow gradually more colorful and three-dimensional as she approached the large curve that was Fraternity Row. No one was in sight, as Saturday night partygoers slept off their indulgences. The area exuded a hushed masculine energy that lured her closer.

She stopped when she could see the row of two-story frat houses stretching in an arc before her. Doug's was near the opposite end of the curve, and she scanned its silent windows, taking a deep breath to suppress the fluttering beneath her ribs.

She resumed riding around the curve, but before reaching Doug's house she cut down a side street and covered the short distance to the parking garage. She glided through the entrance and traveled slowly in the cool dampness, making figure eights up and down the rows of silent cars, climbing each ramp to the next level until she saw the familiar curve of Doug's sports car peeking out between two anonymous vehicles.

Her internal agitation accelerated as she approached. She could not determine whether the car was beckoning to her like a friend who missed her company, or laughing at her. There was little space between the vehicles, so she parked her bicycle and walked along the passenger side, peering inside the low window. Spotless, as usual, offering no hint of any recent activity.

She touched her hand lightly to the edge of the roof and caressed it softly, as if it were Vader's velvety neck. It was cold and uncaring. Black. Masculine. His.

Vindi's hand slid down the side of the car, as she collapsed to the cool concrete floor. She sat on one hip, leaning her head and hand against the smooth metal door. *Why, Doug? Why don't you want me?*

Her body was weak and lethargic against the weight of gravity. She felt moisture in her eyes, but there were no tears, no sobs, not even sorrow—only numbness. She was inert, immobile. When she closed her eyes the blackness became a void where time did not exist.

Eventually she fought her paralysis by curling her fingers, and was comforted by the dull squeak of her fingernails against the polished surface. She inhaled deeply, noting that her lungs still worked, and concentrated on taking slow, steady breaths. Her listless mind began to function as her awareness emerged from the gloom into a sudden burst of illumination.

*No. The question is, why did I think I was in love with him? When did that happen?*

Her thoughts accelerated, as images crowded her consciousness. Bike rides. Jujitsu. Talks at the duck pond. Christmas at his house. Hugging by the pool. Her head on his chest, his arms around her...feeling so safe and protected. On the swing...the warmth of his body. Safe. Protected. The kiss at her car...so gentle and loving.

That was it. She examined it from every angle in her mind. His eyes filled with concern. His gentle touch on her shoulders. The way he placed her hands on his chest. She felt safe, protected, loved. The kiss. The gentle kiss of love.

A single tear escaped from one eye. None followed. She felt a chill spreading through her thigh, and the hardness of the cold, concrete floor. She opened her eyes to filtered sunlight and walls of painted metal that surrounded her.

*I am so stupid! Falling for the charms of an alpha male! I'm not in love with him...it's just his attraction...his strength...feeling protected...and loved. What every female instinctively wants. He knows it...consciously or not. He knows how to make us feel loved and protected.*

*How many times has he done that before? With how many women? Even now. He is so practiced. And I fell for it!*

*I was willing to be one of his conquests...just to feel his closeness. His love. Pah! You idiot. He finally got to you!*

She lifted her head and gazed at the shiny blackness of the car where her clenched hand rested. So cold. So uncaring and mechanical. *It's a machine that goes where its engine takes it. It has no feelings. It is not thinking about you, and it is not going to comfort you.*

Vindi rose and rubbed her face and eyes. She mounted her bicycle and rode down the aisle to the main exit row, then turned to the ramp and pumped the pedals vigorously up the remaining level to the rooftop of the garage. There were few cars present; she sped past them, skidding to a halt at the corner opposite Fraternity Row. She disregarded the view and closed her eyes, as the turbulent breeze cleansed the air that wrapped around her. She raised her face to the sun, visualizing photons of energy penetrating her skin in a blanket of radiant warmth and filling her body with calm light.

She finally turned and exited the parking garage in a controlled descent, then passed the frat houses without looking at them, continuing her leisurely ride toward her apartment. This time she studied each campus building that she passed, contemplating its design and function as if seeing it for the first time.

Vindi participated in mixed class at the dojo on Monday. Doug did not appear. That afternoon Alejandro met her after anthropology class and invited her to go dancing again that weekend.

"No, thanks. I had a great time, but I'm not ready to do it again right now."

"We can do something else."

"No, I can't say right now."

Doug did not show up at the dojo on Wednesday. After class that afternoon Alejandro approached her again. "Vindi, have you been to any of the basketball games?"

"No."

"You really should come with me to the game tomorrow night. It will be like a midseason playoff against our main rival, and there will be some special presentations at half-time. My cousins and I are going, and I happen to have an extra *ticket.*" He stretched out the word, almost singing it.

Vindi laughed at his attempt to build up a weekly basketball game into something special in order to entice her. "I would like to see a game…but there is something we need to discuss."

"What is that?"

"I made a mistake last week, and I appreciate that you didn't take advantage of it. I don't usually do things like that. I just don't want you to be expecting anything."

"I am not expecting anything from you."

"We both know that is not true. I'm telling you this now because I don't want you to think I'm a tease. I know there are plenty of other girls you can go out with. So, do you still want to invite me?"

"Of course! You make it sound like we are war adversaries." He smiled.

"We are," she said seriously. "Didn't you read last week's anthropology assignment?"

The basketball game actually was an important one, and students who could not attend were riveted to their televisions. Doug lounged in front of the large screen at the frat house with several buddies. Just as the third quarter began, one of them pointed. "Look! There's Vindi!"

She had caught the eye of a camera operator, who zoomed in on her momentarily as she laughed and cheered.

"Wow, she's looking good!" another observed. Doug said nothing, but studied the spectators whenever they were in view, searching for another glimpse of her. It happened near the end of the game, when the home team scored to take the lead. The camera scanned the jubilant crowd, then focused in on Vindi, who was jumping up and down and cheering; then she exuberantly hugged her companion.

"Who is that with her?" one of the boys asked.

"That's Alejandro," another replied. "Oh, yeah, I've heard about him. He's been making the rounds through all the hot chicks, and they go crazy over him...seems he's a real Casanova. It figures he would end up with her."

"Casanova was Italian...this guy's a Don Juan," a third corrected.

"He's a dog!"

"I bet she doesn't flip *him* when he gets aggressive!"

"Well, Josh, looks like you lost your chance with her."

"Yeah, as if I ever had one."

Doug stood and left the room without a word.

Doug parked outside Vindi's apartment complex where he could see the front entryway. He remained in his car, listening to the final moments of the basketball game on the radio. When it ended he half-listened to the post-game chatter while he continued to watch and wait.

Eventually a rowdy group approached the apartment entrance, talking and laughing. Vindi's blonde head was unmistakable among the dark-haired Latinos. She and Alejandro went inside; the others loitered near the doorway, conversing loudly in Spanish.

Doug checked the time on his phone, wondering whether to confront them in her apartment. The guys outside did not know him, so they had no reason to try to prevent him from entering the building. But once he got there, what would he do? His heart pounded and he began to breathe rapidly, as if he faced an imminent threat.

He waited, drumming his fingers on the steering wheel, then checked the time again. His hand grasped the door handle. Suddenly he saw Alejandro emerge from the outer door and rejoin his companions. As they moved away, he rushed into the building and up the stairs, bypassing the elevator.

He arrived breathless and agitated at Vindi's door, and pounded harder than he had intended. It took a moment for her to open the door. Her eyes widened when she saw him, but her expression was passive.

"Hi," she said coolly.

He brushed past her as he entered, scanning the room. "So, you're dating Alejandro." His tone was accusatory. "How long has that been going on? What's he going to do…get rid of his friends and come back?"

She did not answer, but stood and watched him circle the living room as if sniffing out an enemy. He eyed the fading rose on the side table, then moved to the CD player, where the Latin trio music was playing softly.

"You're listening to Spanish music, too?" He snorted. "He's got his mark all over this place!"

"Would it make you feel better if I let you pee on the furniture?" she asked sarcastically.

"Not funny, Vindi."

"Oh, I find it quite amusing." She spoke calmly, but did not smile. Her voice then became stern. "Go away, Doug. Your primitive display is not going to accomplish anything. You don't own me, or my egg, so take your cave-man possessiveness and go." She held the door open. "You can let me know when you want to talk with your advanced human brain." He looked at her and hesitated, but words would not form. He left with a scowl.

Doug fumed as he sat in his car, watching the building's entrance. Students came and went, but Alejandro did not appear.

Hours later he awakened in an uncomfortable position when he heard voices outside the car. The sun had already risen and students were walking past him toward the campus.

*Damn!* He punched the steering wheel with the heel of his hand.

*Chapter 17*

# Decision

"You look like crap!" Sensei observed as he invited Doug into the dojo. He had come in early after receiving Doug's distressed call. Doug was unshaven, looked exhausted, and was wearing the wrinkled clothing he had slept in. They sat on a bench in the mirrored training room.

"Let me guess," Sensei said lightly, "...it's a woman."

"Of course it's a woman!" Doug jumped up and paced restlessly as he talked. "You know Vindi...how she's always happy and sparkly...friendly, and nice to everybody." He paused.

"Yes."

"Well, she comes off as this happy-go-lucky free spirit who is wise...experienced...and in control. Then the other day she tells me this story about her life...all these traumas and awful conditions she has had to deal with...you'd never know it to look at her." He paused again. "I thought I knew her, but I was only looking on the surface...deep down, she is so much more."

Sensei waited silently, as Doug continued his agitated back and forth motion.

"First she tells me that she's hardly kissed a guy except for me...and then she starts kissing me, and throws herself at me...and...I couldn't do anything! I practically ran away from her!" He sat back down on the bench and leaned forward, with his forearms resting on his thighs, staring at the floor, tapping his heel.

"Why do you suppose you did that?"

Doug let out a sigh, sat up and looked at him. "That's what's driving me crazy! I had this feeling that she was baiting me...that it was some kind of trap! And another part of me was thinking that she's so innocent and vulnerable...she needs to be protected...especially from guys like me!" He leaned forward again, and shook his head. "What is going on with me?"

Sensei paused, then spoke gently. "It sounds like you care more about her than you do about your own pleasure. And that scares the hell out of you."

Doug pondered that for a moment. "That's not all." He continued more calmly, still staring at the floor. "In the past two weeks I've gone out with every girl I've ever been interested in, and I haven't been motivated enough to get it on with any of them. I don't want to kiss them, and I can't even tolerate listening to them talk! All I can think about is Vindi, and wondering who she is with."

"You've got it bad."

"What?"

"You're obsessed with Vindi. Or as some people would say…you're in love."

Doug sat up rapidly and met his gaze with a scowl. "No…I can't be! I'm going to be a bachelor until I'm at least thirty. This doesn't fit my plans at all!"

"That's why you're resisting it so much, but it won't make it go away."

"But what happened to my instincts to spread my genes around?"

Sensei chuckled. "You still have them, but they're in the background right now. There's a new drug in your brain making you feel like you're only half a person. Vindi is your other half and you feel terrible, like something is missing, when you're not with her."

"That's exactly what it feels like!" He jumped up and clenched his fists, flexing his entire upper body. "She told me last night that I don't own her, but I feel like I have to keep other guys away from her. If I even think about her being with another guy, I want to smash his face in!" He smacked his open palm with his fist as he exhaled forcefully with a growl.

Sensei waited silently, as Doug calmed and sat back down, crossed his arms over his chest and glared at the floor. After a few moments his face and shoulders relaxed and he looked up at Sensei. "So…I'm…in love. Does this mean that she's my soul mate? That we are destined to be together forever?"

"Not at all, even though that's what most people think, because that's what it feels like. No, it is not destiny, or fate, making you feel this way about her. We call it love, but the type of love that lasts is not a part of this process. You will get over this obsession eventually, and will get your selfishness back...and your instincts to pursue other women. Only then will you find out what your future with Vindi will be."

"What do you mean?"

"What you feel now is a chemical rush in your brain. I call it an obsession, because it compels you to want her. It may last for a month, or for several years, but it will eventually fade away. We interpret this sensation as love, and feel like it will last forever. After the chemicals dissipate we often feel like love has ended. But it is only then that we can see the real person behind the obsession, and know whether there is compatibility and respect for each other that is the real basis for a lasting love."

"Are you saying that I have to act on this obsession?"

"You don't have to...but is there any reason not to? Have you made a commitment to anyone else?"

"Absolutely not!"

"Then one option is to go with it and see what happens. The other is to keep fighting it. You'll be miserable for a while, but you'll eventually get over it."

"What should I do?"

"You'll have to figure that one out for yourself."

"What if she doesn't feel the same, and she rejects me?"

Sensei chuckled again. "That has been man's dilemma since the cave man put away his club!"

Sensei got up and left the room. Doug sat motionless, scowling at his image in the mirror, but he found no answer in his disheveled reflection.

Vindi returned home at the usual time after her last class in the afternoon. Within a few minutes there was a knock on the door, and a large bouquet of multicolored roses scattered among spring flowers was delivered. The card read: *"See text."*

Almost immediately she received a text signal on her phone. It was from Doug.

*"Vindi I'm sorry. I know I don't deserve it but I'd like to talk to u with my advanced human brain. May I come over at 10 am tmrw? I'd like to take u somewhere special. Optional overnight stay."*

She stared at the note, her lips forming a tight line as she considered her decision. Did she want to see him?

*Yes!*

Was she going to let him get to her with his charm?

*Well...*

*You know what is going to happen.* She argued with herself. *You're going to be in love with him all over again.*

*Well, so what? Maybe it's time to feel what it's like. Even if...*

*Right. Even if he uses you for his pleasure, then moves on.*

*I know it will hurt. But other girls do it, and they survive. It's all part of the life experience, isn't it?*

*If you want it to be.*

*I want it.*

She texted back: *"Ok."*

She was ready when he arrived Saturday morning, and stood back as he entered the room. His half smile looked more seductive than apologetic. "I'm sorry, Vindi…again…for being a jerk…again."

She focused on his eyes, resisting the urge to run to him and press her face against his muscled chest. "It's okay," she whispered.

"Do you want to take a little trip? I haven't been there before but I think you'll like it. I'd like to go somewhere, away from here, to talk to you about some things. I've been sort of…in a fix lately, and I…need your advice."

She scanned his face, puzzled and concerned. There was none of the usual arrogance. He looked deflated, troubled, sincere.

"I'll get my bag."

As they were leaving, Vindi observed Doug surveying the apartment, and noted his look of satisfaction in seeing the cheerful flowers prominently displayed on the countertop, and verifying that the single red rose was gone.

During the drive they talked blandly about classes and the upcoming semester. They stopped for lunch, and then continued their drive up the mountain. The scenery changed from summer to winter, and they were soon surrounded by snow. The route was unfamiliar to Vindi; it led them down a long winding drive to a nondescript cabin nestled among tall pine trees.

As they entered the doorway Doug instructed Vindi to close her eyes; he led her forward several paces, then sat her down on a small sofa. When she opened her eyes she let out a gasp.

She was looking through a wall of glass that overlooked a motionless mountain lake. The surrounding snow-tipped pine trees, deep blue sky and scattered puffy white clouds were suspended over their upside-down reflections in the smooth mirror surface.

"Oh, it's so beautiful," she whispered as he sat beside her. Her self-control dissolved as she leaned against him and hugged him tightly. She could no longer suppress the growing desire and devotion which had prompted her attempt at intimacy just to feel his closeness, and she pressed her face against his chest, trying to sink into his being.

The single tear she had shed in the parking garage erupted into a cascade of emotions that tumbled and collided like roughly chopped logs with raw, sensitive edges being swept down a raging river. Pain and confusion over his rejection. Sorrow over his subsequent absence. Happiness in their reunion. Apprehension about his present intentions.

He held her and caressed her hair lightly as she wept. She could feel his bewilderment, but was unable to tell him that her tears this time had nothing to do with painful memories of the past, and everything to do with him.

Eventually the tears came to an end, but she continued to hug him tightly. She lifted her face and felt his gentle touch as he stroked her eyelashes. She moved a hand to his chest, then slid it up his neck to the back of his head and pulled his face to hers.

His lips barely touched hers before he resisted, held her wrist and backed away. "Vindi. We have to talk."

She allowed her arms to fall limply as he took her hands in his and surrounded them with his warmth. Her head was bowed and her eyes almost closed as she stared down at nothing.

"I know what you're doing," Doug said softly. "The same thing you did the last time. You're offering yourself to me with no strings. You're willing to let me treat you like a weekend fling. I couldn't accept it then, and I don't accept it now."

He reached forward and lifted her chin gently. She gazed at solemn eyes she had never seen before.

"There's a reason I haven't been around for the past two weeks. I've been fighting something inside me. It seems I've lost my instinct to spread my genes, and...I have fallen in love...with you."

Except for a slight parting of her lips Vindi was motionless, frozen in time. Her shocked eyes fixated on his as she heard him continue to speak. "I have no desire for other women...all I can think about...and all I want...is you."

The voice stopped. Doug was gazing at her. His face—that handsome face, with the rugged chin shadowed by dark follicles of masculine hair; the trio of dark eyes, lashes and brows sculpted into the center, and the swirl of black hair framing the forehead—was being offered to her. He wanted her. He loved her.

Vindi inhaled sharply as she covered her face with her hands and bowed her head as explosions of light saturated her brain. The drug of love was painful, but a good pain—a wonderful pain. She adapted rapidly to its heat and light—already it was the core of her being that had always been present. She had no memory of how she had ever existed without it.

She looked up at him—the man she loved—whom she had always loved. The meaning of her entire life had been waiting for him, and now was fulfilled.

His gaze did not reflect her joy, but was troubled as he pulled an object from his pocket and whispered, "I have something for you."

He gently pulled one of her hands forward and placed a small black velvet box into her palm, keeping his hand cupped over it. "This ring is a symbol of every part of me, and I give it to you. You own me now. There is no other woman in my life or my mind...only you. You can do whatever you want with the ring...wear it...flaunt it...throw it in a drawer. I will be whatever you want me to be...your friend...exclusive lover...someday your husband...you tell me."

She tried to look at his hand on hers, but it was a blur. He really was hers. The euphoria of her love—her life's fulfillment—would not be contained; it escaped within the teardrops that clouded her eyes.

He took her other hand and held it gently. She looked up, surprised to see that his expression remained troubled. His voice was sorrowful. "I know it might be too late. I might have already missed my chance because of my stupidity. But I want you to know that whatever you decide…I love you, and I am unconditionally in love with you."

He pulled his hands away and waited, as she stared at the box and the hand that held it, wondering who it belonged to and why it was not glowing with the golden light she could feel radiating from the rest of her body. It looked like an ordinary hand as the fingers closed slowly around the box. She could feel the soft velvety surface over the firm object that filled her palm.

She opened her hand; the box was still there. She picked it up and placed it into Doug's hand, and saw his worried look deepen. "Am I too late?"

Her lips curved into a smile as she touched her left palm gently against his cheek, and her eyes met his. "Don't you know? I have been in love with you for a long time."

His face morphed into surprise as she pulled her hand away from his face and pointed to her fourth finger with a sly smile. He extracted the ring from the box and slid it onto her finger, then kissed the back of her hand. She stretched out her arm and watched the large center diamond and smaller surrounding ones sparkle in the sunlight that streamed through the window, creating pinpoint fireworks of light around the room as she rotated her hand.

"It's beautiful." She placed her hand on his face again, this time with the diamonds glistening on her finger. "Thank you," she whispered. "I love you."

Doug caressed her face with his fingertips, then held her chin lightly as he leaned forward and touched his lips gently to hers. The kiss was tender, loving—giving everything and demanding nothing. Vindi's hand stroked his neck, then slid down to his chest as she pressed her lips to his.

She was surprised when he backed away. "There's one more thing," he said softly as he lightly touched her hair. "You're not ready to let go physically...I can tell by the way you put your hand on my chest when we kiss." He placed his hand over hers and held it against him. "You don't have to worry about pushing me away, because I'll be the one backing off. I want you to know that my love for you has nothing to do with sex, so that's not going to be a part of our relationship for a while."

She looked at him with bewilderment. "But...how can you do that?"

He chuckled. "Blame it on whatever chemicals are filling my brain. I've totally lost my desire to have sex with any other women, or even to look at them. And my feelings for you are not about that. I want you...in every way...but what I want most is to protect you. I feel such a compulsion to keep you safe...to make sure no guy gets too close to you or makes you feel uncomfortable. I won't allow it...even if that guy is me."

Vindi rested her head on his chest, as he wrapped his arms around her. She had never felt so secure, so loved.

"My God, I love you so much," Doug breathed as he hugged her. "You're a goddess on a pedestal, and I'll spend the rest of my life caring for you."

They held each other as the room around them melted away. The sunlit mountains, the blue sky, the planet beneath them faded from their reality as their awareness floated in the bliss of their own private universe.

Eventually Vindi slid her hand up Doug's chest to his neck, as she lifted her face and gazed into his eyes. He stroked her hair, then touched his lips to hers with a kiss that united the swirling energies that surged through their bodies, sealing the connection with the passion of their devotion and respect for one another.

After a moment Doug paused, rested his cheek against hers and whispered into her ear, "I guess you can't escape the power of Swedish rice porridge."

She laughed, and they kissed again.

# Epilogue

## The alpha male

Doug is not consciously aware that he is an alpha male.

What is an alpha male?

Scientists use this term to refer to the highest ranking animal in a group. Alpha is the first letter of the Greek alphabet. Next are beta, gamma, delta, and last is omega. These are all terms that are used to refer to the rank of individuals within a group.

Chimpanzees and some wild dog and wolf packs have an alpha male who rules over the entire group. The alpha achieves this status by fighting and intimidating other males. He is in charge of leading the group on the hunt, and to breeding and resting grounds. He is rewarded with first access to food and females. In some groups the alpha is the only male who gets to mate with the females and pass on his genes.

In some human groups, males may battle with each other to attain a higher rank, but Doug did not have to physically fight his male classmates to become a leader. In fact, he did not consciously do anything to achieve his status. The genes he was born with gave him good looks and an early maturation, which attracted female interest at an early age. His intelligence and high economic status—exhibited by the clothing he wears and the car he drives—make him even more desirable to his female peers. This success boosts his confidence, creating an upward cycle of superiority.

Human societies, such as high schools, are made up of many separate groups, and there are rankings in each group. Todd, who is gamma or delta compared to Doug, may be alpha among his circle of friends. Quinn is beta when he is with Doug, but is probably alpha in other groups. The females would also have similar rankings in each of their social groups.

*Natural selection*

The characteristics, or traits, that give Doug his status are those that appeal to the females around him. He has what girls want. Yet, as he complains to Vindi in their discussion at Sequoia, the girls that want him often make him work to get what he wants from them, which is sex. She tells him it is because the evolutionary instincts of males and females are different when it comes to sex.

What does evolution have to do with sex?

First, what is *evolution*? Evolution does not mean that humans descended from monkeys or chimpanzees that exist today. A "missing link" of a chimpanzee turning into a human will never be found.

The word *evolution* can be defined as *any process of formation or development.* Examples are: *the evolution of a language; the evolution of the computer.* One could say that Doug *evolves* throughout the story as his attitudes and perceptions change, little by little, over time.

The *evolution* of the various species of plants and animals on earth refers to specific types of change and development over millions of years. It is often illustrated by a tree which branches from one type of organism to others as changes occur.

In the evolutionary tree humans are considered to be a separate species from monkeys, chimpanzees and gorillas. All of these are part of the group of mammals called primates. Through *natural selection* primates *evolved* (changed over time) into the separate species we see today.

Scientists believe that the last common ancestor of humans and chimpanzees existed around fifteen million years ago. It is sometimes referred to as an ape, but that term does not refer to apes that we see today.

*Natural selection* can change a population of any living thing as long as it passes on its genetic material when it reproduces. This is why evolution depends on sex.

When Charles Darwin developed his theory of *natural selection,* he did not know about genes or chromosomes, but he noticed the results of genetic differences, which he called traits. In his journey to the Galapagos Islands off the coast of Ecuador, he was able to study birds and mammals that were isolated from the rest of the world.

Darwin recorded the characteristics of various species over several generations, and realized that some traits changed throughout the entire population over a period of time. The new traits were *adaptations* to the environment that helped individuals of the population survive. It took him many more years to develop the theory of evolution to explain what caused these changes.

Darwin wrote his theory of natural selection as a four-step process:

1. Individuals of a population will have different traits (such as body and beak size, and color of feathers or fur).
2. Some of these traits are passed from parent to offspring.
3. Most populations have more offspring each year than local resources can support, so many of them die.
4. The individuals who possess traits that help them survive will have more offspring, and the trait will be passed on.

*A 20th century example of evolution: Darwin's finches*

Darwin brought mammal and bird specimens back to England from his journey to the Galapagos Islands, and presented the bird specimens to the Geological Society of

London at their meeting in January 1837. John Gould, the famous English ornithologist, studied the birds and reported that the specimens which Darwin had thought were blackbirds, grossbeaks and finches were actually all finches which had undergone various changes that were so established that they represented twelve new species. This gave Darwin insight into the process of natural selection.

After 1973, Peter and Rosemary Grant and their colleagues studied Darwin's finches in the Galapagos Islands. They found that ground finches tended to eat seeds that were varied sizes. The individual finches in the population had varied sizes of bodies and beaks. Small beaks could handle only small seeds, whereas large beaks could handle both large and small seeds. When rainfall was plentiful, all sizes of seeds were available, and all of the finches thrived and reproduced.

From 1976 through 1977, a severe drought struck the islands, with virtually no rainfall for over a year. This caused a rapid decline in the production of the seeds. One of the plants to make it through the drought produced seeds that were too large for the birds with a small beak to eat. Many birds died as a result of the drought. The scientists tracked which birds died, and found that smaller birds and those with smaller beaks were the majority of those that died.

After the rains returned and new generations of ground finches were produced, the scientists discovered that the average body and beak size had increased from the previous generation. This occurred because the birds with larger beaks were able to survive and reproduce, and they passed on their genes for large beaks.

This is an example of evolution of a species through natural selection.

Vindi referred to the process of natural selection as *survival of the fittest,* which is appropriate, because the individuals with the adaptations that help them survive have a better "fit" for their environment, and they will produce more offspring to pass on their genes.

But the genetic mutations do not occur in response to environmental changes. They occur randomly. If a mutation makes it more difficult for its host to survive, it may not be able to reproduce, and the trait will not get passed on and will disappear. On the other hand, if a mutation helps its host survive and thrive, it is likely to get passed on to further generations. As time passes, more individuals in the population will have the trait that gives them a survival advantage.

## *Instincts*

*Natural selection* creates changes in *physical traits.* It also creates changes in *inborn patterns of behaviors* that can make individuals more successful at surviving and reproducing. These are called *instincts.*

Birds follow their instincts when they migrate. Animals follow their instincts when they hunt for food and care for their young. Humans follow their instincts when they enter into relationships with each other.

Unlike animals and birds, humans can analyze their feelings and behaviors. Yet, like Doug, humans rarely recognize when their behaviors are guided by their instincts. All we know is that we feel a strong *motivation* or *impulse* to perform a certain action. Our instincts create this motivation through hormones and other chemicals that flow throughout our bodies and brains. Scientists have learned some of the specific effects of various chemicals, but still know very little about the complex processes that trigger and control these functions.

## *Sex drives*

A member of a population could have all the best traits for his environment, but he has to do two things to pass along those traits: he has to survive, and he has to reproduce. So it makes sense that after millions of years of natural selection, all species on the planet are driven primarily by two common instincts: the instincts to *survive* and to *reproduce*.

An individual with a strong sex drive is likely to have more offspring than one with a weak sex drive, so more of its genetic traits will be present in future generations. One of those traits will be the strong sex drive. So strong sex drives should be common in all species.

In both males and females of every species, the sex drive compels them to seek each other out and get together for mating. They do not think about what genes they are passing on, or about whether they are going to create offspring. They just follow the instincts that have been developed by natural selection.

With modern birth control methods, humans now can make conscious choices to use sex for reproduction when they want it to occur. They can also choose to avoid sex to prevent reproduction. But many times humans follow their instincts to have sex and end up creating offspring without thinking about or planning it, just as animals do, and just as our ancestors did throughout the ages.

As long as genes keep getting passed to future generations through sex, humans will continue to be motivated by their instincts to have sex.

*Female versus male sex drives*

Doug gets confused because girls are attracted to him, but are not as interested in having sex as he is. Vindi explains that females have different motivations for sex because they bear the consequences of going through a pregnancy and caring for the infant. "It's the egg," she says.

Vindi is correct. Most of the differences between male and female *sexual strategies* arise because females pass their genes through a (usually) single egg that is created about once a month, and males pass their genes through millions of sperm that are continually replaced.

Eggs are scarce, while sperm are plentiful. This is why males of most species have to compete with each other for access to eggs to reproduce themselves.

While females bear the consequences of a pregnancy, a male can reproduce with nothing more than a one-night stand—his genes could get passed on with no further effort on his part. His reproductive instincts stimulate hormones that create a strong desire for sex. He does not want to create a baby; he just wants to have sex. If he cannot attain his ideal of a young, beautiful woman, he may settle for that which is available to him at the time. The more casual encounters he has, the more offspring he may have (whether he knows about them or not), and his reproductive instincts have succeeded.

A female should have no trouble getting sperm, so she can and should be selective in which male she chooses to accept. After all, adding weak genes to her egg will not provide much reproductive success, especially when she has to endure nine months of pregnancy before she can get better genes the next time.

How do females choose the best mate?

A female will want healthy offspring, so she will look for signs of good health in a potential partner. This would include youth, strength, and whatever features are considered to be attractive to a particular culture and individual. Doug passes this test.

Her instincts will also guide her to look for a partner who can protect and provide for her and her offspring. Physical strength and intelligence would have traditionally been important in this regard. In modern times, financial success has become an additional indicator of this ability. Doug passes these tests also.

As Vindi points out, females are also motivated to seek an additional critical feature in a partner—a commitment. Scientists use the term *parental investment* to describe how much time and effort each parent gives to the offspring. Mothers have a large PI during the pregnancy, and in caring for the infant after birth until it is able to survive to some degree on its own. Although it is possible, especially in our modern age, for offspring to survive without significant PI from the father, it would have been much more difficult in the early days of humans when these instincts developed.

This is the test that Doug fails in his relationships with the girls he dates. He fails because he is following his own instincts, which motivate him to seek as many opportunities to reproduce as possible. The females that pursue him may hold back from giving him the sex that he wants because he is not giving them the commitment they want. Doug recognizes this as the "war between the sexes."

*Short-term versus long-term mating strategies*

Doug actively practices short-term mating throughout most of the story. This can be defined as anything from a one-night stand to a six-to-twelve month relationship.

Throughout human history, both men and women have practiced both short-term and long-term mating under certain conditions. Their instincts would motivate them to pursue these opportunities only if they increased their reproductive success at some point in time.

As Vindi pointed out, males and females have different strategies in seeking a mate. Scientific studies have been performed to test whether the predictions based on evolutionary instincts are correct. The best examples of these were reported in a 1993 paper by Buss and Schmitt (see *References*). Most of the information was obtained by asking 75 male and 73 female college students questions which they rated by a point scale. Results from these and additional studies will be indicated by a bullet.

Because males can reproduce with no more parental investment than the sex act itself, they should be more motivated than women to pursue short-term mating, and they should seek more partners.

- When surveyed, five times as many men as women reported they were currently seeking short-term sexual partners.

*Male short-term mating*

Doug is not consciously aware of how his instincts have developed throughout primate history to make short-term mating a successful strategy, but his instincts help him accomplish four specific goals: 1) maximizing the number of partners he can have sex with; 2) identifying which women are sexually available; 3) identifying which women are fertile; and 4) minimizing commitment and investment.

Maximizing the number of sex partners:

- When asked how many sexual partners they would ideally like to have over a series of time intervals, men wanted three to four times as many partners as women wanted. For example, men reported wanting approximately eight sex partners over the following two years, whereas women reported wanting approximately one. Over the course of a lifetime men reported, on average, wanting more than eighteen sex partners, whereas women reported wanting four or five.

- In a separate study, an attractive man or women approached strangers of the opposite sex on a college campus, said they found them attractive, then asked one of three random questions: a) would you go out with me tonight? b) would you come over to my apartment tonight? c) would you go to bed with me tonight? Of the women approached, the percent that consented to each question was a) 50 percent, b) 6 percent, c) 0 percent. Of the men approached, the percent that consented were a) 50 percent, b) 69 percent, c) 75 percent. [This means that 25 percent of men would be interested in having sex without investing time and resources on a date.] This type of study has been repeated over the years with similar results each time.

• When asked to judge acceptable characteristics of potential short-term and long-term mates, men's standards for a short-term mate were significantly lower than for a long-term mate, except for the characteristic of *physical attractiveness* (this is discussed further in "identifying women who are fertile"). Scientists believe this is a strategy to increase the number of potential sex partners.

Identifying women who are sexually accessible:

• When asked to judge acceptable characteristics of potential short-term versus long-term mates, men favored partners with evidence of *promiscuity, sex appeal* and *sexual experience* for short-term mating, but did not like these traits for long-term mates.

• The characteristics of *prudishness,* and *apparent low sex drive* were disliked by men for both short-term and long-term mates. *Lack of sexual experience* was disliked by men in short-term mates but was mildly valued for long-term mates.

Identifying which women are fertile:

- The characteristics *good looking* and *physically attractive* were reported by men as strongly desirable for both short-term and long-term mates. [Instincts for what is considered physically attractive would have developed to select mates who are fertile.]

- The characteristic *physically unattractive* was reported by men as undesirable in both short-term and long-term mates.

Minimizing commitment and investment:

- The characteristic of *wants a commitment* was reported by men as strongly desirable in a long-term mate, but strongly undesirable in a short-term mate.

## *Male long-term mating*

Scientists who study evolutionary psychology recognize that men can "fall in love," causing them to switch from a short-term to a long-term mating strategy, at least temporarily. They believe this process developed because it resulted in

LOVE INSTINCTS: *The Romance of Sex*

increased survival of offspring due to the combined efforts of both parents.

In long-term mating a man confronts a different set of problems: 1) finding women with high reproductive value (able to have many children over a long period of time); 2) ensuring he is the father of any offspring; 3) identifying women with good parenting skills; 4) identifying women who are willing and able to commit to a long-term mating relationship; and 5) finding good quality genes.

Finding women with high reproductive value:

In long-term mating a man monopolizes a woman's ability to produce offspring throughout her lifetime. This gives him an advantage in the number of offspring he produces, but only if she can bear many children over many years. Scientists refer to this as having *high reproductive value*.

A man's instincts should guide him to prefer women with high reproductive value. They do this by stimulating a physical attraction to women who are young and healthy.

- In many separate studies men consistently give physical attractiveness greater importance than women do in seeking a long-term mate.

- In 37 cultures men who were surveyed consistently preferred marriage partners who were younger than they were.

- As men get older, they prefer mates who are progressively younger than they are.

- Actual data shows that men marry women who are younger than they are, on average, in every country worldwide for which data exists. Brides are an average of three years younger than grooms. In the U.S. men marry women five years younger in a second marriage, and eight years younger in a third marriage.

- Causes of divorce worldwide include old age, infertility and sexual refusal on the part of the woman [all result in low reproductive value].

Ensuring he is the father of any offspring:

In most non-human mammal species, females are able to get pregnant only at certain intervals. Some female primates advertise when they ovulate with large, red genital swellings, while others emit pheromonal scents. Their male partners know when to have sex with them and protect them from having sex with other males.

Humans are unique among primates in that the female ovulation is hidden. This presents a problem for the human male. He cannot keep other males away from his partner one hundred percent of the time, so how can he be certain that the offspring he supports is his? A male who invests his time and energy into another male's offspring will pass on fewer of his own genes, whereas a male who has developed instinctual methods of avoiding such a situation will have greater reproductive success.

Male sexual jealousy functions to guard a mate and keep other males away from her. A male's instincts should also guide him to select a mate who will be faithful to him.

- Men reported being more distressed by imagining their partner having sex with another person than imagining their partner forming a deep emotional attachment to that person.

- When recording heart rate and facial frowning, men reacted more when imagining their partner having sex with another person than imagining their partner forming a deep emotional attachment to that person.

- The characteristics of *faithfulness* and *sexual loyalty* were seen by men as neither desirable nor undesirable in a short-term mate, but were near the maximum in desirability in a long-term mate. *Faithfulness* was the single most valued characteristic by men for a long-term mate.

- The characteristics of *promiscuity, sleeps around a lot,* and *unfaithful* were reported by men as desirable for short-term mates, but as undesirable for long-term mates.

- Data shows that the most frequently cited cause of divorce worldwide was sexual infidelity, and infidelity by the wife was far more likely to lead to divorce than by the husband.

## *Female short-term mating*

Women do not have a problem with finding willing partners for sex, but they must be selective in finding a partner who is able and willing to support their offspring. They also want to get good genes. But women traditionally have had problems with the practice of short-term mating. If they are sexually promiscuous, they may be less favored by men for long-term mating. In addition, contact with multiple men puts them more at risk for being abused physically and sexually.

The reproductive benefits females may obtain in short-term mating include: 1) immediate extraction of resources, 2) the ability to evaluate long-term prospects, and 3) gaining increased protection.

Immediate extraction of resources:

In many societies men are expected to bring gifts such as food or jewelry to their mistresses, and women may decline sex if these gifts are not presented. Prostitution is a form of short-term mating.

- The characteristics *spends a lot of money early on, gives gifts early on*, and *has an extravagant lifestyle* were reported by women as more desirable in a short-term than a long-term mate.

- The characteristic *is stingy early on* is reported by women as undesirable in a long-term mate, but significantly more undesirable in a short-term mate.

The ability to evaluate long-term prospects:

Short-term mating for men is a way to increase their number of offspring, because all they do is provide sperm. Because a women carries the pregnancy and sperm are plentiful, short-term mating does not help her in this regard. Her benefit in short-term mating is to evaluate the characteristics of a potential long-term mate. This predicts that, unlike men, the characteristics women seek in a short-term mate should be similar to what they seek in a long-term mate.

- The characteristic *already in a relationship* was reported by women as moderately undesirable in a short-term mate; in contrast to men, who reported it as only slightly undesirable for short-term mating.

- The characteristic of *promiscuity* was reported by women as moderately undesirable for a short-term mate, in contrast to men, who reported it as close to neutral (neither desirable nor undesirable). [A man's promiscuity signals to a woman that he is pursuing short-term relationships and is less likely to commit to a long-term relationship.]

Gaining increased protection:

Scientists believe women would have traditionally benefited from short-term mating by gaining protection from aggressive men.

- The characteristic *physically strong* was reported as desirable in both short and long-term mates by women more than by men.

- Physically strong was reported by women as more desirable in a short-term than a long-term mate. [Long-term mates are committed to protect their partners; short-term mates are not, so a physically stronger short-term mate can deter abuse from other men at a lower cost to himself.]

*Female long-term mating*

Evolutionary theory predicts that women will select men for long-term mating on the basis of the *parental investment* they are willing and able to provide.

For long-term mating, a female's instincts guide her to identify men who: 1) are *able* to invest resources (time and money, in modern times) in her and her children on a long-term basis; 2) are *willing* to invest resources in her and her children on a long-term basis; 3) have good parenting skills; 4) are willing and able to commit to a long-term relationship; 5) are willing and able to provide physical protection; and 6) have good quality genes.

Able to invest resources in her and her children:

- Surveys across several cultures confirm that women, more than men, desire characteristics in long-term mates that correspond to good financial prospects. Wording used included *ambition, good earning capacity, professional degrees, wealth,* and *social status.*

- In a separate survey the characteristics *has a promising career, has good financial prospects, is likely to succeed in profession, is likely to earn a lot of money,* and *has a reliable future career* were reported by women as more desirable in a long-term than a short-term mate. Women also valued these characteristics in a long-term mate more than men did.

- Scientists wondered whether females answered survey questions in this manner because, as a group, they had less access to financial resources, and had to depend on their partners for support. So they performed additional surveys of women who were financially successful and compared their answers to women who were less financially successful. They also compared these answers to those of men who were and were not financially successful. There was no difference in the results obtained compared to previous studies mentioned. Women with more financial resources actually valued them in mates *more* than did women with fewer resources. [This indicates that the preference for a mate with financial resources is based on instincts guiding them to seek male parental investment, not based on actual financial need.]

- The characteristics *financially poor, lacking in ambition* and *uneducated* were reported by women to be very undesirable in long-term mates but only mildly undesirable in short-term mates. Women reported these characteristics as significantly more undesirable than did men in both short-term and long-term mates.

- Causes of divorce worldwide include the failure of a man to provide resources to the woman and their children.

Willing to commit to a long-term relationship:

- Women reported being more distressed by imagining their partner forming a deep emotional attachment to another person than imagining their partner having sex with that person. [This suggests a risk that his financial resources will be used in an alternate relationship].

- When recording heart rate and facial frowning, women reacted more when imagining their partner forming a deep emotional attachment to another person than imagining their partner having sex with that person.

## *The drug of love*

Vindi began to feel her love for Doug, then repressed it when she felt that he had rejected her. Was she or was she not in love?

When she learned that Doug loved her, she was struck with a sensation of euphoria, as if she had taken a drug. She actually was experiencing the production of chemicals in her own brain.

Scientific research has identified that several brain chemicals, including *norepinephrine, dopamine, seratonin, oxytocin* and *vasopressin* are involved in the feelings and behaviors we experience when we are in love. Brain chemicals are involved in thoughts and emotions, so it should be no surprise that the sensation of being in love is related to the release of chemicals.

As Sensei pointed out to Doug, the chemical effect of love is temporary, and may or may not be associated with a lasting love for a particular partner. How can we tell the difference?

Vindi and Doug explore that question in their next adventure, in a dramatic way.

# References and additional sources

Epilogue source:

*Sexual Strategies Theory: An Evolutionary Perspective on Human Mating,* David M. Buss and David P. Schmitt, Psychological Review 1993, Vol. 100. No. 2. 204-232.


Suggested further reading:
[These are books the author is familiar with; there are many, many more]

Explanations of evolution, written for the general public:

*The Greatest Show on Earth: The Evidence for Evolution,* Richard Dawkins, 2009.

*Shadows of Forgotten Ancestors,* Carl Sagan and Ann Druyan, 1993.

*The Third Chimpanzee: The Evolution and Future of the Human Animal,* Jared Diamond, 1992.

*The Blind Watchmaker: Why the Evidence of Evolution Reveals a Universe Without Design,* Richard Dawkins, 1986.

*The Selfish Gene,* Richard Dawkins, 1976.


Discussions about evolutionary psychology:

*The Moral Animal: Why We Are the Way We Are: The New Science of Evolutionary Psychology,* Robert Wright,

1994 [written for the general public].

*Evolutionary Psychology: An Introduction,* Second Edition, Lance Workman and Will Reader, 2008 [more scientific depth].

Reference texts [basic science knowledge helpful]:

*What Evolution Is,* Ernst Mayr, 2001.

*The Book of Life: An Illustrated History of the Evolution of Life on Earth,* General Editor Stephen Jay Gould, 1993.

# Message from the author

Hi, Friends,

I grew up in Fort Wayne, Indiana, and moved to Florida to attend college and escape the cold winters. I earned my B.S. and M.D. degrees from the University of Florida, longer ago than I care to admit. I am Board Certified in Family Medicine, and currently enjoy living and providing patient care in South Carolina.

The topics of anthropology and evolutionary psychology are among my many scientific interests, and I have done extensive reading about them for many years. I believe that by having an understanding of our origins and how we are motivated by our instincts, we can have more successful relationships with other humans in our lives. And that is what life is all about, is it not?

I hope you enjoyed Vindi and Doug's story, and possibly learned something about yourself in the process. Please share your thoughts and comments on the site where you acquired the book, and/or at www.facebook.com/loveinstinctsbook.

In Vindi and Doug's next adventure they explore the meaning of romantic love. Is it love, or is it an obsession created by our own brain chemicals? How can you tell the difference? The anticipated publication date is November

2012. To receive previews and updates, you can "Like" our Facebook page at www.facebook.com/loveinstinctsbook or join our Contact List at www.loveinstinctsbook.com.

Happy reading!

*Jan McBride, M.D.*

Book 2 of the *Love Instincts* series:

# Love Instincts:
## *The Obsession of Love and Sex*

*A love story about how
human brain chemicals can
impersonate love*

Anticipated publication date: November 2012